NORTHERN EXPOSURE

Letters from Cicely

A BOOK BY ELLIS WEINER

Based on the Universal television
series "NORTHERN EXPOSURE"
Created by Joshua Brand & John Falsey

Mandarin

This book is a work of fiction. Names, characters, places and incidents are either products of the author's imagination or are used fictitiously. Any resemblance to actual events or locales or persons, living or dead, is entirely coincidental.

A Mandarin Paperback

NORTHERN EXPOSURE

First published in Great Britain 1992
by Mandarin Paperbacks
Michelin House, 81 Fulham Road, London SW3 6RB

Mandarin is an imprint of the Octopus Publishing Group,
a division of Reed International Books Limited

A CIP catalogue record for this title
is available from the British Library
ISBN 0 7493 1334 X

Printed and bound in Great Britain
by Cox & Wyman Ltd, Reading, Berks

PART ONE

THE
BIG
SLEEPLESS

Dear Mom,

Thanks for the pastrami. I know how inconvenient it is for you to schlep all the way down to Katz's from midtown. I mean I know you were in the City anyway for that matinee, but still. (If, God forbid, you ever visit me here—AND DON'T. YOU'D HATE IT. GUARANTEED.—there's a guy you can discuss musicals with. He's an ex-astronaut, which means he's the opposite of Jewish. But you have *Gigi* in common.

Anyway, I appreciate it. Although you could just as easily ask them how they pack it for Federal Express and then do it yourself with a couple pounds of lean from Ginsberg's. As for me, I'm fine. It's not spring yet, but they tell me it will be soon, which means the meadows around my house will be blooming with a million wildflower blossoms and the sky will turn a deep vibrant blue. Could you throw in a jar of Kosciusko mustard next time? Thanks. Do they make a coarse grind, a country-style, anything like that? Thanks. My best to Pop.

Oh yes, and thanks for the sweatshirt. I wear it all the time.

Love,
Joey

Mr. Steven Cohen, Esq.
129 W. Sumner
Pittsburgh!, PA

Dear Steve,

Before we go any further: jump to the end of the letter and look at my name, which I artfully omitted from the return address. I'll wait here.

3

Yeah—Alaska. Surprised? How do you think *I* feel? But first: So you're in Pittsburgh! They say, contrary to what they say, it's nice. And you're a Legal Services attorney. I'm impressed. But not all that impressed, since I'm the medical equivalent, at least for four years.

This is not exactly where I expected to end up after med school. But I reject that. This is by no stretch of the imagination "ending up." It is a stint of public service in return for value received—ie, the state paid my med school tuition, and in return I serve as in-house doc for four years in a sub-Arctic hellhole. Okay, it's not that bad. A sub-Arctic heck-hole. It's like going from ROTC into the Army, except the food is worse. Actually I've already been here two years, so I plan to get used to it any day now.

I'm writing because my mother sent me an old, dead, moss-green Camp Indian Head staff sweatshirt from our summer camp days. Because I'm a good son, I tried it on. Small? The sleeves stop halfway down my forearms. I look like one of those depraved hillbillies you see on Appalachian documentaries on PBS, and you think, "Thank God I don't look like *that*." (Is "hillbillies" politically incorrect? I meant, "Lower-Class, Rural, Gene-Pool Challenged Americans.")

Anyway, the shirt made me think of you, so I thought I'd say hello. I don't usually do things like that (i.e., "say hello") because I usually don't have the time or energy. But I find myself awake now at 4:18 AM and not a bit sleepy. Which is very odd. So I called my mother (it's after 8:00 AM in NY—they're up) and got your address, which she had on file from your mother. Yes, like the old tv commerical used to say: "Without mothers, life itself would be impossible."

Let me stop on that thought-provoking note. Please write back, thus proving you got this. And if you didn't get this, write back

4

and let me know, and I'll send it again. Meanwhile, it's almost 4:21, and I feel fine.

From Out of the Past,
Joel Fleischman

PS—I know. At camp we were seventeen. Now we're—well, *you're*—thirty. (Me, not quite.) Sorry.

JF

. . . .

MARCH 1

Dear Phyl,

Okay, I know I wrote you three months ago, just after you moved to Minneapolis, and said let's stay in touch. You wrote back very promptly. And I proceeded not to write. But you know how it is. You get distracted and busy. (You especially, with the baby. SHE'S SO CUTE! Can I have another photo?)

So, I apologize for dropping the ball and hereby offer my new idea: let's *really* stay in touch. I mean it. How many college roommates does a person have in her lifetime? Okay, it's an arbitrary connection. But what isn't? You don't get to choose your parents, you don't get to choose your classmates, you don't get to choose the people you fall in love with—all connections are arbitrary, now that I think of it. Does this make sense? The weird thing is, it's about 3:00 on Sat. night/Sun. morning, and I feel like it's noon. I haven't slept all night, but I don't really feel the need to. So I'm catching up on letters—yours is the first, I swear—and feeling very . . . *thoughtful.*

So, here's an update. Work: fine. Winter is always slow, of course, but it's coming to an end, and biz has been good. The plane has only minor problems that I can fix for cheap, and I'm saving for a new one.

Men: disaster. No, I take that back. Not that I'm seeing anybody. And not that I don't miss . . . well, you name it: love, sex, a relationship. But also I sort of *don't* miss them. I have

5

friends. There's a guy here, we're a little like quarreling siblings, but with an undertone of . . . something . . .

Sound vague? It *is* vague. I don't approve of him, but I kind of like him, but I don't actually "like" him, but I sort of care about him in a detached, uncaring way. Clear?

Maybe it's the hour. Maybe it's the lack of sleep, although frankly I don't feel tired. Anyway, I'll stop here. PLEASE write back, and I promise never to let it lapse again. And give the baby a kiss for me. MORE PICTURES! And hello to Jonathan.

Love,
Maggie

. . . .

3/1

Dear Tim—

You're breaking my heart. The traffic is "horrendous" in White Plains? It's "next to impossible" to find a "really first-rate pool man"? At least you can buy a *bagel* when you want to.

Anyway, thanks for the reprints. Although I don't know how relevant "Intensive Cephalosporin Treatment Schedules for *Staph*-Based Forms of Acute Pyelonephritis Infections" will be up here, where most people's idea of medical intervention is to knock back a double bourbon and then go out in the woods and scream at some trees. It's mainly nuts and bolts medicine here in Alaska, i.e., some nut walks in with a severed arm and you bolt it back on.

Meanwhile, in answer to your question, I do *not* "scope out" the "babes" up here, because we do not have "babes" in our community. The closest we'd get to a "babe" would be if a giant blue ox were to wander down Main Street, which hasn't happened yet but isn't entirely out of the realm of possibility. (We do get a moose. Once a month. The same one, every time. And yet he never speaks! Maybe he's shy.)

Didn't I mention this town has a population of about 860? Tops, total, all-inclusive, the entire populace, encompassing

6

every age, sex, race, and creed. So there are about as many "babes" as there are Thai restaurants.

By the way, note that this is the frontier; they really do have "creeds" up here. Weird ones, but they are definitely creeds. One guy believes that dogs are reincarnated as cats. "That's why so many people have cats," he tells me as I remove and bandage an ingrown toenail. (This is what I get in my "practice." Ingrown toenails, wives stabbing their husbands with vegetable peelers, a woman asking if I can give her pet porcupine a facelift. Instead of a lab coat I should wear a barbecue apron with big letters reading FOR THIS I WENT TO MED SCHOOL?)

Anyway, the cat man. "The Egyptians worshiped the cat," the guy tells me, thumbing over his shoulder as though it just happened in the backyard. "So by now, all the dogs of the previous era have come back in feline form."

Like an idiot, I engage him in rational discourse. "Wait a minute," I say. "Where did all the cats come from that the Egyptians worshiped? Whose dogs were they the reincarnations of?"

Immediately he says, "The dogs of Atlantis."

This will be the title of my Alaskan memoirs, if I live to write them. *The Dogs of Atlantis.* I find myself on the receiving end of such theorizing all the time and am starting to believe some of it.

Anyway, 860. I've seen more people in line at the fish counter at Zabar's. So, out of 860, how many decent (eligible, attractive) women do you suppose can be assembled?

There is one, but—never mind. It would take three pages to fully explain my ludicrous relationship with her. In any case, I'll see her tomorrow—which is actually today, since I'm writing this at 5:00 AM, having somehow not felt the need to sleep all night. No drugs, no coffee, no all-night cramming for a histology final in the morning. Odd? You bet.

Anyway, she's an air taxi pilot, owns her own plane, etc. Sexy? No, but *admirable,* right? And kind of sexy, in a way. Certainly sexier than any of the other cabbies I've encountered in my life.

She's flying me 200 miles north, further into the taiga or tundra or whatever it is, so that I can amputate an oil rigger's finger that got crushed when he tried to open a can of Bud with an axe. Don't ask. I mean yeah, they have pop-tops on their beer cans up here, but people get bored during the long winter. Real bored.

Wasting His Precious God-Given Medical Talent,
Dr. Joel Fleischman, M.D.

. . . .

1 MARCH

Editor
Stereo Age
350 Madison Ave.
New York, NY

Dear Sir:

It is not my normal practice to write to editors of magazines, but as I seem to be unnaturally awake here at dawn on March 1, I have decided to take this opportunity to go on record as objecting to the comment by your critic, Mr. Gene Fanelli, when he says that "the most American of all musicals" is *Guys and Dolls.* Isn't he aware that a key scene of *Guys and Dolls* takes place (albeit offstage) in Cuba? Which, as I can attest from having seen the island from high earth orbit, is not even a part of *Latin* America. It is a Caribbean nation. So how "American" is that? Although don't get me wrong, Mr. Frank Loesser's musical is one of the greatest, and a particular favorite of mine.

Nonetheless, in terms of Americanism, other musicals clamor to be cited. What about *The Music Man? What about Fiorello!?* What about *Hello, Dolly!?*

But finally, what about *Oklahoma!?* I ask this, not only because I am a native Oklahoman, and because that show's intermelding of song and story set new standards for the form, but because—and I'm vulnerable, expertise-wise, on this next assertion—I believe this Rogers and Hammerstein masterpiece was the first show to include an exclamation point in its title, which, as I'm sure Mr. Fanelli is aware, became something of a sine qua non for musical titles for decades to follow, as is evidenced in the titles above. (!)

> *Yours truly,*
> *Maurice Minnifield*

. . . .

Dear Shanna,

Hey, many thanks for your provocative, intriguing, and I guess I should say *challenging* letter. I'm extremely gratified that you like the radio show. I'm also frankly incredulous that you're able to receive it all the way out in Seward. And yes, it's great to be thought of as a competent, even stimulating deejay, although I'm afraid I'll have to put out the yellow warning flag when you describe me as "the most important person in the universe." I mean to say, yes, I do like to talk in an improvisatory way about certain philosophical and religious subjects, but then so do most barroom drunks. (Maybe that's where I get it; my Dad was chemically dependent on the sauce.) So while I'm glad you find the chat interesting and even relevant, let's keep things in perspective. I realize, too, that keeping things in perspective is no way to have a peak experience. But unless there is perspective, every molehill looks like a peak.

Having said that, I should probably now address your main point. While I'd like to say that, yes, I do remember leaving my body on the night of last December 16th and encountering yours on the Astral Plane, I, in fact, have no such memory. You say we "embraced one another as kindred spirits," and "discussed the mythic resonance and Tantric meaning of the Parcheesi board." I wish I could remember such a discussion—it sounds interesting. Finally, you say your etheric double accompanied mine as it returned to my body, which, you say, was "clad in red tartan-plaid pajamas and was lying in bed beside a girl named Marcie," for which you "forgave" me and where, by way of proof, you

9

"initiated lovemaking" that "proceeded on both the Astral and the physical planes" until our mutual delight and satiation.

Shanna, while I've always wanted to initiate lovemaking on a plane, the sad and sobering truth is, I don't own any tartan-plaid pajamas. In addition, the last time I even knew a girl named Marcie we were both seven years old, and if my etheric Astral double is logging flight hours and discussing board game metaphysics, it's news to me. Your first reaction will be, "that doesn't mean it didn't happen," and I agree. It does mean, I'm afraid, that I will be unable to take conscious, temporal-body, material-world credit for fathering the child with which you say you are three months pregnant. I would suggest that you search your heart, mind, soul, and random access memory for the identity of someone who can—and should. Not that it isn't flattering to be asked.

So thanks for the kind words, and, if it's any consolation, I will try to play more Blind Faith. As they only made one album, repetition is a constant pitfall.

Best wishes,
Chris in the Morning

. . . .

Dear Woody,

I finally read a review in a magazine of that biography about you by Eric Lax. It left me with a few questions. Do you have to be Jewish to have anxiety? And what's the difference between anxiety and worrying about things? We have a Jewish doctor in our town, so maybe I should ask him. He usually seems anxious about one thing or another. But is that because he's Jewish, or a doctor? Doctors know more about what there is to worry about than normal people.

Come to think of it, is that why so many doctors are Jewish? They're anxious already, so they might as well go ahead and be doctors, and learn all the things there really are to worry about?

I think this would make a good movie, but of course you know best.

Your friend,
Ed Chigliak

....

MARCH 2

Dear Tawni,

Man, only March, and I'm climbing the walls. At least in Saskatoon there was indoor stuff to do to get away from all the snow. Cicely's okay, but there's not much here. Outside, the plows shove the snow into piles at the sides of the road, so whenever you go anywhere it's like you're a cow running through this white chute with nothing on either side except walls of snow. By the time you get to your destination you expect it to be a branding pen or a slaughterhouse or something. On the other hand, I'm so busy working I don't have much time to go outside.

Holling says to find a hobby, like learn a foreign language. Right! Plus, what for? The people I know who speak French speak English anyway. I mean, what am I going to do, go to France?

Meanwhile, I mentioned all this to Dr. Fleischman, that New York guy who moved here like barely two years ago. And he said, Learn to appreciate reading, and really get into it. But, I mean, you know. I like reading, and so forth, but what about having fun?

Holling says that's why so many Alaskans drink. So I said, "Well, suppose I learn to drink?" He says, "You can try it, but it's not all it's cracked up to be." So we decided on a compromise. I'm going to learn to drink drinks with labels in foreign languages—sweet thick sippy drinks like Cointreau and Courvoisier. So far they taste like medicine, but maybe I'll get used to them. At least I can pursue this inside.

Gotta go.

Luv ya,
Shells

PS—I wrote this at 4 in the morning. Holling and I stayed up all night, for the second night in a row. It is Monday night, and we haven't slept since Sat. night! We do the deed, and then we sit around. We write letters, we watch tv, Holling looks at photography magazines, I read *Mademoiselle* etc. Then we just get up and open the Brick like normal! And everyone else seems to be having the same experience. It's like the Twilight Zone. S.

. . . .

Dear Diane,

It's me, Joel Fleischman, writing from Alaska. That's right: Joel Fleischman. (That's right: Alaska.) Thank your lucky stars we never got involved at Columbia. Because if you lived here, you'd be home by now.

Instead, sensibly, you live in Baltimore, where people don't brag if their homes feature electricity. I'm writing to you, not only because we were lab partners in Chem 101 and dated an unforgettable once (I'm still sorry about that soy sauce, by the way)—but because you're the only Ph.D. in psych I know, and I need some insight.

Note the date. It is Monday, March 2. It is actually 2:45 in the morning of Tues., March 3, and I have not slept since the previous Saturday night. NO ONE IN THIS TOWN HAS. And I mean no one, since sooner or later everyone in Cicely, AK (pop. 850 plus or minus) shows up at the local bar/cafe and talks to (or eavesdrops on) everyone else, and the results are in. NO ONE IN CICELY CAN SLEEP. Weirder still, NO ONE WANTS TO. Which is to say, NO ONE IS TIRED, SLEEPY, IRRITABLE, OR IN ANY WAY, SHAPE, OR FORM MANIFESTING SYMPTOMS. People parade through my office like it's the customs office at Kennedy Airport. They tell me they can't sleep and ask me for "something" (they mean: sedatives). But when I ask them if they're suffering, they laugh! *I* laugh! We're all up all the time, laughin' and scratchin' and doin' our Klondike "thing," and no one can explain it.

12

But did I mention that I was almost killed yesterday? A professional pilot named Maggie O'Connell flew me to a pipeline maintenance station up north. And it was weird: she (who, like everyone else, hasn't slept) looks alert and fine, as do I. We get in the plane. We taxi, take off, and here let me note that I enjoy these small-plane hops across untracked wilderness every bit as much as I enjoy being mugged—we take off, and about a minute later, O'Connell starts to look all droopy-eyed and starts swaying around in her seat, and her hands fall off the "steering wheel." She mutters, "Gee, Fleischman, I'm suddenly so sleepy," and starts to *doze off!*

The plane dives, and O'Connell manages to snap out of it, and we spend the whole trip struggling to remain conscious. We arrive at the station and drink three cups of coffee-scented mud. I do what I've gone there for (amputating a finger. Don't knock it if you haven't tried it), and we take off again. The only way we survived the return trip was by singing old Bee Gees songs. ("Stayin' awake . . . Stayin' awake . . .")

But when we got back, we were alert and normal again. (!!!)

You could feel it as we landed. The sleepiness dissolved, just lifted, like Judy Garland waking up in the field of poppies in the Wizard of Oz. How can this be? How can an entire community not require sleep? And not feel the effects of an already truly humongous and steadily escalating sleep deficit? Medically, of course, this is impossible, so I'm begging you for input. Is this a psychological phenomenon, or what? Obviously, the incident with the plane trip suggests that the effects of this are localized, that when we leave the town our normal sleep requirements reassert themselves.

Is this a kind of mass psychological *folie* state, a sort of gigantic instance of group hypnosis?

Which, no, is not probable or persuasive. So you tell me. And please answer fast. If this keeps up, there may be big career gold to mine up here. And don't worry, I'll cut you in. (So, of course, mum's the word.)

Stayin' alive,
Joel

Dear Mother,

Thanks for asking, but no, I will *not* be joining you for a tour of Tuscany next month. Much as I would like to see Tuscany, and even much as I might want to see you. But not the two at the same time. Because I know what you have in mind. First it's, "Isn't Siena beautiful?" Then it's, "How can you go back to that awful Alaska?" As though the one necessarily means the other.

Look, I respect the big changes you've initiated in your life. (I think you underestimate how hard it is for Jack and me to adjust to it, but maybe by definition that's not your problem. Fine. Maybe.) And I guess I'm even touched by your desire to try to teach me not to make the same mistakes you (think you) made. But was it really so bad, being Dad's wife and our mother? Or does it only seem so now that you're free to discover the rest of the world?

But you've always been free to do this. Who told you to go to those awful Democratic Ladies Auxiliary teas and listen to Cissy Reynolds decree (week after week) that the milk goes in BEFORE the tea and the sugar? When—as I told you from the time I was in seventh grade—it's a matter of common sense, not to mention basic chemistry, that if you put the tea in first, and then the sugar, the sugar has a chance to dissolve in the hot tea before the everything is cooled down by the milk.

"No, dear," you would smile at me. "This is the way it's done."

Says who? Cissy Reynolds? Or is that the point, the whole gross Grosse Pointe point? That you *were* free to bag the whole thing and didn't know it, or—worse—did know it but didn't have the nerve?

In any case, please try to get used to the fact that I LIKE it here. I LIKE flying my plane, I LIKE wearing jeans and a down vest all the time, I LIKE all the wildness and strangeness of this place. Not "have gotten used to" or "have learned to make the best of" or "feel I should give it a chance." "Like."

Which is why, I suppose, I took it personally when you burned down my house. Is that narrow of me? Okay, I'm sure it was an accident. Although even you, in your newly liberated frame of mind, must admit it looked . . . iffy. But fine. Iffiness between mothers and daughters is okay. What kind of world would it be if a mother can't iffily torch her own daughter's dwelling?

But that's my point! You didn't have to do that. I've *already* broken out of the life you wish you had broken out of. I HAVE had the nerve. That's why I'm here! So when you come and "accidentally" reduce my home to ashes, I wonder what the meaning is.

I'm writing this having just got back from flying Joel Fleischman (famous doctor/non-boyfriend) to a logging camp, where he amputated the crushed finger of a guy who tried to open a can of Bud with a trimming axe. Did a nice job. (Fleischman, not the logger.) I asked the patient why he did it, why he didn't just use a can opener. "That would have been too obvious," he said. That's why I like it here! Never mind.

Love,
Mary

MINNIFIELD COMMUNICATIONS
CICELY, ALASKA
907-555-8610

DATE: 6 March
TO: Dr. Robert Barlow
     NASA—Planetary Sciences
     Houston, TX
FROM: MM
VIA FAX. NUMBER OF PAGES INCLUDING THIS COVER: 2

Dear Bob:

Thanks for the fast detective work. Let me see if I have this right, and by the way, I appreciate your eagerness to go public with this, but just hang on a few more days.

You're saying this whole phenomenon probably has some connection with this recent crop of sunspots. The spots give rise to solar flares, which create ripples in the solar wind, which in turn induce changes in the earth's magnetic field. This generates current in rock formations with high concentrations of iron, which could be inducing a secondary magnetic field, which could be affecting the brain waves of every man, woman, and child in the greater Cicely area.

Hell, I'll buy it. Beats anything I have to offer. All I know is, nobody in this town sleeps any more. If you ask me, it's a mixed blessing. It's nice to be able to do more, to use the night productively. But if you stay alert and vigorous all night, you're going to need one or two more meals per day. I'm starting to put on weight!

I'll be in touch. Keep this under your hat until you hear from me. And thanks, buddy.

Maurice

. . . .

MARCH 5

Dear Cynd,

Sit down. You are not going to believe this. Remember when you were here? And Wayne came to get you? How normal everything was? Things are SO WEIRD now. *Nobody sleeps.* I have been totally awake, nonstop, since last Saturday night. Everyone in town has.

The Brick is now open all day and all night, but Holling and Dave and me can't possibly run it by ourselves. The only reason I'm able to write to you is Holling hired Ed Chigliak to help out, so I'm on break. And it's not just that people sit around drinking and eating peanuts from midnight til breakfast. I mean, if you're up, you get hungry, right? So we need a night-shift cook now, I mean, Dave is flipping burgers 24 hours a day, and the quality suffers.

In my opinion, this is not natural. But I ask myself, "Shelly, do you feel like a mutant or anything?" and my sincere answer is, "No, I don't." Not that I have unlimited energy. It's like my brain doesn't need to sleep, but my muscles do get tired. After you do a day's work, you want to rest, but not necessarily sleep, ok? That's what it is. So we *sit.*

I don't know how long this will go on, but if you feel like visiting, definitely come on out. Just bring stuff to do. Or can you do short-order cooking? Burgers, scrambled eggs, stuff like that? Just kidding. (But really not!)

Love,
Shelly

....

Dear Steven,

Up here in Cicely, Alaska, people have stopped sleeping. Everyone stays awake twenty-four hours day and night, and no one seems tired. Our local doctor, Dr. Fleischman, says that if we keep this up, and there are no bad side effects, it's "like doubling people's life span."

Wouldn't this make a great movie? Maybe a documentary, with interviews with everyone, asking them what it's like to be awake. Or maybe a fictional story, in which a man and woman are in love, and somehow not sleeping comes into it. Or maybe some evil threat menaces the community, only what it doesn't know is, everyone can band together to defeat it because they have so much extra time.

Just a suggestion.

Your fan,
Ed Chigliak

Classified Department
Anchorage Times
PO Box 4489
Anchorage, AK

Gentlemen:

Kindly run the following classified in your Help Wanted
column for a period of six days, not counting the Sunday edition.
I have enclosed a check for $35 as per your usual rate:

> WANTED: SHORT-ORDER COOK. Must know basics—
> burgers, chili, breakfasts, sandwiches, etc. For day
> shift, 7 AM to 4 PM. $6/hr, meals free, plus unlimited
> consciousness. Call H. Vincouer, The Brick, Cicely.
> 555-2910.

For your information, the phrase "unlimited consciousness"
was urged on me by several of my customers. Particularly a Mr.
Chris Stevens, who is a disk jockey and an artist, so I assume he
knows what he is talking about. I don't really understand it
myself, but Chris claims it is classified ad shorthand for the fact
that in our town, no one sleeps. So an employee who works the
day shift can still enjoy an evening and a night of normal
wakefulness, thus ensuring himself a full day's life. It's only two
words. If it attracts the attention of a good short-order cook, I
figured what the hell.

> *Yours truly,*
> *Holling Vincouer*
> *Prop., The Brick*

Dear Jack,

Guess what. Mom wants me to tour Tuscany with her in
April. As though it's that easy, right? The ink on the divorce

papers isn't dry—it may not even be wet yet, for all I know!—
and she's recruiting me to her side. I don't like it. It's not fair to
me—or to you, either. If anyone is going to Tuscany, it should
be all of us, like a family.

Wouldn't *that* be a nightmare. In Italian, too.

Am I nattering on? It's because that no-sleep thing that I told
you about on the phone last week is still with us. Does it mean
that now I have 24 hours a day in which to move passengers and
freight, log flight hours, and generally improve what Dad would
call my "financials"? As we used to say in Paris, au contraire: I
can't fly at all.

The second I leave Cicely's airspace, I practically pass out.
The missed sleep descends on me like an avalanche. It happened once, and only the hysterical screams of my terrified
passenger woke me up enough to finish the flight. So I'm taking
some time off, hanging out, and helping out around town. Maybe
this weird thing will pass soon, and I'll be back in business.

By the way, the terrified passenger was our very own Dr. Joel
Fleischman, the NY MD, for whom you'd think this period of full-
time wakefulness would be a godsend. More time in which to
feel superior to the entire state of Alaska! More time to bug his
parents to send him mail-order pastrami while he waits for his
"real" life to resume! More time to harrass and whine and carp
at yours truly about . . . about more and more!

You'd be wrong. The hilarious irony—at least, I find it hilarious; Fleischman, typically, does not—is that he's busier than
ever. Patients troop into and out of his office night and day. Poor
Marilyn (his assistant). At least I *assume* she's suffering, although it's always hard to tell how she feels about things.

One reason Fleischman is so busy is the noticeable increase
in interpersonal conflict throughout the town. People seem edgy.
Husbands and wives hit each other with hammers, or pour that
second cup of boiling coffee "accidentally" on each other's
hand instead of in the cup.

Apparently, without sleep, spouses get on each other's nerves
simply by being in each other's face for so many hours of the
day. Because think of it: when that ancient, adorable couple

stands up on "Donahue" or "Oprah" and announces that they've been married 72 years and everyone applauds, does anyone ever point out how much of that time hubby was away at work? Does anyone mention that during a third of that time (24 years), the happy couple were unconscious, with their backs to each other?

Or do I have a negative view of marriage because of the example set by Mom and Dad? You make the call.

More later. Believe me, I'll write again.

Love,
Mags

. . . .

3/9

Major Maurice Minnifield
c/o Minnifield Communications
124 Main Street
Cicely, AK

Dear Major Minnifield:

With reference to my service as state-appointed physician for the town of Cicely, Alaska:

No doubt you are aware of the ongoing anomalous condition in the town, in which all residents and visitors are able to survive and, indeed, thrive without their normal nighttime sleep period. However, what you may not be aware of is the fact that, coincident with this phenomenon, there has been a sharp, indeed, a *severe* upturn in the number of patients seeking medical consultation and service. The attributability of this latter state of affairs to the former is totally indisputable.

This being the case, I hereby request that the term required of me to serve as Cicely's resident physician be reduced on a prorata basis. Since now each day in Cecily equals, in duration of awakeness and amount of work performed, two days, I request that my term be shortened accordingly. For example: should this anomaly persist for an entire year, then, adding that year together with the two I have already served, and adding to that total this proposed "year's worth" of "nighttime" service, I would consider my four-year obligation fulfilled.

Yours truly,
Joel Fleischman, M.D.

cc Rep. Peter Gilliam

. . . .

10 MARCH

Dr. Joel Fleischman, M.D.
c/o O'Connell
RFD 6
Cicely, AK

Now Hold On, Son—

I appreciate your state of overwork, but look at it from our point of view. If under normal circumstances you went through a day here in which you had *no* patients, how would you feel if we extended your tenure with us by an additional day? Sound fair?

You catch my drift. This awake-all-the-time deal is simply the luck of the geophysical draw, Joel. I have it on good authority that this whole aberration is caused by sunspots. You think the good people of Alaska are going to feel they've got their money's worth of investment in you if we grant you time off because of solar flare-ups ninety-three million miles away? Ever hear of force majeure? Ever hear of acts of God?

You've overworked. I can appreciate that. Take a day off now and then. Better yet, do what Holling and Shelly are doing: work at "night" and pursue healthful recreation by day. Now that nobody sleeps, it's all the same to us Cicelians. Hell's bells, son, you're sitting smack dab in the middle of the most gorgeous country God ever nailed together. Take up a sport or a hobby. You name it—skiing, skating, ice boating, archery, hunting—

must I go on? We've got it all here in beautiful Cicely, on the Alaskan Riviera. Get out of the office and breathe some air. Your patients will understand.

Request denied.

Sincerely,
Maurice Minnifield

cc Rep. Peter Gilliam

....

Dear Aunt Sylvia,

How are you? I have not slept in eleven days, but I feel fine. The whole town is that way. Nobody can explain it. But I was wondering: maybe you would feel stronger if you came and visited us. Ma and Pa say it's okay. They're awake all the time, too, so you three could have a lot of long talks. You'll have to get someone to drive you into town, though. We can't come pick you up. Whenever someone from Cicely leaves town, they fall asleep.

Love,
Marilyn

....

10 MARCH

Dr. Bob Barlow
NASA—Planetary
Houston, TX

Dear Bob,

Now please, Bobby, don't rush me. If this anomalous condition lasts, I guarantee you will be the first to be granted unlimited research access to the whole town. If it stops, well, I'll owe you one. But I want to manage the development and exploitation of this thing carefully, and proclaiming the official arrival of a NASA scientist of your stature would let the cat out of the bag and the genie out of the bottle. Stick with me.

I can't tell you how odd it is. You talk about mankind being creatures of habit: everyone goes through their usual daytime routine, goes home, eats dinner or whatever, does their after-dinner ritual, reading or watching tv or listening to music, playing cards, visiting, drinking . . . waiting for bedtime . . . and then nothing happens. You sit there like a fool, wondering what to do next.

Invariably I wander over to the local bar, and that place is more jammed than on New Year's Eve. At 2 AM! When half the people, hell, ninety percent of the people, there have to start work the next day at six, seven, eight o'clock. Of course it's pitch black out—daylight is at a premium this time of year anyway, I mean night falls at 3:30 in the afternoon—but we all loiter around, drink and talk and eat like it's Happy Hour and we're revving up for some prime-time fun!

I've asked our local medic, a Jewish fellow from New York, so he's up on things, about possible negative complications. He tells me he has no idea. "We're in terra incognita here, Maurice," he says. "This whole phenomenon is so off the scale, so totally abnormal and anomalous, that it's any man's guess." I can't decide whether that's reassuring or not.

Tell you whose work has picked up, though: Ruth-Anne Miller. Runs the local General Store—which means the Post Office *and* the library. It turns out that, with so much time on our hands, everyone has taken to writing letters. She says the volume of outgoing mail is four times normal, which I can vouch for personally, since I've been brainstorming and firing off proposals to beat the band.

I know you're eager to fly up with equipment and personnel. As soon as things are under control, I'll give you the green light.

Maurice

National Science Foundation
1800 G. Street N.W.
Washington, DC

Gentlemen:

Kindly forward to me all appropiate application forms for scientific research grants, specifically those concerned with the psychological and neurological bases of sleep disorder. Time is of the essence.

Please excuse the xerographic nature of this query, but I am presently engaged in field work in Alaska and my computer is back in New York. Thank you.

Sincerely,
Joel Fleischman, M.D.

American Psychological Association
New York, NY

Gentlemen:

Kindly forward to me all appropiate application forms for scientific research grants, specifically those concerned with the psychological and neurological bases of sleep disorder. Time is of the essence.

Please excuse the xerographic nature of this query, but I am presently engaged in field work in Alaska and my computer is back in New York. Thank you.

Sincerely,
Joel Fleischman, M.D.

American Academy of Neurological Studies
874 E. 42nd St.
New York, NY

Gentlemen:

Kindly forward to me all appropiate application forms for scientific research grants, specifically those concerned with the psychological and neurological bases of sleep disorder. Time is of the essence.

Please excuse the xerographic nature of this query, but I am presently engaged in field work in Alaska and my computer is back in New York. Thank you.

Sincerely,
Joel Fleischman, M.D.

Squibb Pharmaceuticals
P.O. Box 4000
Princeton, NJ

Gentlemen:

Kindly forward to me all appropiate application forms for scientific research grants, specifically those concerned with the psychological and neurological bases of sleep disorder. Time is of the essence.

Please excuse the xerographic nature of this query, but I am presently engaged in field work in Alaska and my computer is back in New York. Thank you.

Sincerely,
Joel Fleischman, M.D.

Proctor and Gamble, Inc.
1 Proctor and Gamble Plaza
Cincinnati, OH

Gentlemen:

Kindly forward to me all appropiate application forms for scientific research grants, specifically those concerned with the psychological and neurological bases of sleep disorder. Time is of the essence.

Please excuse the xerographic nature of the query, but I am presently engaged in field work in Alaska and my computer is back in New York. Thank you.

Sincerely,
Joel Fleischman, M.D.

MINNIFIELD COMMUNICATIONS

CICELY, ALASKA

907-555-8610

10 March

Mr. Steven Jobs
NeXT Corporation
Redwood City, CA

Dear Mr. Jobs:

First, my credentials: Maj. Maurice Minnifield, president and CEO, Minnifield Communications. Also former A-level flight-grade technician, National Aeronautics and Space Administration. In a word, astronaut, retired. Noteworthy mission: Project Mercury, Earth orbit. Also decorated Air Force pilot, Korean War. None of which ought to mean a thimbleful of diddly to you, sir, but I include it just so you know I've had some technological as well as real-world experience.

I would like to advance a business proposition. I've chosen you, from all the other luminaries of the computer field, because I believe that you (like myself, if I may say so) are a man of vision. Besides, who else is there? Gates? A tough competitor, you'll give him that, but in the end, a nasty boy, with a vindictive streak. Scully? A slick suit with a hidden agenda, and I withdraw the question. Wozniak? MIA. Canion? Out. The fellows over at IBM are famous for their anonymity. And come to think of it, whatever happened to what's his name—Noland Bushnell?

No, sir, there is only you. And there is me. Pygmies, Mr. Jobs. Even at NASA, and especially here, in Cicely, Alaska, I was and am surrounded by visionary pygmies, if you take my meaning. A man has a view of the horizon; he points to a thing—an exciting thing, a thing of promise—and says, by God, there it is, let's go get it; and those around him look down at the dirt and call it "reality." I know you agree with me, so I'll get to the heart of the matter.

For years now I've been gleaning from the general-interest press an impression of your vision concerning what the computer could and should be in our society. If I may say, it's a magnificent conception. I hope you won't be offended if I add that I appreciate its vagueness. After all, it's at the blurry margin of the familiar that the extraordinary takes shape. The unknown is, by definition, ill-defined.

May I venture a leap into that undefined vagueness with the following proposition? You expound on the idea of the computer

27

being THE integral appliance of the future household. I seem to remember an interview somewhere in which you posit a day when we will all use the computer with the casual unself-consciousness that a six-year-old today displays toward the telephone. To explore this concept, you could be and presumably are experimenting with advanced models of computers in simulated domestic settings.

My point is, why stop there? Put it this way: Of what use is the telephone, if only one six-year-old has one? For your idea to have its fullest expression and undergo its most meaningful trial, a *neighborhood* of "telephones"—i.e., computers—must be established, hooked up, and running interdependently. A neighborhood—or a town.

That's where I can help. I represent the town of Cicely, Alaska, on the so-called Alaskan Riviera. Population a small, controllable 850 plus or minus. Number of households: call it around 500—a number, Mr. Jobs, smaller than the freshman class at many high schools. And yet here is a fully operational community, with its local economy, its social ebb and flow, etc. In a word, we are talking about a COMPLETE SOCIAL ENVIRONMENT.

You see where I'm leading. I'm about to suggest that you equip every household in Cicely with a unit of your most experimental machine, link them up not only to the national and international phone system but to each other, then stand back and take notes. I will not say our town is hermetically sealed from the rest of the world—indeed, I predict the opposite. Some day. But for now, a hard-wired Cicely, humming with NeXT computers, could be of significant mutual benefit. You get a living, breathing Petri dish in which to study the life of your cybernetic vision. I get some killer publicity for my town. Nobody loses. Everybody wins.

Let me anticipate your objections. Red tape? It doesn't exist. The (defacto) mayor is a friend of mine, and there is almost no other government. Reluctance of the local populace? There may be some, but while Cicelians can be ornery, they're also massagable. Inaccessibility to you and your people? A slight problem, but soluble, and remember that our remoteness is the beauty part. Adequate power sources? In place. Unsophistication of the residents, where you've got to teach them how to use the product? *Our biggest asset*—otherwise you're preaching to the choir.

Look, son, anyone can shove some IBM PS/2s into a development of Ken and Barbie ranch homes, boot up Windows, and call it "friendly." Or throw a couple dozen Macs at a bunch of ice-cube tray condominiums and claim it's an experiment in cybernetic futurology. Balls, if you'll excuse my French. Envision, instead, our one-traffic-light town with each quaint Mom and Pop store, each hand-built house, each wood-stove-heated cabin and clapboard Victorian containing at its throbbing nerve center one of your sleek black gleaming cubes. Isn't that beautiful? With HDTV on the display, *Joy of Cooking* on CD-ROM in the kitchen, with modems and mouses for all. You'll have magazines lined up for a mile and "60 Minutes" begging on their knees.

There is another aspect of Cicelian life that I am not at liberty to disclose at this time. Suffice to say, Mr. Jobs, if it pans out, your machines will get more of a workout than you have ever dreamed possible. I hope I've whetted your appetite for more details. I will be able to provide same when the whole situation is confirmed.

Attached is my card. I know you're a busy man. Hell, I'm a busy man. Let's be busy together and make us a future. Call me.

Sincerely,
Maurice Minnifield
CEO

Mr. Tony Petrillo
Ads Infinitum
1000 Saguaro, Suite 514
Santa Fe, NM

Dear Tony,

Man, am I glad we stayed in touch. I'm appealing to you, in your triple capacity as 1) a poet of the Southwest desert whose work I genuinely admire, 2) the guy who introduced me to The Hero With a Thousand Faces back in '86, when I staggered into Taos from the San Jemez mountains and offered in barter carpentry work for your Creative Writing Workshop, and 3) a Real World adept who started his own ad agency and still finds time to write. I am largely as I was when last we wrote, in Cicely, doing the radio show, making the sculptures, evolving according to some master scheme not revealed to me as of yet.

But dig it, brother: my whole town has stopped sleeping.

We all just stay up, night and day, and have done so since the first of the month. No exhaustion, no irrationality, no bleary eyes. Maybe a touch of peevishness, interpersonally, but otherwise, our waking day is now 24 hours. Which is why I appeal to you. You're versed in the literature, a man of the world and a man of the word. So: is there any precedent for this, in myth, legend, or Bazooka comics? And can we get away with it?

As re the former, I frankly dunno. As re the latter, I have big misgivings. The cause of it all seems to be sunspots; Sol, our stellar adolescent, suffers an outbreak of acne, and we mortal fools down here lose sleep over it. So the (as we have learned to refer to it) "anomaly" is, if only technically, "natural." But so is leprosy. And while it's amusing and amazing to play all-night hands of bridge or actually to start and finish a game of Monopoly without getting up from the table, still: what about dreams? Can we really survive without them?

On the assumption that we can't, and that now is the time for all good dj's to come to the aid of their community, I have commenced playing lullabies over the radio. I also read bedtime stories—not *Where the Wild Things Are*, as I do during Meltdown Mania, no, this time it's beddy-bye classics like *Goodnight Moon.* Duly revamped for Alaskan adult audiences, it is now called "Goodnight Moose" and includes the line, "Goodnight deer and goodnight beer . . . Goodnight pipeline and goodnight 'Nightline' . . ."

I do this, not because anyone is complaining that they want to sleep, but because I can't help feeling that we're flirting with disaster by denying this primal need. It's a public service that lacks a public. Still, I'll keep trying. Any thoughts? Write or call any time. Don't be afraid of waking me up. Regards to your wife and kids, too.

Supremely conscious,
Chris Stevens

....

MARCH 12

Dear Jeff,

So you found me, eh? I assume my mother told you on the phone what she tells everyone else (and me) when she refers to my current situation. Just remember to read this to yourself in her patented adenoidal Jewish/Queens drone: "Jo-el is giving checkups to Eskimos at the North Po-el." This is a gross distortion of the truth, which is already horrible enough. They are not Eskimos. They are Inuit Indians. And we are hundreds of miles from the North Pole.

But it *is* Alaska.

Remember those tv ads? The sleep cruise ship plying the crystal waters . . . a gigantic dazzling white glacier looms up ahead . . . and suddenly, a Glen Campbell-type guy sings, in a big majestic echo chamber, "A-lass-KUUUHHHHHHH . . ." Well, when it comes time to picture my setup, don't picture that. Instead picture a small town in the mountains, lots of woods and meadows, deer in your backyard, bear in your back door, a

31

native population of Indians, a non-native population of eccentrics and loners and visionaries and wackos, and about ten feet of snow each winter. Which starts around Columbus Day and lasts until further notice.

(FYI: The state of AK paid for my med school tuition, so I owe them four years of service as a doc in a remote area. Sort of like indentured socialism.)

Which means, alas, that I will not be able to attend your thirtieth birthday party, since circumstances prohibit, etc. Oh God, the thought of returning to NY, of walking into Posner's House of Seven Bagels on 133rd, of standing there in that horrible flourescent lighting, with the fresh ryes and pumps sitting in those plastic bins and the air so thick it must weigh fifty-six pounds per cubic foot—sorry. I'll try to control myself.

Of course, now you live in the City, and can buy and sell bagel shops at will. How *is* the investment banking biz? Is there any money left in the world? Will there be some available when I return to N.Y., and commence living in a manner to which I hope some day to become accustomed?

(I was just staring out the window, thinking about that Advanced Chem seminar we took the summer after 11th grade. Remember? When we introduced ourselves as brothers to those girls? Told them our names were Florenz and Ehrlenmeyer Flask? Somehow, even as they laughed in our faces and told us to get lost, I knew I would go to med school, and you knew you would go to Wharton. And now look! You're living a dream come true! And I'm living a waking nightmare!)

So I'm sorry I can't make it. Happy birthday in advance. And in case you start experiencing an end-of-youth life assessment, take comfort in the fact that you're still not old enough to be President, you have your health, and you're not examining beaver teeth in Alaska.

> *Putting the Alas Back in Alaska,*
> *Joel F.*

DOCTOR Jennifer Kelly
Department of Sociology
University of Michigan
Ann Arbor, MI

Dear Jen, or rather, Dear DOCTOR,

Congratulations on getting your Ph.D., which I happen to know about thanks to a highly placed source who shall remain nameless but is my mother. What's next? Tenure, right? I'm sure you'll get it. If you need a letter of recommendation, feel free to xerox the following:

> Jennifer Kelly (aka "Jen," "Jens," "Kennifer Jelly") has been a sterling individual and a dear friend of mine ever since ninth grade at St. Anne's Upper School, where she majored in helping me not get in trouble with the sisters, field hockey, Harrison Ford worship, and advanced makeup application. She is eminently qualified to get tenure at any university, is probably a great teacher, and was excellent as my mother when I played the bratty, murderous title role in our production of *The Bad Seed*.

Bear in mind that while I rejoice at the news of your success, secretly it makes me miserable. All my friends are either getting married, Ph.D.'s, or pregnant! Is life passing me by? Normally I don't think so, but life these days isn't normal. I can't fly—I'll tell you why some other time; it's weird—so I feel useless and at a loss.

Which isn't my usual emotional state, I assure you. Like I wrote you three years ago (!!), I fly an air taxi. In my plane, soaring above the Alaskan landscape, I feel privileged and exhilerated. THAT'S my idea of normal: crusing along, ten thousand feet above everybody else, able to swoop in over this staggering landscape—mountains, lakes, glaciers!—and take care of myself no matter what happens. Even macho creep passengers—less common than you'd expect, really—don't bother me with their "clever" jokes about their joy sticks. But if I'm grounded . . .

Well, I'm trying to take it easy, but you know me: busy, bustling Margaret. So it's hard. Oh hell, this mood will disappear once I get back in the air. Meanwhile, write back! And congratulations. Send me your thesis! I promise to read it. (This promise does not extend to understanding it, however.)

But I'm forgetting something. Namely: are you still seeing what was his name? Kevin? Or am I hopelessly behind the times? Answer fully, be specific, and show your work. Then I'll tell you my story. Such as it is. Which, now that I think of it, is sort of hair-raising.

Intrigued? Good.

> Love,
> Maggie

. . . .

MARCH 12

Dear Francis,

I finally saw that documentary about you which your wife shot while you were making *Apocalypse Now.* My favorite part was when Marlon Brando gave some lines I couldn't understand and then gulped and said, "I swallowed a bug." That was great! Did you write it? Or did Brando improvise? Probably the two of you kind of worked it out on the set. Too bad you had to cut it from the final version.

I had no idea making that movie was so hard. No wonder when you shot your next movie, *One From the Heart,* you didn't even come out of the editing trailer to the set. I don't blame you.

Keep up the great work.

> Your fan,
> Ed Chigliak

March 13

Inmate Earl David Bentine
#28449006
Lompoc State Prison
Lompoc, CA 93436

Dear Earl,

Yo, glad to hear you're getting by. It seems to me one thing holds true in the Big House that applies also to life on the Outside: you do it one day at a time.

I want to congratulate you on the program of self-education you say you are pursuing in the joint and to wave off any credit you want to bestow on me. I'm no example to anybody, man. I'm just a soul trying to reconcile the demands of mind and body on this travel through time. Still, I'm glad our correspondence has sparked some nascent curiosity in you.

As for your conundrum, it is familiar to me and has brought many a perplexed evening's discussion at the local cafe. The question is, "If God can do anything, can He make a stone so heavy He can't lift it?" You say, "It can't be answered, it's a Paradox." I agree—for a minute. The next minute I find attractive an alternate answer, one more grounded in time. Namely, yes: He creates it, and He can't lift it. "Shit, man," he says. "That sucker's heavy."

But then a moment passes, and a new situation presents itself. I'm not here invoking the so-called Copenhagen Interpretation of quantum reality, which suggests—and I'll get into this in a different letter, it's highly arcane, mind-bending stuff—that an infinite number of universes is constantly being generated every moment by the decay of subatomic particles throughout the universe. I mean that, a minute later, God reconsiders. He says "Hey, hold on. I'm *God,* God damn it." And He goes on to lift the stone with one Hand. The left one. Because, as my Catholic friends used to joke, "Jesus was crucified and went to Heaven, where he sits on the right hand of God." Ouch!

Does that resolve the paradox? You tell me. I look forward to your next letter. Meanwhile, take it easy. Perseverance furthers.

Yours,
Chris Stevens

. . . .

MARCH 13

Internal Revenue Service
Anchorage, AK

Gentlemen:

I am in receipt of your letter to me of February 25, in which you request information with regard to what I've paid my employees in salary and benefits over the past twenty-three years. I would love to give you this information, but I simply do not know. People who've worked here have come and gone, and some have come back again and then gone again. I suppose I've paid these various individuals four or five dollars an hour, but probably in the early days it was much less, considering that a dollar bought a lot more back then.

Currently I employ three people. One is Dave, the cook, who I pay seven dollars an hour. As for benefits, he can have all his meals free. I have also hired Ed Chigliak at that same rate with those same benefits. I have a classified ad out for another cook, as we are now open twenty-four hours a day.

My other employee is Shelly Tambo, but as she and I are cohabiting on a personal basis, I don't really pay her. I just give her money.

I hope this answers your question.

Yours truly,
Holling Vincouer
Prop., The Brick

. . . .

14 March

Mr. Chuck Williams
℅ Williams-Sonoma
P.O. Box 7456
San Francisco, CA 94120

Dear Mr. Williams:

I have been a satisfied customer of your catalogue cookware operation since I moved out here to Alaska in 1972. It didn't take a genius to perceive that the availability of quality cookery items and ingredients in a state with a total population smaller than that of San Francisco was less than nil, and many is the time I have thanked whatever deity is out there for your excellent wares and crackerjack service. I say all this, quite frankly, by way of buttering you up—I use the term advisedly—in preparation for what I concede is an audacious request.

I am about to ask you to send me an appreciable amount of cookware and ingredients for free.

Before you scoff or consign this to the circular file, hear me out. Due to circumstances that quite frankly you would not believe, I find myself with a surplus of time on my hands. Now, as an amateur chef, I have always fantasized, as I am sure many have, of conducting a cooking class. Nothing fancy, nothing elaborate—just some basic lessons to instill in others an appreciation for the fundamentals of real cooking. Blame it on an innate tribal desire to pass on skills and expertise to others, blame it on ego—hell, blame it on the bossa nova: all I know is, it's something I've wanted to do for a long time.

I now find I have the opportunity. I have what I assume will prove to be a willing customer base, consisting of a handful of curious people whose time weighs heavily on their hands. But I need the equipment: pots, pans, utensils, and so on, as specified on the attached list.

I am asking you to donate these items, not because this is a nonprofit operation or a benefit for charity—it's neither—but because it's good business. These people, once they learn that it takes exactly as much effort to put a real chicken in the oven as it takes to put a godawful frozen dinner in the microwave, will be ready to cook. And they'll need equipment for their homes. And they will be unable to buy the stuff in stores out here.

Which means that they will be sitting ducks for endorsement of your products. Send me a carton of catalogues and I'll hand them out like Halloween candy. With every class that graduates from my course, you will be gaining six, eight, ten customers for life. Hell, the first class alone should buy enough Grande Cuisine starter sets and Silverstone muffin tins and Barbier Dauphin Tomato Paste to pay back your initial investment. The rest—if you'll pardon the expression—is gravy.

I know arrangements must be made with regard to delivery and shipping and so forth. Please call or write me at the attached address. Meanwhile, if you should ever desire to see what real natural beauty is, it would be my honor to have you as my guest up here in beautiful Cicely, on the breathtaking Alaskan Riviera. Feel free to call at any time.

Yours truly,
Maurice Minnifield

. . . .

3/14

Steven Cohen, Attorney
Pittsburgh, USA

Dear Steve,

Nice letter, but are you kidding? "Who do I like for President"? I like Seve Ballesteros. He's handsome, he's suave, he has a sense of humor, he's Spanish, and he's a great golfer. Who I'll get is another matter.

Is that "immature"? Sue me. Up here, in wacky Alaska, I'm discovering parts of myself I forgot even existed. Remember back in 7th grade, when you "decided" what your "personality" would be? The chickens come home to roost up here—only they've turned into eagles and owls.

You realize there are aspects of yourself you had forgotten about or decided were less important than being cool, or hip, or attractive, or, you know, *acceptable* to your peer group. And they start to reassert themselves. Because why stifle them? Up here it's very hard for anyone to find a convincing, credible peer group. Everyone's too focused on being themselves to be anyone else's peer. Is this a good thing? Yeah, I think it's probably a good thing. Unless the self you're busy being is totally insane.

Which brings me to what happened last month, when I went shopping in Anchorage.

I decide to take a few days off. It's early February, when life was still normal. And it's prime time winter; the only thing I can compare it to is summer on Pluto. So for a change of pace I decide to go into Anchorage—pig out at a real restaurant, get some clothes and some books and CDs. Because I'm pampering myself. That's what you want to do in Alaska during the winter, when you feel like you're *really doing very well* if you just get out of bed.

Plus, in this dark and gloom and general foggy cruddy murk, you start to feel . . . sad. Depressed. Sorry for yourself, and sick of life. Because ask yourself: Where did human life begin? AFRICA! Where it's warm and humid and green, and people don't eat mooses. So on the very evolutionary level we're way off course up here.

Being Jewish, of course, I'm going to pamper myself with a nice dinner (i.e., food), and then buy some entertainment to bring back home (culture). You have to fly to Anchorage to maximize your time. The local air taxi pilot (I told you about her. Maggie O'Connell? From Grosse Pointe? Cute, touchy, neurotic—don't get me started) says she can't fly me to the city itself, but she can drop me off at the airstrip in a town called Good Mule. I say okay. She does, and I do indeed fly into Anchorage on one of the few intrastate airlines. (Of course, since the state is as big as one-fifth of the entire continental US, "intrastate" can mean flights longer than from NY to Chicago.)

I cab into the city, grab some new clothes, nice pamper-y lunch, some paperbacks, and the pièce de résistance, a spree in a record store. Not that "records" exist any more, but you know what I mean. Now, on my limited income, a single CD is a major purchase, but I've given myself permission to buy three. Which comes to, you know—with tax, forty bucks. I browse, I dither, I pick up and put down, I beg for permission to buy four or five and I sternly refuse. Finally I have my three, and I go to the cash register.

The guy there looks like he was dragged from a medieval dungeon and told to work the register. Totally emaciated, gaunt, stringy hair, dirty gray sweatshirt—and he's muttering. To himself. "Goddamn Elliot. Tell *me* how to do it . . . Goddamn son of a bitch . . ." And so on. I, naturally, am unfazed. I get this in

New York on a daily basis. Men in business suits walk down Park Avenue talking like this to themselves. I plunk the disks on the counter and pull out my wallet.

"Goddamn Elliot," the guy says to me. "Look, man, just take the goddamn things, okay, just split, man, I don't care."

"Who's Elliot?" I ask, trying to strike the sympathetic note. "Your boss?"

"Yeah, my boss, man, okay? Just take 'em."

Tempting? You bet. But I'm feeling solid, I've given myself permission to spend the money. I need the full social nourishment of a culturally validated commercial exchange. I WANT to pay.

"Come on," I say. "If Elliot finds out, you'll get fired."

He yells, with maximum insanity: "I DON'T GIVE A DAMN, MAN. JUST TAKE 'EM, OKAY?"

I look around. The place is deserted, so there's nobody to take over for Mr. Nutbar here, nobody to slap him on the back and say, "Hey, Tim, how's about you take your medication and I'll wrap this one up." No, just me and the skinny guy still muttering about Elliot, who suddenly pulls out from under the counter A SEMI-AUTOMATIC HANDGUN, and I see the whole scenario unfolding in grisly slo-mo: he shouts, points, I hold up my hands in feeble protest, and BLAM BLAM BLAM, little Joel is blasted into picturesque smithereens. What would you do? I grabbed the disks and ran.

Five blocks later I pull up, panting, and take stock. Well, I've got the CDs. Maybe I should have left them, but it serves Elliot right, employing psychopaths so he won't have to give them a health plan. And I'm forty bucks to the good. (I TOLD YOU YOU SHOULD HAVE BOUGHT MORE, my greedy self says.) I'm standing in front of a bar; for the hell of it, I go in and talk to the bartender.

"That music store up the street," I say. "What's the owner's name? Elliot something?"

"Susan Hampton," the guy says.

"Who's Elliot? Like a husband, or the manager—?"

41

"Damn if I know. Never heard of any Elliot. Susan's owned it for years."

This is a perfect Alaskan story—the gun, the lunatic, the fact that "Elliot" was probably the name of a beaver the guy saw last year—except for one thing. The story isn't over yet. Not by a long shot. Look for the thrilling conclusion in my next letter.

Not pampered nearly enough,
J.

....

MARCH 15

Dear Aunt Martha,

Happy birthday.

Love,
Marilyn

....

16 MARCH

Dear Tyler,

I am in receipt of your letter and want to thank you for asking me to give you my thoughts on what happens to astronauts after their flight missions cease. It's a good question, and I've had a lot of time to ruminate on it, since my last mission was in 1971.

Since that time I have been involved in numerous commercial enterprises, some in the communications field. In 1974 I purchased the license for an AM radio station, currently broadcasting on a daily basis. In 1975 I began a daily newspaper, currently in weekly publication. I have also invested in several satellite telecommunications ventures, with mixed results. In addition I invested in a rather sizeable parcel of undeveloped virgin wilderness comprising approximately fifteen thousand acres. It is my belief that this land will one day undergo extensive development for industrial, recreational, and residential or tourist-entertainment uses.

42

I was attracted to these ventures by virtue of my experience as an astronaut. While orbiting the Earth I had, as many astronauts do, something of an epiphany. I was moved almost to tears by the great beauty of our planet. But while many astronauts report an impression, upon gazing at planet Earth, of its fragility, I looked down on that radiant blue-white opaline globe and had no sensation of fragility at all. I thought that world looked healthy and thriving and able to take whatever Man could dish out. People who have never seen Earth from space believe that it looks frail, and endangered, and overdeveloped. Well hell, if you'll excuse the expression, I've been there, and I thought it looked not developed *enough*.

There was something in that glimpse of Earth's scale and splendor that shook me to my core. I had found my medium and my calling, which was bigness. And I knew that when I resigned my post at NASA, I could no more settle for a desk job working for some governmental agency, or a glad-handing socializing greeter job for some big corporation, than a lion tamer could settle for selling stuffed toys. I came out of that Mercury capsule determined to do big things in a big way in a big place.

And so I moved to Alaska, because I knew that this was one place I could find a landscape and potential commensurate with my goals and desires. I have been here twenty years now, and I have no reason to amend or alter that conception.

In closing, I want to thank you once again for asking about this, and I hope that you and your fellow second-graders in Mrs. Flimner's class will find it useful.

> *Yours truly,*
> *Maurice Minnifield*

....

Dear Tony,

Many thanks for your letter of the 14th. And you're right, of course: whatever the neurological function of sleep is, we apprehend it via dreams. Physical rest aside, what we get from it is immersion in the unconscious.

So I've altered my strategy. Rather than trying to lull the town asleep—a notable failure—I have decided to bore it into submission. Over the radio—which I now commandeer almost all day and night, stopping only for meals and an occasional beer or two—I read the most excruciatingly tedious documents I can get my hands on: opaque sociological texts, brain-numbing magazine articles, the *Congressional Record*. To keep myself sane I also chant, for minutes at a time, the sacred monosyllable OM, alternating with the "Preliminary Trance Formula" ("You are increasingly relaxed . . . your eyelids are like lead . . .") from a really stupid book on hypnotizing people for fun and profit.

Then, just when I sense the onset of laryngitis, I clam up completely, and subject the town to a marathon festival of New Age trance-music: meandering piano noodles, fairy-tale harp recitals, muted quasi-jazz suitable for dentists' offices. (After twenty minutes of it, like Graham Greene, you *ask* to have your teeth pulled, just to feel alive again.)

Not that any of this works, of course. Not that people don't revile me in public and demand more uplifting musical selections. Not that my boss, a can-do ex-astronaut, doesn't glare at me and administer the occasional tonguelashing. I won't be able to do this much longer.

Meanwhile, thanks for the interest in "Goodnight Moose," a copy of which is attached. Keep those insights coming. I need all the help I can get.

Best,
Chris

GOODNIGHT MOOSE
A BEDTIME POEM FOR INSOMNIAC ALASKANS

In the great big state

There was a little town

44

And a wild white goose
And a big brown moose.

And there were three grizzly bears giving out scares

And two little beavers
And short-wave receivers

And beautiful lakes
And caribou steaks.

And eagles and fishes
And satellite dishes.

And a deejay starting to play "Nighttime's the Right Time"
And the Alyeska Pipeline
And a quiet old lady who was tuning in "Nightline."

Goodnight goose.
Goodnight moose.

Goodnight whites, Indians, Aleuts.

Goodnight Aurora
And Fauna and Flora.

Goodnight deer
And goodnight beer.

Goodnight huskies
And immigrant Russkies.

Goodnight stars
And goodnight bars.

Goodnight deejay
And "Nighttime's the Right Time."
Goodnight nobody
And goodnight pipeline.

And goodnight to the old lady
Turning off "Nightline."

Goodnight permafrost, taiga, tundra
Goodnight biscuits of Gold Medal Wondra.

Goodnight mountains
Goodnight air
Goodnight Alaskans everywhere.

Goodnight oil
Goodnight sea
Goodnight, sleep tight, Cicely.

....

MARCH 17

Dear Jack,

Our letters crossed in the mail, so here I am to answer
yours:

I know I'll have to come down to G.P. soon so we can talk about (sigh) dividing up all the stuff once Mom and Dad sell the house. But can it wait? This whole divorce thing is still too new to me. I'm not yet ready to talk about the *assets*. Surely the house won't sell *that* quickly. If it does, call me and I'll come down.

If it's any time soon, you'll have to scrape me out of the plane. I'd conk out for days (I think) if I left Cicely. So that's another reason to delay—until I get my normal sleep life back.

Meanwhile, nobody even takes a nap around here. It is extremely bizarre, because you go from one thing to the next without that sense of pacing and rhythm you normally get from ending one day and beginning another.

Here's another bizarre turn of events: I'm tending bar! I needed a job. And since I can't fly, and the whole town now hangs out at the local cafe all night as well as all day—which means they need help—your sister is now serving up Moosehead and Prinz Brau and the occasional boilermaker. I like it, actually. Although it has its share of annoyances. Like last night, when Dr. Joel Fleischman (I may have mentioned him. From New York? Comes equipped with a natural superiority *and* unbelievable arrogance?) came in and proceeded to rag me in his "witty" (read: half-witty) way. Sample dialogue:

> JF: So, O'Connell . . . expanding your repertoire of professional skills, I'm impressed.
>
> ME: What'll it be, Fleischman.
>
> JF: So curt, so short, so brusque! I may have to inform Mr. Vincoeur that his help is a quart low on customer relational finesse.
>
> ME: Fleischman, you don't have to bother to impress me with your vocabulary. I already know you got a 714 on your verbal SATs.
>
> JF: Hey, how did you know that? Who told you? Did Elaine tell you?
>
> ME: You did, Fleischman. It was one of the first things you said after we met. And you want to know what my sincere reaction was?

47

JF: What . . .

ME: How refreshing. To see such a good vocabulary in the possession of such a jerk. And you'll be happy to know that in the two years you've been here, I have seen no reason to revise that assessment. You do have a good vocabulary. And you are a jerk.

JF: Oh yeah? And what did you get, O'Connell?

ME: 632.

JF: I rest my case.

ME: So do I. What'll it be.

JF: Beer.

And so on. Of course this is all very amusing, for now. But if it persists, and I really can't fly, I don't know what the hell I'm going to do. One answer would be, move out of Cicely to where things are normal. Which I guess is what's called for if I want to keep flying. If I choose to stay, I'd have to take up some indoor profession. The good news is, I'll have twice the normal workday to get up to speed in it, right? For now, I'm using that time writing letters. It's supposed to be therapeutic.

Don't tell the folks. That's all I need.

Love,
Mags

. . . .

March 17

Dr. Michael Robertson
Wilson Institute of Neurological Studies
Philadelphia, PA

Dear Dr. Robertson:

I obtained your name from Dr. Howard Bateman, a classmate of mine from Columbia Medical whose father, apparently, is your uncle's golf buddy. So far it sounds like a conspiracy theory, but from such labyrinthine connections is history forged. By the way, when, during our phone conversation, Howard told me that you were one of the most eminent neuropsychologists around, I was in a position to personally confirm that assessment, having read several of your papers in *JAMA*.

By now Howard will have briefed you on the situation out here, so I won't recapitulate the background. Suffice to say, it's still going on. Cicely's epic all-nighter is now seventeen days long and counting. During this time a steady stream, at times resembling the mighty Mississippi, of patients has flowed through what we all laughingly call my "office," evincing all kinds of problems—especially stabbing. Stabbing is big here—but not much pathology. Unless you call cabin fever, exacerbated by nonstop awakeness, a disease. Stress, yes. But where's the fatigue? Where's the exhaustion?

This phenomenon must be studied. And I am in the perfect position to do so. Howard told you of my credentials, so let me only add that I have been privileged to be Cicely's resident physician for two years and have an excellent working relationship with the patient population. All I lack is a control; no one in town seems unaffected, but then, I have not made a careful search. (Did I mention, by the way, that this has affected me, too?)

I am prepared to launch a systematic study of this unusual phenomenon. But I require two things. One is a grant or fellowship to pay for materials and personnel. (I have at present one assistant, who is rapidly becoming overwhelmed by the work load. I have contemplated hiring another, but lack the funds to do so.) The other is the explicit sponsorship of an established authority, whose imprimatur would lend credibility to a situation that is, let me assure you, utterly incredible.

That's why I'm writing to you, Dr. Robertson. The implications of what is happening in Cicely are staggering. This situation demands the fullest possible scientific scrutiny. But that in turn requires money and support.

May I look to you for either or both? In either case, you would have my undying gratitude.

Yours truly,
Joel Fleischman, M.D.

....

KNOWLEDGE IS POWER AND
BOOKS ARE ITS CURRENCY

Dear Friend,

This Letter has been around the world nine times. It is not about Money or Religious Subjects. It is about Knowledge, which is the only way to Peace and Self-Knowing. This Letter was started by Prof. Fleynn Stodterflygnniak of Finland in 1985. Since then it has been in many countries, and all who have taken part in it have benefitted.

To promote Knowledge and increase Understanding both of oneself and the World, send a book of any kind to the first name on the list. Do not send pornographic material. Then strike the first name and add your name and address to the bottom of the list. Then send a copy of the Letter to seven friends.

THE LETTER WORKS. DO WHAT THE LETTER SAYS. YOU WILL RECEIVE MANY BOOKS IN A FEW WEEKS. DO NOT BREAK THE CHAIN.

Please note that Pedro Arganaraz in Uruguay broke

the chain, and several days later he died. Mirelle Chandon in Marseilles threw the Letter away and had terrible luck. Then she retrieved it. She sent it out as instructed and three weeks later received many fascinating and worthwhile volumes.

OTHERS ARE DEPENDING ON YOU. DO NOT BREAK THE CHAIN.

....

MARCH 18

Dear Tawni,

I got this today. Cyndy sent it—she's married to Wayne, who moves his lips when he reads hockey scores, so the books are definitely for her. I know these things are silly, but my cousin once did one, sent out ten dollars, and got forty dollars back a few weeks later. I think it's illegal, but what the heck.

Anyway, this one is for books, which I think is legal. And it's funny, because now that I have all this free time, I decided to read more. But the only local library we have is Ruth-Anne's general store. When I asked Ruth-Anne for something to read, she looked very sad, shook her head, and said, "Shelly, all I have left is this copy of Henry Kissinger's memoirs. Either that or the *World Almanac* from 1977." I took the almanac, big surprise.

It turns out that this no-sleep thing has made a lot of people want to read, so all her stock is gone. (She's out of light bulbs, too!)

So I'm stuck with this almanac. Which I would send, but I want to finish it. I told Holling I wanted to enter this chain letter, but didn't have anything to send. He dug around in the back room and came up with something. I know the letter says, send any book you want as long as it isn't pornographic, but do you think it'll be okay if we send the "Instructions for Use" booklet from one of the blenders?

Anyway, here's the letter. I'll understand if you toss it. I showed this to our local doctor and he totally laughed in my face!!

51

"Come on, Shelly," he said. "You don't actually believe those things work, do you?" When I told him about my cousin, he said, "What happened to him was a fluke. The secret of these things is that they depend on a constant, geometric expansion of the base population. This has what, seven names?" He started scribbling some numbers on a napkin. "Seven to the . . . twelfth, thirteenth . . ." Then he laughed and waved the napkin at me. Like I'm supposed to be able to read math! "Shelly, if everyone did this, and sent a book, and sent out seven copies to friends, if would only take twelve or thirteen rounds of this to exhaust the entire population."

"Of Alaska?" I said.

"Alaska? Of the world! Of planet Earth!"

I felt my eyes open wide. "Wouldn't that be great!?"

"Great shmate! It would be impossible! You're sending out an item of value with very little chance of getting anything in return! It's a sucker bet!"

Well, that's his opinion. Plus it's easy for him to talk. He has all these medical textbooks to read. What about the rest of us? So hey, send someone a book (it can be one you've read already) and who knows? Maybe you'll get something nice back.

Love,
Shelly

. . . .

MARCH 18

Mr. Benton T. Culpepper, Esq.
1455 Ninth Ave. Suite 3A
Anchorage, AK

Dear Mr. Culpepper, Esq.:

I have received your letter to me dated March 14 of this year, but frankly I do not know what to make of it. You say you represent Mr. Arthur B. Marone, who was in my restaurant The Brick on or about February 27. And apparently Mr. Marone was poorly treated by my staff, resulting in "grievous physical and psychological/emotional harm to Mr. Marone with the upshot that he is unable to perform his customary professional duties, resulting in a severe abridgment of his being able to earn a living." Then you say Mr. Marone is suing me for damages.

I have to tell you, Mr. Culpepper, that I have no memory of who Mr. Marone is or what if anything happened to him. We get lots of customers at the Brick, and many of them leave in a condition in which they are unable to perform their customary professional duties or earn a living. But the next day they sober up, and that's that.

If you can provide anything to jog my memory, that might help me to recollect this incident. Otherwise, I think you and Mr. Marone may be suing the wrong establishment.

Thank you very much.

Yours truly,
Holling Vincouer

. . . .

18 March

Panhandle Provisions
2399 Gastineau Ave.
Juneau, AK

Gentlemen:

Attached please find a preliminary list of items I would like shipped Federal Express to the address below. The idea is that I am inaugurating a cooking class for which I have thus far enrolled twenty-seven people. If you knew the nature of my customer base here in Cicely—I mean in terms of its limited size as well as its even-more-limited sophistication—you would be as thunderstruck as I am. I mention this because if this gratifying enthusiasm keeps up, I will want to discuss with you the possibility of quantity discounts. Several specific notes:

1) The olive oil should not be Extra Virgin, but should be Italian and not Spanish. My goal is to help these people form good habits without becoming unnecessarily obsessive.

2) If you can't provide the shallots in the quantity called for, for God's sake tell me. Don't string me along.

3) Parsley should be broadleaf Italian. Curly is most decidedly a fallback option.

4) Corn starch may be freely substituted for arrowroot.

5) Stale cinnamon, rancid almonds, dried-up garlic, soft potatoes, slimy onions, and droopy celery will be returned immediately for credit. I may not be the chef of the Baranof Hotel, but I assure you I know the difference between a springform pan and a Maidenform bra.

Thank you, and I know you join me in looking forward to a mutually profitable long-term relationship.

Yours truly,
Maurice Minnifield

. . . .

MARCH 18

Dear Peggy,

CONGRATULATIONS! It's about time. Everyone knew you and Phil were 2-gether 4-ever, so how come it took you guys six years to set a date? But never mind, I withdraw the question. (With my track record, I have no right to ask such a thing.) Instead it might be better to say, at this late date, why bother? But wait. Don't tell me. I forgot—you want k.i.d.s. (FYI: So do I, but no, there isn't anyone at the moment.) So great, I'm really happy for you.

Although I hate you, too—you're moving on in life, reaching major plateaus (plateaux?), and I'm spinning my wheels. But don't listen to me. I just feel bad because I haven't flown in more than two weeks. It's like swimming: do it regularly, and when you cut it off cold turkey you feel creaky and cranky. As to why I haven't flown, call it atmospheric anomalies.

So to make ends meet I've taken on a series of part-time jobs. Sometimes I tend bar. Sometimes I work in a general store. Sometimes I TALK ON A RADIO SHOW AND PLAY MUSIC. None of which feels right in that work-related way, but it's a stopgap, so what the hell. Actually I feel unanchored and brittle. I MISS MY PLANE!

I've marked the wedding day on my calendar and I can't wait to see you both. Give my best to Phil. And the hell with six years of cohabitation—WEAR WHITE!

Love,
Maggie

PS—Of course, since you two HAVE been living together for that long, instead of shacking up with your boring old new husband on your wedding night, let's have a slumber party like we used to! We can do it all: have pillow fights, scarf Mallomars, play CS&N (&Y!!) records, play What Is Your Wish?, and generally stay up all night. (I'm getting very good at that.) Okay, I'll tell you what: Phil can join us. Deal? M.

Steven Cohen, Atty. at Esq.
Pitt., PA

Dear Steve—

Man, it's cold. I mean I know that it can get cold in NY, and
I know how the buildings in Manhattan can channel the wind
into gale-force tempests that increase the chill factor by whatever
it is—but this is Alaska, pal, and it is FRIGID. It almost makes
me wish I smoked.

I remember going to Jets games with my father on freezing
Sundays, and we'd be sitting there—not running around playing
football, remember, just sitting there, which is *the coldest thing
you can do*—and Dad would light up one of his El Productos.
I'd stare at the flame from the lighter and the glowing tip and
ask him, "Dad, does smoking make you warmer?" Because it
had to, right? You're wielding naked fire, you're taking into your
body the product of this blatant act of combustion—and he'd
say, "No." Every time. I never really believed him.

Anyway, back to my shopping story. Which I am delighted to
recount, not the least reason for which being I have some time
on my hands these days, and you know me: I love to hear myself
write. So: Remember the maniac, the grumbling about "Elliot,"
the hand gun, the me running for my life with three new CDs?
With their Estimated Cash Value of forty bucks?

I'm in Anchorage, and it's time to fly back to Good Mule,
where O'Connell is supposed to pick me up. But one of the
things about the Alaskan winter is, snow isn't the only story.
There's ice fog, which descends like a gigantic wad of (freezing)
sterile cotton. So when I board the plane and hear some passengers and crew muttering about "the fog," I start to suspect the
worst. Said suspicions are promptly confirmed when we are told
that Good Mule is fogged in, and there's no way to land.
Remember, too, that these intrastate flights are like IRT locals—
they stop everywhere, half the flight time is spent landing and

taxiing and taking off. So what can we do? We have to go on to the next destination.

A drag, but not a fatal drag, I assume. I'll have to call O'Connell, tell her to skip this flight, and I'll call her from the next town when I know when my return flight can get through. Naive? Check it out:

Next stop, Yakutat. Small town with an air strip that is utterly fogged in, forget it, no can do. We keep flying to—

Haines. Medium-sized town. Principle attractions: Indian arts and crafts, bald eagle preserve. Plus the name makes you think of underwear. All this, except for the thinking about underwear, will be denied me, because the fog is impenetrable, worse than ever. We keep flying to—

Juneau, the capital. Big area, the second largest city in the— get this—*world*. Not, of course, that I could tell—the airport is closed, the town is closed, the world is closed. What can we do? You got it: we can fly out of the state altogether and seek sanctuary in fabulous—

SEATTLE. Which is a very nice city, actually. True, Joel did not intend to visit Seattle on this trip and did not have even his shaving kit with which to provide the most basic forms of personal hygiene and grooming . . . but fine. I'll do Seattle, stay in a hotel overnight, live it up. Hey, I'll spend the extra $40 and— yes—I'll pamper myself! In a city where the burgers are beef and not caribou! Will this be luxurious or what?

Sadly, the answer is, "what," since Seattle is entirely, completely fogged in. Nobody comes in or goes out. We're still flying, and by now the question of fuel becomes, if only passingly, of theoretical interest. Or so I assume. What are we going to do, refuel in midair like a B-52?

"Got a little bit of ground condition downstairs," the captain says in that I'm-so-competent-I'm-bored way they have. "Let's see if we can't set her down in Portland."

Oregon, at least; not Maine. Or at least not yet. We fly on. Everything in the kitchen and the bar has been consumed; the guy next to me has set up his six little empty Smirnoff bottles like bowling pins. Everybody greets every new failed attempt to land with hearty good-natured laughter . . . I want to say to these people, "Anybody ever hear of gravity?" We cannot keep doing this indefinitely.

Twenty minutes later we're over Portland. Did you know that it rains a million days out of the year there? The rep on Portland is very lush, you can grow anything, but of course, the rain, the humidity, you see . . . Anyway, what with the present combination of cold, humidity, winter—Portland is closed.

We finally landed, three hours after taking off, in Las Vegas, Nevada.

So, savor the flavor: I set out that morning to go shopping for a day in Anchorage, I'm assuming I'll be back in Cicely in time to have a nightcap at the Brick which closes at midnight, and I'm in *the Nevada desert*. And all my fellow passengers, and the crew, chuckle warmly at this, as though it's just another amusing, lovable quirk of the wacky, bracing Alaskan lifestyle! So I've got my soft travel bag, stuffed with my new clothes, my new books, my new CDs; I'm wearing layers up the wazoo, Thinsulate this and Goretex that, wool sweater and flannel shirt, PLUS my L.L. Bean Arctic Hell-style goose-down/seal-skin/moose-hide/fur-lined Ice Station Zebra autograph model parka . . . and I'm going to do Vegas?

I go to the general info desk and discover that the next flight back—to Juneau—is tomorrow morning. Well, okay, it has to be a long time anyway, so the fog can lift. Am I going to grab a cab into town? I can't bring myself to do it. What for? To wander through Circus-Circus like a zombie and watch grandmothers in Day-Glo jumpsuits shove coins into slot machines? I mean, yeah, I've been known to put down a few sports bets, play a few hands of poker . . . but not tonight. I'm not in the mood. And in Las Vegas, you'd better be there either for a convention or to gamble. So I decide to sit it out. I'll read. I'll eat dinner. I'll make a few phone calls, even. And I do that and look up, and it's only 10:20 PM. Now what?

In the lobby of the airport there are slot machines. So, strictly for recreational purposes, I break a ten into quarters and put one in. One. The wheels turn around, I get two cherries—four quarters back! I'm hot! So I put another one in and lose. But the feeling of winning is still fresh, I'm still vibrating from it, so I put another quarter in, pull the handle. And lose. So now it's a challenge, right? I have to prove to the gods that not everything about this return trip is destined to be bad.

I forgot that you can't "prove" anything to the gods. They're the gods. You're the putz.

I stood at that slot machine and systematically gave it money, quarter after quarter, like I was hand-feeding a sick animal. And of course in the midst of this I look to my left and see, yes, a grandmother in a Day-Glo jumpsuit with a plastic cup from Burger King full of coins feeding her machine and pulling the handle and saying, "Oh darn" every time she lost. Which was every time.

This went on, of course, until I had not only lost my entire forty dollar savings from the record store—oh darn—but ten more as well. Fifty bucks—for what? Frustration, tedium, and that dirty feeling you get when you hang around public places too long? GODDAMN ELLIOT! I finally gave up at about 1:30 in the morning. I took a nap on the seats, which would have been a prescription for disaster and an invitation to a mugging, except that all the other passengers from my flight were there, and believe me, nobody from Las Vegas was going to mess with our group of deadpan, weather-worn Alaskans, all of whom were tired by now and had long ago established a secondary support beachhead in the cocktail lounge, and who generally looked like Night of the Living Dead costumed by L. L. Bean.

The next morning we flew back. O'Connell met me at Good Mule, exuding her customary charm ("My god, Fleischman, you look awful"). Still, it wasn't entirely unpleasant to see her. She flew me back to Cicely and we landed without incident.

Get it? On one end, free CDs. On the other, weather so bad you have to fly to Las Vegas and lose all your money before you can come back. Alaska giveth with one hand and taketh with the other and slappeth you around with the other.

But forget all that. What's with the Knicks?

Joel

Mr. Benton T. Culpepper, Esq.
1455 Ninth Ave. Suite 3A
Anchorage, AK

Dear Mr. Culpepper, Esq.:

Thank you for your letter of March 20. It was useful in reminding me and my associate, Miss Shelly Tambo, about your client, Mr. Arthur Marone, and the so-called incident in which he suffered physical and psychological damage. As I recall it, he entered The Brick in a bad mood. Surly and argumentative. Maybe that is his customary nature—I wouldn't know. I do know, since Shelly waited on him and she reminded me, that he proceeded to order a hot chocolate. She brought him the hot chocolate, and he proceeded to taste it and then claim that it wasn't hot enough, wasn't sweet enough, and wasn't chocolatey enough. She apologized and took it back. Then she made another cup, which she presented to him, and he had the same complaint.

Shelly then told Mr. Marone that that was the mix that we used, but she could doctor it up for him. He

THIS IS SHELLY TAMBO TYPING TO YOU ON HOLLING'S TYPEWRITER. THAT ARTHUR MARONE GUY IS AN OBNOXIOUS CREEP. I HAVE SERVED HOT CHOCOALTE TO PEOPLE LIKE A MILLION TIMES AND EVERYONE THINKS ITS GREAT. ITS SWISS! THEY KNOW HOT CHOCOALTE!

SO THIS GUY SAYS ITS NO GOOD. I SAY FINE. I TAKE IT BACK, AND ADD HERSHEY'S SYRUP TO IT, I MEAN, WHAT MORE DO YOU WANT!!! PLUS I HEAT IT UP UNTIL IT IS *BOILING*, OKAY? YOU CAN'T GET ANY HOTTER THAN BOILING.

I TAKE IT TO HIM, AND HE IS JUST SITTING THERE, LOOKING SOUR AND READY FOR A FIGHT. I GIVE IT TO HIM, AND HE TASTES IT, AND MAKES THIS TOTALLY OBNOXIOUS FACE, AND SAYS ITS NO GOOD. I SAY LOOK. MAYBE YOU JUST AREN'T IN

THE MOOD FOR HOT CHOCOALTE? HOW ABOUT A CUP OF TEA? HE SAYS NO, I WANT HOT CHOCOALTE

Please excuse Miss Tambo, but you have to understand, she herself was very upset by this incident, not only because Mr. Marone was criticizing her ability to make hot chocolate, but at the time we were extremely busy on account of a busload of French journalists had stopped in Cicely and everyone was ordering lunch in F

SO I SAY OK. I TAKE IT BACK, AND JUST AS I'M ABOUT TO TAKE IT BACK TO DO GOD KNOWS WHAT ELSE TO IT, HE SUDDENLY STANDS UP! AND GUESS WHAT HAPPENS? HE HITS MY TRAY AND THE HOT CHOCOALTE SPILLS ALL OVER HIM! BECAUSE I MEAN WHAT DID HE EXPECT?! AND HE STARTS YELLING OH MY GOD, I'M BEING BURNED, I'M DISFIGURED, I'M SUFFERING THIRD DEGREE BURNS ON MY EPIDERMISS!

LISTEN. HE STOOD UP ON PURPOSE. YOURS TRULY, SHELLY TAMBO. PERIOD.

In any case, that is our recollection of the incident. We gave him a damp towel to clean up with, and I offered to pay his dry cleaning bill. Otherwise, as Mr. Marone had no apparent difficulty getting back to his car and driving away, I assumed he was fine. So you can see it was a common accident and no cause for a lawsuit.

Yours truly,
Holling Vincouer

....

MARCH 24

Dear Phyl,

First, yes. I agree absolutely. Starch the avocado, make all the sweatshirts butterscotch, and tell Raoul to sing "April in Paris" or you'll revoke his hair.

Now: The New York doctor? The Right Obnoxious Doctor Joel Fleischman? Well, he has a regular nurse, but his office has been mobbed for three weeks, and I knew she needed help. And since, you know, I wasn't flying . . .

Anyway, that distant yappy barking you heard, down in L.A., around 10:30 AM today? That was the sound of one Fleischman laughing. I will NEVER EVER again take the initiative to do something nice for that *child.* Here's what I'm talking about:

I stuck my head into his office at ten-thirty this morning and, as usual, he was on his guard. "What do you want, O'Connell?" he said with typical charm. "I'm inordinately busy, plus I'm dying to get home because I'm expecting an important letter today from a very prestigious neurologist from Philadelphia."

He wanted to provoke me, and, naturally, he succeeded. "Fleischman," I said in my best patient-teacher-to-immature-student tone, "I am terribly impressed that you have a neurologist for a pen pal, although I don't recall asking about it. I just came with a suggestion."

"Oh, dandy. A suggestion. Just put it in the box. I encourage all my patients to tell me how to do my job." He threw his pen down. "What is this, the shop floor of an Oldsmobile plant? What kind of suggestion? No, let me guess—inaugurate a series of labor-management volleyball games."

"It's Marilyn. She's overworked."

"And I assume you have the proper OSHA forms for me to fill out?"

"Fleischman, I came in here to help you—"

"I don't need your help, O'Connell." He began to get agitated. "What I need is an explanation for why none of us have had to change our bed linen for three weeks. What I need is a partner who can handle this patient load while I go do something recreational. What I *need* is some decent food and a tv that gets the Knicks so I can have a bit of escape during the few hours I'm not being called upon to remove splinters or mediate domestic disputes. And what I really need is another receptionist, so Marilyn can take a break and go home and spend some time with her Aunt Sylvia who, for some unfathomable reason, has decided that now was a good time to move into chez Whirlwind."

"I know. That's why I'm here. For Marilyn."

He shook his head, took his glasses off, rubbed his eyes. "What—I don't get it. You're here—?"

"To help Marilyn. To be your—" And I had to stop, and look away, and stall, and shrug. "—second receptionist."

Silence. He scratched his head. "You? I mean, I know you can't fly, and we're all suffering from some latent form of schizophrenia that I'm sure we're going to pay for later, but . . . you work . . . for ME?"

I started to leave. "You're right. It's absurd. Never mind."

"No, no . . . wait." He looked pensive, nodded—you know how men will milk a situation when they are "amused"? and just do it to death? that sort of thing—and said, as though granting me a favor, "No, O'Connell, I have to admit, the idea has some merit. You're intelligent . . . presentable . . . responsible . . . Of course, you realize you will have to make a sincere effort to mitigate some of the more off-putting, not to say, *obnoxious* aspects of your personality . . ."

I had had enough. I leaned over the desk toward him, "Fleischman," I said, "Ruth-Anne needs help at the store. Holling wants me to run the day shift. Beryl even asked if I could run the laundromat all night. Everyone needs extra help. I will have no trouble getting work, I assure you. So bear in mind that you're not doing me a favor. And unless you treat my offer with the respect it deserves, I will start to feel that I am doing *you* a favor. Then I will decide not to do it."

Again silence. And what's so infuriating about him is that he knows damn well I'm right. Of course he relented. He always does in the end. Which is what makes every new display of attitude so tedious and such a waste of time. "Okay, O'Connell. You're right. I'm just tired. Not sleepy, no, that would be too much to ask. But tired. So no offense intended. The job is yours if you want it. Argue with Maurice over salary and benefits."

"I'll take it."

I held my hand out. He blinked, looking like a myopic squirrel, and shook it. At least his handshake was firm.

Hey, it's a living.

More later,
Maggie

....

MARCH 24

Mr. Benton T. Culpepper, Esq.
1455 Ninth Ave. Suite 3A
Anchorage, AK

Dear Mr. Culpepper, Esq.:

I am in receipt of your letter of March 24, in which you offer to drop the suit and to "settle" for a sum of ten thousand dollars. Frankly I do not know what to say. It's true that getting hot chocolate spilled on you can be a bad experience. I am not eager to hire my own lawyer and meet Mr. Marone in court, but $10,000 is a lot of money. At least it is to me. I'm afraid you will have to give me some time to think about this.

Yours truly,
Holling Vincouer

....

24 MARCH

My Dear Selena,

I hope your Austin address is still current and that you won't mind this intrusion into your happy domestic life. But it occurred to me that in a few hours I will be up to my elbows in gnocchi, and naturally my thoughts turned to you. To you and to the brief time we spent together those many years ago. And so, since letter-writing has lately become a regular activity not only with me but my entire community, I succumbed to the impulse to take computer in hand.

Now we have been in haphazard touch over the years, and I have come to look forward to your annual Christmas card and to the unusual or exotic recipe you invariably include with it. So I'm going to take that fact as proof that a longer and more personal letter from me will not be unwelcome in your home.

That the inspiration behind all this is gnocchi will not surprise you. It was you who taught me to cook and more importantly to appreciate good food. Until I met you, I was a gastronomic cretin, a cave man for whom the freeze-dried ice cream and stew-in-a-tube they gave us on space missions could have served as acceptable daily fare. I got steak-and-eggs before a mission and considered it gourmet cuisine.

But you changed all that. When that LTV p.r. gal told me I had a one o'clock interview with a feature writer from the Sugar Land Courier, I was ready to sneak out the service entrance and head for the nearest saloon. But Ling Temco Vaught was paying for my services, paying for the hotel and expenses, and I knew the space program needed all the good publicity it could get. So I ordered my lunch just before you showed up, in your crisp white blouse and neat blue skirt . . .

And you were what? Barely twenty-five? It helped that you were slim and trim and pleasant to look at, because frankly, Lena, your questions were yawners that had mold on them from a year previous. Then my lunch arrived, and the smart-alecky waiter wheeled it in and took off the big silver dome, and I asked your permission to eat. Which you gave, of course. So there I was, tucking in to this well-appointed meal on its fancy wheeled cart, with this pretty news gal peppering me with cliches. But I noticed your eyes straying more and more to the platter, until you sat back and pointed.

"Please excuse my asking," you said. "But what do they call that?"

"That, little lady, is a seafood salad," I said, every inch a pompous patronizing fool.

"Do you mind if I taste it?" you asked. Today, of course, I understand how a person fond of cooking may not want to eat anything, but he (or she) wants to taste *everything*. It's a matter of detached scientific curiosity. But at the time I didn't know that; I thought you were hungry. And this was annoying, no two ways about it. But I was so flabbergasted and exhilerated by your audacity—some could call it downright bad manners—that I handed you the teaspoon and said go ahead. You did and shook your head and bit your lower lip in a sign of deep disappointment.

Then you won my heart.

"Major Minnifield, you risk life and limb in a tin can to bring our nation glory and extend the boundaries of human knowledge," you said. "And this supposedly deluxe hotel in big cosmopolitan Houston can't do better than that for its seafood salad? And us so near the Gulf with these fine shrimp, too. That is a scandal. May I?"

You gestured to the food, and for all I knew your may-I referred to sending it back or chucking it out the window. But before I could say anything you took the parsley (which I had always disregarded as a food or an herb, thought of it as being sheer decoration, like a ribbon on a birthday present), tore it up with your well-manicured fingers, sprinkled it on the dish in question, then stuck your fingers in my iced tea—incredible!—and scooped up the lemon. Squeezed same over the salad, plucked up the tiny crystal salt and pepper shakers, and proceeded to apply them in a rapid fusillade of prestigitation like a stage magician, a flurry that made your bracelets jingle and your carefully lipsticked mouth tighten up in concentration.

I tell you what I should have done. I should have fallen down on my knees then and there and begged you to marry me. But instead I got huffy. "Now hold on, sweetheart, this is just fine the way it is—"

"Major, I think you'll like that better," you said. And held out a forkful and hand-fed me like a baby.

Well, it was bliss. Of course, I realize today that you put parsley and lemon juice on a rusty cam shaft and it'll come out palatable. But to the 37-year-old Maurice Minnifield, this was music of a divine order. That inert, undistinguished aggolomeration of scallops and shrimp and celery suddenly became a chamber concerto of brightness, transparency, and flavorful harmonics.

Do you recall who said what next? I do. I looked at you with new eyes and said, "Pardon my asking. But are you married?"

And you said, "Not at the moment."

That is how the six most satisfying, not to mention delicious, months of my life began. But much as I'd like to dwell on it further, I see I have work to do. My students will be here soon, and I intend to pass the torch to them.

My regards to your husband. Tell him I remember anew what a lucky man he is.

All my love,
Maurice

....

MARCH 25

Mr. Arthur B. Marone
338 McKinley St.
Anchorage, AK

Dear Mr. Marone,

I hope you don't mind, but I took the liberty of looking your name up in the Anchorage phone book. Since you are the only Arthur B. Marone listed, I assume you are the same man who had the hot chocolate experience at my restaurant, The Brick, in Cicely, last month and who is thinking of suing me. Now I know it's probably unwise or illegal or unethical for me to write directly to you, but frankly I am nearing the end of my rope. What I want to do is to ask you to drop the lawsuit.

I know you ordered a hot chocolate and were dissatisfied with it. All I can say is, I'm sorry. I also know that somehow you got hot chocolate spilled on your suit and on your epidermis. Once again, all I can do is offer you my heartfelt apology. I can also add the apology of Miss Shelly Tambo, the young lady who waited on you.

Is it really necessary to sue? Can't we talk about this on the phone like two men of good faith? My number is 555-2910. Please call me collect at any time of the day or night, and let's discuss this.

Thank you very much.

Yours truly,
Holling Vincouer

. . . .

MARCH 26

Dear Phyl,

It's too soon for me to have received anything you've written in response to my previous letter—the one in which I applied, in the face of almost overwhelming obnoxiousness, to work as Dr. Joel Fleischman's alternate receptionist—but things have developed in a rather interesting way, so I thought I'd keep you informed.

I started work today on the 5-to-midnight shift. Fleischman gave me a cursory tour of the filing system. At least he started to, but half a minute into it we both gave up. It turns out that Marilyn has organized files, patient data, etc. in a completely baffling way, with little Indian symbols on the folders only she can read. Oh well.

So I man the desk for the steady stream of customers. I know that after a moment's reflection you'll be wondering, "How many patients can a doctor in a small—microscopic, really—town have at midnight?" It's a long story. Just accept the fact that nobody sleeps in this town—literally—so nights and days are indistinguishable except for the absence or presence of daylight.

I admit the first patient, a big beefy logger with a beer belly out to here. And, dutifully, I follow him into the doctor's office. Because isn't that what I'm supposed to do? Hover crisply and assist "Doctor"?

Fleischman looks at me with that inimitable blend of defensiveness and arrogance. Try it in the mirror. It's a real skill. "What."

I spread my hands in innocence and smile. "Nothing. I'm here."

"I can see you're here, O'Connell. My question is, why?"

I was stunned. "To . . . help. To assist. Isn't that my job?"

"You're a *receptionist*, O'Connell," he says in a nasal sneer. "Your job is to *recept*. Now excuse me please?" He turns to the patient. "So. Roy. The knee go out again?"

Now these loggers are a mixed lot. Some will talk your ear off, and others say ten words a year. This was one of the latter. "Got a pain in my gut."

"Uh-huh . . ." Fleischman looks at me, sees I'm still there, rolls his eyes. "O'Connell, don't you have to sit at the desk and do your nails or something?"

Knowing it will work, I say, "I want to watch a professional at work." It does. He shrugs and turns back to the patient.

"What kind of pain?"

"Sharp, in my stomach and lower."

"When did this start?"

"This afternoon."

"Any idea what might have brought it on? Some questionable food, a sudden jolt of stress—"

"Something I ate."

Silence. Finally Fleischman prods him with, "Well, come on, what did you eat?"

"Monopoly pieces."

I couldn't help myself. I said, "Houses? Or hotels?"

Roy looks at me, absolutely deadpan. "Both. Plus the top hat, steam iron, and the little whatchamacallit."

Fleischman said, "The *dice?*"

"Roadster."

I say, "Aren't those pieces made of metal?"

Roy shrugs. "Tin," he says in a minimizing tone, as if to say, tin is so soft, it's practically food. "Houses and hotels are plastic."

Fleischman's face is scrunched up in—something, I don't know, horror or disbelief. "How many houses and hotels did you . . . did you eat?"

69

Roy looks away, shrugs. "Five or six houses, couple-three hotels."

"Not to pry . . . but can I ask why? Just couldn't wait for the popcorn to cool down?"

"My wife. She keeps winning. I buy everything I land on, and she still ends up with all the railroads. I buy Park Place, she gets Boardwalk, I figure, fine. Then boom, she ends up with all the light green properties. North Carolina, all those. Breaks my back. Kitty builds up in Free Parking, I never touch it. She lands on it like she owns it. Finally I just had enough."

BANG! Fleischman slams his fist on the examination table, jumps up, and starts roaming around the office. "I can't do this," he says to the walls. "This is not MEDICINE as I have been TAUGHT it in the INSTITUTIONS of the MEDICAL PROFESSION in NEW YORK CITY. This is NOT medicine. This is being STRAIGHT MAN to a bunch of RUSTIC FREAKS and MARRIAGE COUNSELOR to HOMO ERECTUS. I do my HOMEWORK. I read the LITERATURE. I try to keep UP. And for WHAT? To treat people who ingest TIN GAME TOKENS and PLASTIC HOTELS?"

"Fleischman—"

"What am I supposed to write him a prescription for? Drano?"

"I'm sorry, Fleischman," I say, "If this man's malady doesn't suit your image of yourself as a healer of worthy men of affairs. Did it ever occur to you that he must be really hurting for him to come in? That his type is whole orders of magnitude more stoic and disciplined when it comes to pain than your type?"

"My type, my type, what does that mean, my type—"

"Narcissistic intellectuals who think that all other people are nothing more than extras in *their* star vehicle."

"Please, O'Connell, spare me the—" Then he's suddenly stunned by a realization and turns to Roy and says, "Do you believe this? *She's* lecturing *me?* The woman is in my employ! I am her *boss.*" He turns to me. "This is the first patient. Is this how it's going to be? Every patient is going to provide a theme for you to criticize my professional competence and take cheap shots at my personality?"

"This isn't about you, Fleischman. And it isn't about me. It's about Roy."

"Roy will be fine. I'll take care of Roy. But I'll tell you what is about you, O'Connell. I'm about to deliver your first job review. And guess what?"

"I won't give you the satisfaction. I quit."

"That dovetails nicely with what I'm about to say. You're fired."

I know I should have kept my mouth shut (which is what Marilyn does and is the secret of her success), but there's something about him that provokes and irritates the hell out of me. And what about Roy's feelings? Although he sat there like a totem pole figure the whole time.

But it's just as well. Who sits at a desk and does their nails? Who has nails to do?

Love,
Maggie

. . . .

MARCH 26

Dear Lou,

How are you? How are things in Skagway? And are you coming out here so we can go after salmon in Katmai, or am I going to have to catch them myself? On second thought, maybe that's the best idea. I still have that scar you gave me when you cast too close and your hook bit my side. Shelly touches it and makes a face. She says it's "sexy," but I don't think she means it. She doesn't look turned on. Actually she looks kind of put-off.

Anyhow we're fine here, but we've got a problem. You've been in this game as long as I have, maybe longer, so I wonder if you could offer some advice.

A few weeks ago a customer came in, ordered hot chocolate, and kept sending it back. Finally he stood up, knocked it out of Shelly's hands, and claimed he was burned. Now he's suing us, but is willing to settle for ten thousand dollars. I've written to him personally and asked him to call and discuss it, but he just

71

called back (collect) and said he was deeply traumatized and might require psychiatric counseling.

In all the years you've owned The Fremont has anything like this ever happened to you? I'd hate to have to go hiring a lawyer just because one ornery man decides to try to earn some easy money. But I'd hate worse to have to pay ten grand just to get him off my back. I'd appreciate hearing what you think about all this. Many thanks, and my love to Helen.

Holling

....

Dear Phyl,

Me again. I got your first letter since this working-for-Fleischman thing began, and of course it's pathetically out of date. Here's the latest, but first: Definitely *not*. Tell Raoul it's *his* job to slice the pancakes, and window sills are no excuse.

Now: Remember how I quit moments before I was fired? So I went home, wrote my previous letter to you, and went over to the Brick. I'd been tending bar there, and the owner was glad to have me back. It's indicative of how weird things are in this town that he was absolutely unfazed by all my coming and going and changing my mind.

So I started working the bar again, which is open night and day. People who haven't taken on a second job or plunged into a hobby now use the 24-hour day/night cycle to do their one job. The result is a complete shattering of the idea of routine and schedule. There's something wild and giddy about it, with an undertone of cheating and menace. Like we're all having a breathless time on a runaway train heading for a cliff.

At least everyone else is wild and giddy. I'm sort of glum. Not flying, bickering with Fleischman, not in a relationship (not that I "need" one, but still . . .). Have you ever had the feeling that you're ready for something . . . DIRE? Anything, just to blast you out of the doldrums? Well, I am reflecting on just that feeling, when who should shuffle in from the street but you-know-who, looking sad and regretful in that puppy-like way that makes me want to go oh-poor-baby and then smack him.

"O'Connell, I was thinking . . . I mean I wasn't thinking, but Roy said something . . . Maybe you were right. Maybe I was being unprofessional." I smiled pleasantly and said nothing. "So, I was thinking . . . if, you know, you still needed a job . . ."

"Do I look like I need a job, Fleischman?"

"Mmm, no. Not really. Okay. Can I have a beer?"

I drew him a Pyramid and put it in front of him. Then I said, "However, it would certainly be in the community's best interests to have a doctor whose office was fully staffed."

"Especially in these anomalous times," he said.

"Exactly," I said. "Because of the situation. That prevails."

"And the increased pressure on all of us therefrom."

"Exactly. So yeah, okay. I'll come back."

"You will?" He gave that smug little smile men reserve for when they win bets. "All r-i-i-i-ght . . ."

Which I have. Because if I live to regret it, I figure, Hey. I can always blame it on the sunspots.

Fully employed,
Maggie

....

MARCH 30

Mr. Benton T. Culpepper, Esq.
1455 Ninth Ave. Suite 3A
Anchorage, AK

Dear Mr. Culpepper:

I have recently been made aware of a most disturbing fact concerning your client, Mr. Arthur B. Marone. It turns out that he is in the habit, and you could almost say, the profession, of making trouble at restaurants and then threatening to sue. Ask him if he is familiar with a place called The Fremont Cafe in Skagway. If he says he is not, he is telling an untruth, since Mr.

Lou Carpentier, a friend of mine, owns and operates The Fremont and identified Mr. Marone by name strictly from my description of him.

For this reason I am going to decline your offer to settle for ten thousand dollars. Furthermore, I am advised by Dr. Joel Fleischman, M.D., who is from New York, that if you persist in this harrassment, I will have grounds to take legal proceedings against your client. It is

(NOT ONLY AGAINST YOUR CLIENT, JACK, BUT AGAINST YOU YOURSELF. I HAPPEN TO HAVE ONCE BEEN ENGAGED TO AN ATTORNEY AND I KNOW WHAT I'M TALKING ABOUT. Also: Mr. Vincouer is from a very old and venerable Yukon family; the chances are good he'll be acquainted with, if not directly related to, any judge you try to stage this farce in front of. Second: Miss Tambo is a very attractive and well-spoken young lady. She'll have judge, jury, and bailiff eating out of her hand while you're busy trying to flash your Rolex to let everyone know how successful you are. Third: We have a secret witness—okay, he's not secret, it's Holling's friend Lou—who is prepared to testify, under oath, that your client has tried to pull this exact same scam in a different town. Maybe you represented him in this. Check your files. Then do yourself a favor, Mr. Benton T. Culpepper Esq., if that really is your name: drop back and punt. Or face a countersuit that will severely inhibit your being able to pursue your own professional duties, i.e., e.g., viz., it will result in your disbarment. Have a nice day. JF, M.D.)

Thank you, Joel. Mr. Culpepper, I think that says it all.

Yours,
Holling Vincouer

....

31 MARCH

My Dear Selena,

Many thanks for your reply and for that one photo. Believe me, you look fine, fine. Just lovely. I recognized you immediately, and all I can say is, if you think you've put on weight, you

74

should see me! As for your request to hear about how my cooking class went, if you want the short version, I can sum up the entire experience with these words: I tried.

You'll note the tone of melancholy seeping in already. Put that down to a confluence of factors, starting with frustrated creativity and ending with having my kitchen and living room more or less devastated by a mob of ingrates and Philistines. I'm going to go on like this for a page or two, but don't worry—unless my tether snaps and I go drifting off into the deep space of self-pity, the result shouldn't be anything you can't show your husband or, for that matter, your three fine kids. On the other hand, I've already had about one brandy more than my system's configured for, and the bottle's at hand, so anything can happen.

My students were about two dozen citizens from Cicely: men and women, teens to seniors, Anglos and Indians and whatnot. Now before we go any further you have got to appreciate how remarkable that kind of a turnout is for a town with about 850 people, most of whom are content to eat caribou burgers from dawn til dusk and dropped out of school ten miles before algebra.

But people have time on their hands these days, so the kitchen was crowded. Some were there out of idleness; some were there out of boredom; some were there for entertainment or a free meal (although it wasn't free, exactly, since I charged everyone six dollars a head for supplies. But you can see I wasn't making a penny.) . . . And a few were there to learn to cook. The lesson was gnocchi and sauce bolognese, i.e., meat and potatoes, but with flair.

Well, flair be damned. You try saying the word "gnocchi" to a roomful of intimidated Alaskans. I got giggles and blank stares, until inspiration struck and I amended it to "Italian potato dumplings." The relief in the room was palpable. But it was downhill from there. When I encouraged them to mash up the boiled potatoes on the table, they looked at me like I was insane. When I instructed them on how to sprinkle on the flour, they turned to each other with little smirks. When I gave each of them a plate of the mash and had them form little gnocchi

75

bundles, they either stared at it with a look of distant dismay, or rolled it into small marbles and *then* stared at it, or balled the stuff up and ate it.

Excuse me while I pour another two fingers.

There. Now.

When I browned the beef and then mixed it with white wine, they yelled out as though I had really gone crazy and was just wantonly making a mess. And of course we had to let the beef cook down, so there was plenty of time to wander through my kitchen and living room and den and flop onto the chairs and couch, handle the memorabilia, turn on the tv and fiddle with the satellite control, and so forth. I found myself lecturing to a lone polite survivor, poor Ed Chigliak, who I know is perfectly happy to eat Beefaroni until Doomsday. Finally the sauce was ready, I had stirred three brimming cauldrons of boiling gnocchi while my home was destroyed, and I invited my pupils to file past and serve themselves. Five did, twenty-two declined and went home. Of the five, two expressed pleasure, and one asked if I would cook this again for him tomorrow if he paid me another six dollars.

I miss you, Lena. I miss the meals we made, the love we made, the time we spent without saying a word, just deveining shrimp in the kitchen. I promised myself I wasn't going to say this, but the brandy has given me permission, so here goes: when I said I loved you that last night in Austin, I meant it more than I have ever meant anything else before or since. And when you said that you loved me, I felt like I could have dropped dead then and there and not felt cheated by life.

But when you said you could not bring yourself to come with me to Alaska

I mean I understood, of course I understood, this country, I mean hell, look at it, and it was wilder twenty years ago, like outer space, just as you said,

See, the point is, that was the *point.*

Well. A person asks, Do I regret it? Of course I regret it! But I don't *regret* it. What

I had better stop now. This is a big house. Very big house. And it gets bigger when I drink too much. So you take care, Lena

All my love,
Maurice

. . . .

3/31

TO: DR. MICHAEL ROBERTSON
     WILSON INSTITUTE OF NEUROLOGICAL STUDIES
FROM: JOEL FLEISCHMAN

VIA FAX—NUMBER OF PAGES INCLUDING THIS COVER: 1

Dear Dr. Robertson:

I am absolutely thrilled and delighted you are taking time off from your busy schedule to visit us here in Cicely. Bring clothes suitable for a coolish Eastern spring. Normally our "birdwoman" (pilot) would pick you up in Juneau and bring you out, but she's grounded. Anyone who leaves the town falls asleep immediately. So hire a Juneau service. Bring bagels!

JF

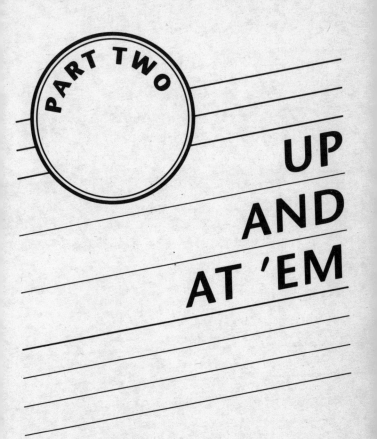

PART TWO

UP
AND
AT 'EM

APRIL THE FIRST

President George Bush
The White House
1600 Pennsylvania Avenue
Washington, D.C.

Dear President Bush,

Like all Americans, I know you are concerned about the role our nation plays in the exploration of outer space. Now that the Russians have given up, it's pretty much left to us. It's a big responsibility, since outer space is the biggest thing there is. But I know we're up to it.

However, we have to be careful. Because if we do too much, other parts of our society suffer. Take when we landed a man on the moon. That was a teriffic thing, even though it happened before I was born. But ever since then, people have used that to criticize everything else in our society. If the waffle iron breaks at Holling's cafe in our town, people say, "If they can put a man on the moon, why can't they make a waffle iron that works?" I try to explain that the people who put men on the moon don't make waffle irons. But no one listens.

I am interested in movies and would like some day to direct a motion picture. I was thinking. Wouldn't it be great to shoot it on Mars? The cast and crew would need space suits and life-support protection and so forth, but the cameras would work. And what an excellent location. I know this is a dream, but still—if we can put a man on the moon, why can't we shoot a movie on Mars?

All this goes to show you how important it is to keep NASA a respectable agency, so people will continue to support it. Well, that's why I'm writing. We have a former astronaut in Cicely, Maurice Minnifield, who goes around wearing NASA patches on his personal clothing. Is this legal? It's true he was once a member of NASA, but now he isn't. This concerns me, because people might see some of the things he does and decide that it reflects poorly on NASA. For example, he gave a cooking class. The food he made was pretty good, but the whole time he was sort of yelling at everyone. They all got annoyed and left. I stayed, but I thought, I hope this doesn't affect the space program.

In closing, let me just say, I like Maurice, and I even work for him. He's an OK boss. But lately he's been getting on my nerves.

Thank you very much.

> Yours truly,
> Ed Chigliak

. . . .

APRIL 1

Dear Tawni—

Things here are getting totally weird.

First, I'm still not sleeping. I mean, an entire MONTH, right? Now some big brain doctor has flown in from Philadelphia to study this thing. Holling says the whole town is going to be asked a lot of questions. But, I mean, why? It's not like it's our fault.

Second, business which was going nonstop has suddenly shut down. It's like at first everyone treated this no-sleep thing like a big party, and we had customers 24 hours a day. Now people figure, Hey, as long as my days are twice as long, I might as well make good use of them. So instead of hanging out waiting for this bonus party time to end, everyone stays home at night, doing hobbies or writing letters. Because if you're not going to go to sleep, there's no such thing as winding down, right? And if you're not winding down, you might as well do something constructive.

I feel the same way. I'm almost finished reading that *World*

Almanac I told you about. Frankly, I don't know why colleges even exist. All the facts in the world are in this one book. So you pay the five dollars. It's worth it! You have to read it more than once to absorb everything, but it sure doesn't have to take four years!

Meanwhile, the mood is getting strange around here. We have a guy, Ed Chigliak, who I think you met. He's an Indian, our age. Last night, when Maurice came by, Ed was sitting at the bar, took one look at him, and said, "I'm young, Maurice. There's still a chance I can get to shoot my movie on Mars. So don't ruin it for me."

Everybody looked at everybody else, and I'm like, huh? Finally, after a few seconds, Maurice says, "Ed, if that's some kind of authentic Native American incantation, I respect your right to incant it, but I can't say as I understand it." Ed made a face and turned away.

But meanwhile, what's his problem? I swear, some people think that just because they go around all year in a black leather motorcycle jacket *without even owning a hog,* they can be creative. It really bugs me.

I hope you sent that chain letter out. I check the mail every day. Nothing yet.

Luv,
Shells

....

APRIL FOOLS' DAY

Dear Bernard,

Things go from weird to worse, brother. Our town has gone sleepless now for a month. I had hoped that a complete lunar cycle would renew our passports to Dreamland, but no such luck. (The culprit, after all, isn't the moon, but the sun.) As you said on the phone, more wakefulness equals more life. OK. But what kind of life? If a nightly spell of unconsciousness is the price we hairy bipeds have to pay for our highly developed brains, then let's fork it over. I would rather buy death on the installment plan at a fixed rate, than face a sudden balloon payment for which I'm not prepared. In other words, what if all this catches up with us in some drastic way?

Grim thoughts. And I'm the only one entertaining them. To everyone else, it's either party time or an endless supply of unexpected study halls. And I take your other point: that if this thing is the result of sunspots, then it's as natural as a thunderstorm. But so is an earthquake.

Still, every time I sidle up to despair, I see what might be called signs of correction. Take this morning. I'm in the window, doing the show, and enjoying my customary splendid view of the town and its denizens. The normal morning traffic is sorting itself out . . . when I spot Holling Vincouer striding manfully up the street, mail in hand, toward the Brick. At that moment, out of Dr. Fleischman's office comes Marilyn Whirlwind.

The two encounter each other in the middle of Main Street. Holling gives some pleasant greeting, and Marilyn stops, looks indescribably offended in that deeply placid, undemonstrative way of hers—and slaps him on the face! Later I asked Marilyn what Holling had said to offend her. She replied, "He said good morning."

Faint glimmer of normality—i.e., reasonable stress caused by lack of sleep—slowly dawning in Ms. Whirlwind's psyche? Or one-of-a-kind aberration not likely to be repeated? I hope the former. We should all be borderline psychos by now; a Marilyn who slaps a man for no good reason is a Marilyn one slap more sane and healthy than the rest of us.

Still, all this free time is helping me catch up on my reading. To paraphrase the immortal Mose Allison: my body's on vacation, and my mind is working overtime. I'd just ask you to join me in hoping that my spirit isn't out to lunch.

More later

Fraternally,
Chris

Dear Aunt Louise,

I have a question for you. When I was growing up and you were teaching me the piano, we used to talk about the feeling one note had for another. If two notes had the same feeling, they were in harmony, and if you played them together, they made a third sound. If they had a different feeling, and you played them together, they made disharmony and an ugly sound. You said the same thing was true of people.

My question is, can a person's note change? I am in disharmony with a man who I used to be in harmony with. He is Holling Vincouer. He owns the local cafe. Suddenly everything about him annoys me. This afternoon, when I went to Ruth-Anne's store to buy paper, he was there talking to Ruth-Anne about books. Holling said, "There's no accounting for taste." This inflamed me with anger.

Can you explain this? Does it have anything to do with our unusual situation? It must. I can't explain my reaction any other way. I have always liked Holling, but suddenly the sight of his plaid shirt fills me with rage. What should I do?

With love,
Marilyn

Prof. Jennifer Kelly
Soc. Dept.
U. Mich.
A A, MI

Dear Jen,

Great letter! But I keep picturing the last time I saw you, i.e., eleven years ago. So I end up imagining a teenage girl in plaid skirt and navy knee socks, teaching college kids who are older than she is. (Remember the day after graduation? Going back in jeans and shirts, just to see how it would feel to walk around school in something besides the *uniform?* School was out, the halls were empty. We turned the corner. Halfway up the hall, Sister Lucille stepped out of her room and just stood there, staring at us, I stopped and gulped, and you said to me, "Our *minds* are still in skirts and knee socks.")

Not after four years of college and six years of Alaska, believe me. Speaking of which, interesting developments around here in sleepy, sleepless Cicely.

I have taken a job as off-hour receptionist for the local doctor, the Physician In Spite of Himself, Joel Fleischman (cf. prev. correspondence). So I was there, in the office, when he arrived this afternoon with our latest celebrity visitor: Dr. Michael Robertson, world-renowned (or so says Fleischman) neurologist from Philadelphia. He runs an important research clinic there. And get this: tall, fortyish, smooth, gorgeous. Black hair with that becoming hint of approaching grey. Clothing courtesy of Ralph Lauren.

In a word, potentially insufferable, but not literally painful to look at. Not that I care, of course. But it was gratifying to see Fleischman, who has been condescending and arrogant and superior from his first day here, suddenly turn deferential. Sort of gratifying, anyway. Also a little sad. But then, it didn't last long, as Fleischman immediately announced the pecking order, as it were.

"O'Connell, this is Dr. Robertson. I'll be working with him, so some of your duties may include helping with our research." Then, as an afterthought: "Mike, Margaret O'Connell."

"A pleasure, Margaret," he said, his brown eyes on mine.

What's your position on cleft chins? I'm for them, in moderation. "Please," I said. "Maggie."

"Maggie it is."

I offered a smile without subtext. "Welcome to Cicely, Dr. Robertson."

"Please. Mike."

"Uh," Fleischman intruded eloquently. "I don't think that level of, of intimacy is wise, uh, Mike. Just to keep the lines of authority straight . . ."

"Come on, Joel," Dr. Dreamboat says, "Alaska is no place to stand on ceremony." Then, looking at me: "Especially with such a beautiful girl. Oops! Sorry. You'll have my head for that. Woman. So, Maggie. Is it Mike?"

"You seem like a nice boy," I said politely. "Sorry. Man. So we'll compromise. Michael."

Still looking at me, Dr. Robertson said, "This one's dangerous, Joel. How do you get any work done?"

Fleischman said, "I wear a blindfold."

Maurice has set Dr. Robertson (okay, Michael) up in a storefront office two doors down. (Maurice is, to no one's surprise, ecstatic that Dr. Robertson is here. "I'm telling you," he was telling us, "this man is going to single-handedly put Cicely on the map. And not just the Fish and Game topo map of caribou migration patterns, either. I mean the tourist map, the convention map, the health-spa-pilgrims' map, and several other cartographic variations I haven't even thought of yet!")

Michael has asked me to show him around and introduce him to the natives. He intends to take a detailed history of every person in town. "It's an ideal research situation," he enthused, as we all had a get-acquainted beer at Holling's. "A self-contained community with fewer than a thousand people. A living laboratory."

Fleischman started to reply, "Yeah, well—"

But Michael smiled at me and said, "That's what's so thrilling about Alaska. All this beauty . . ." (Explicit eye contact.) ". . . and hardly anyone here to really appreciate it."

Are you gagging? The worst part is, even as I blinked back at him in a parody of flirtatious stupidity, I got a buzz. Meanwhile, Fleischman scowled and said, "No! No, I, I disagree completely! There are plenty of people here who appreciate the beauty. I myself appreciate it like crazy every day. Don't I, O'Connell?"

I smiled at him and said, "Like crazy, Dr. Fleischman."

Then Michael said, "One thing does concern me about Cicely,

Joel. Are you familiar with the Rackshaffen experiment?" (I'm sure I spelled that wrong.)

Fleischman suddenly looked alarmed. For all they were including me in the conversation, I could have been a decorative salt shaker on the table. "You don't think it applies, do you?"

"What?" I asked. "What doesn't apply?"

BOTH OF THEM AT THE SAME TIME said, "Nothing." And changed the subject.

Ever hear of it? Ask your sources. I have sources, too, but they treat me like a salt shaker.

Shaken,
Maggie

. . . .

4/2

Richard Marx
c/o Siegel, Vartorella, Berger, & Knapp
812 East 41st Street
NY, NY

Dear Richie—

Moving into second gear with this sleepless thing. Finally. A big-time neurologist from Philly's not only willing to fund some systematic research, but get this: HE'S COME HERE HIMSELF.

Admittedly, at first my feelings were mixed. He'll steal the limelight, control the work, put his name on the paper, claim credit. But I think I know a way around that, a way to secure my fair share of the glory. See, he's an interloper. Whereas these people—I'm one of them. Okay, let's say, I'm as one-of-them as a fast-talking Jew from Flushing who's being held here against his will can be. But at least I have two years' seniority! I know people's names, I know the name of the spouse they've stabbed, I know the endearing names of their pets and their rifles and their flatbeds.

So I'm in the system. But I'm also the local doc, and my patient case load is atypically high. So I'll have to hustle. Most of the complaints from my patients continue to be minor, although I notice the number of bar fights has risen dramatically, which is odd considering that the amount of bar business has fallen off. Local guys in flannel shirts and ZZ-Top beards, who used to drink six, seven beers a night and walk two miles around the pool table, now can be found at home, assembling Heathkit shortwave receivers or putting up wallpaper. But *crankily*, as more and more people seem to be in a permanent bad mood. The local disk jockey, a mild-mannered poet/artist, went off the deep end and yelled at the cafe owner's dippy airhead girlfriend about pistachio nuts.

"Our lives are fragile things, Shelly!" he starts shouting after he gets one of those hermetically sealed nuts with no access-crack. "Given that, and given the apparent impunity with which we all seem to be able to flout the laws of nature these days, is it too much to ask that you weed out these jawbreakers before putting down a bowl of nuts?"

No, it doesn't make sense, and to a Manhattan-based attorney such as yourself, Richard, this smacks of incipient madness. But I found myself doing what everybody else in the vicinity was doing, i.e., nodding indignantly and yelling, "Yeah! Right on! You tell 'er, Chris!"

I too find myself losing patience a lot these days. No pun intended. Is this related to the sleepless syndrome? Has to be. And no doubt will be detected, quantified, and duly theorized by myself and my disting. colleague, Dr. Mike Robertson. Speaking of whom, gotta go make sure Mike's new landlady remembers that the shower in Mike's room is for *his* use only.

Best,
Joel

Amy Levin Cooper, Editor-in-Chief
Mademoiselle
350 Madison Ave.
New York, NY

Dear Amy,

I read your magazine all the time. I think it's great. The regular columns are pretty helpful and answer some of my questions.

The thing is, though, I am a somewhat unusual case. My boyfriend is older than me. I am eighteen, and he is sixty-three. But there must be others like me out there. So my suggestion is, could you do a special issue for girls like us? If you did, here are some questions I think would be helpful in the Q and A section:

1. HELP! My guy often mentions Pearl Harbor. Is she a blues singer, and, if not, who is she? Should I worry?

2. HUH? Sometimes, after we make love, my boyfriend says, "Honey, you're the bee's knees." What does this mean? Do bees really have knees? And if so, so what? What's it have to do with sex?

3. UH-OH! Last night my squeeze and I argued over a movie. I wanted to see *Father of the Bride.* He didn't. I said, "Don't you want to see what it's about?" He said, "I already know what it's about. I've already seen it." But the movie only came to our town the day before, and there was no way he could have seen it. So the question is, Do people get more psychic as they get older? Can they read your mind? Should I be careful of what I think, and so forth?

Maybe older women know all this stuff, but younger chicks like me don't. So thanks, and keep up the great work with the magazine!

Yours truly,
Shelly Tambo

Dear Anita,

How are you? I am quite fine, although that strange situation I wrote you about has not changed. If as you say it's still not affecting you in Anchorage, then I believe it's only happening in Cicely.

As I say, I feel fine. The thing is, though, I wonder about Shelly. And I thought I might ask your advice. Now as I told you when you were here last year, I am absolutely crazy about that girl. She is by far the most wonderful thing that has ever happened to me. Which is not to take away from the good times you and I had in the old days, of course. And I tell her this constantly, I mean, I may not be as demonstrative as some men, but I do not neglect telling her of my love.

Lately, though, she seems to pay more attention to someone else than to me. I don't know if you remember him. His name is Ed Chigliak, a young Indian, Shelly's age. Always wears a black leather jacket. Until recently I thought he was just about the sweetest, most unassuming young man you could ever want to meet. Wouldn't hurt a fly, as agreeable as the day is long (and up here it's pretty long!), and so forth.

But Shelly can't stop talking about him. "Holling," she suddenly said last night while we were reading in bed. "Doesn't Ed's mopey expression just make you want to scream?"

I said, "Well, hon, not really. He only looks mopey. When you talk to him you realize he's actually quite cheerful."

"I knew you'd say that. You're so nice. Maybe too nice."

"It's his personality. I'm sure there are aspects of me that make him want to scream."

"And what about that leather jacket? I mean, is that pretentious or what?"

I looked at her in shock. Because that's what I was. I was shocked. "Shelly," I said. "Where did you learn a word like pretentious? From reading that *World Almanac?*"

"In *Mademoiselle.* Look, never mind. It's just that Ed is getting on my nerves these days in a major way. No biggie."

Anita, this is not like Shelly. And it makes me wonder: Could there be something going on between her and Ed? As I say, they are the same age, and I am acutely aware of the difference between my age and hers.

I have started to examine her behavior for signs of discontent or boredom or what have you, but frankly I don't see any. Still, why does she go on and on about this boy, who she has never had any strong opinion about until now?

I would appreciate your ideas about this. I also intend to ask Dr. Fleischman, who as a physician has some experience in these matters. I would also want to discuss it with another one of our local young men, Chris Stevens, who is something of a philosopher and took Shelly's confession when she was addicted to satellite tv. But for some reason that Chris gets on my nerves so much these days, I can barely look at him.

Thanks for your help, Anita, and I hope to see you again soon.

Love,
Holling

MINNIFIELD COMMUNICATIONS
CICELY, ALASKA
907-555-8610

2 April
Mr. Charles Rouse
10275 Little Patuxent Parkway
Columbia, MD 21044

Dear Sir:

I am a great admirer of your commercial developments, from Faneuil Hall in Boston to Harbor Place in Baltimore, and South Street Seaport in New York. I am especially impressed with the global scale of your accomplishments. Now before you tell your girl to word-process out one of your standard generic thank-yous, let me note here that when it comes to activities on a global scale, I know a bit more than most. As a former NASA astronaut, I have been fortunate enough to gaze upon planet Earth from the ultimate vantage point. So I hope you'll forgive me if I am so bold as to suggest that I feel a certain congruence or kinship with what you do.

I say all this by way of broaching the subject of a business proposition—or no, better yet, call it a concerned citizen's suggestion. Mr. Rouse, I am a resident of Cicely, Alaska, a minuscule town along what many are increasingly calling "the Alaskan Riviera." And it is my firm and fervent belief that one day Cicely will be a Mecca for sportsmen, outdoor enthusiasts, vacationers, tourists—something of a cross between Aspen and Saint Tropez. Well, lately my vision has taken a quantum leap closer to realization with this absolutely fantastical development:

No one in this town, sir, has slept since the end of February. And we don't seem to suffer any ill effects from it, either. Now I realize your first response to this information is disbelief. I don't blame you. In a moment I will present two suggestions about how you can convince yourself that this amazing fact is indeed true, but first I want to tell you why you should care at all. Actually it may already have occurred to you: if Cicely is indeed the place where no one sleeps OR NEEDS to, *then we may be looking at the closest thing to an actual fountain of youth this side of Heaven.*

If not youth, then energy. If not actually energy—because the normal physical activities of life do leave us fatigued in a somatic, muscular sense—then consciousness. And I ask you, sir: is that worth developing commercially, or do I lack the intelligence God gave celery? Is the potential not infinite for conventions, retreats, international conferences, sanitaria, medical research centers—need I go on?

Come see Cicely for yourself. Regardless of what you may think about Alaska, it is anything but a frozen wasteland, and my home—all 14 rooms of it—would be at your disposal. Or, if that is impractical, allow me to send you, when it is complete, the report of Dr. Michael Robertson, of the Wilson Neurological Institute of Philadelphia, PA. Dr. Robertson has come to Cicely to study this phenomenon and no doubt will be forthcoming with a credible and enlightening explanation for it sometime soon.

He takes this seriously. So, too, I might add, does our local physician, a young man, a Jewish young man, from New York. Talk about your institutional validation! This is more than a bunch of wilderness crazymen staying up as long as they can to get their names into the *Guinness Book of Records*. This is an ongoing psychoneurological mystery.

Of course, what I call our "unlimited consciousness" isn't all. The Cicely Experience also includes some downright gorgeous country and a nice congenial local population. Sure, we've got our share of bad apples. There's an Indian gal, works for the aforementioned local doctor, some people might find her laconic, undemonstrative personality and cryptic monosyllabic utterances a tad infuriating, as I do.

But hell, no community is perfect. Look past these occasional, atypical kinds of individuals, and you're looking at not only a first-rate wilderness experience, but a truly amazing psychological one as well—and none of the inconveniences of passports, currency conversions, language difficulties, or pajamas.

In a word, *Alaska*, Mr. Rouse. Our state motto says it all: North to the Future. I look forward to your reply. And if a phone call tempts you, feel free to yield to temptation. Call anytime, day or night. I'll be up.

Yours truly,
Maurice Minnifield
CEO, Minnifield Communications

....

Dear Andrew,

How great to hear from you! Of course I remember you—my brother Jack's freshman-year roommate. From the dorms. We met at our house when Jack brought you home for the Xmas holiday. Was it you who spilled the eggnog on our cat? Oh, who remembers!?

I remember that as a fun time, even if it was ten long years ago. And yes, what Jack told you is true. I'm not currently "seeing" anyone. But it would be a bad idea for you to come up here now, Andrew. Even if you will be in Seattle in three weeks, visiting Microsoft in Redmond with whom (as you say) you have a very special relationship.

You see, I have an extreme case of insomnia at the moment. In fact, I have been awake continuously for almost five weeks. Some doctors think the Rockshaffen Experiment may be relevant. Ask Jack. Plus, the reason I am not "seeing" anyone at this time is that all the men I have "seen" over the past six years have died.

So, it was great to hear from you. Good luck with your software program!

Yours truly,
Mary O'Connell

....

Dear Jack,

PLEASE don't do that again, i.e., give my address or phone number to your old college buddies. I can't STAND your freshman-year roommate. You know that. So I just had to give him the brushoff. He wanted to *stay with me* for a week! He asked me to show him Alaska! I told him I have insomnia, which is true enough.

If he asks you, back me up on this, or you'll regret it come "asset" time.

Meanwhile, is it me, or are all doctors, in one way or another, insufferable?

I ask because my new routine involves exposure to two doctors almost twenty-four hours a day. The diff. between this new life and my old one as a pilot could not be more extreme. As a pilot, I was the boss; as a receptionist (for Joel "Fleischman" Fleischman) and research assistant (for Dr. Michael "Michael" Robertson), I am, respectively, the well-meaning but faintly dippy gal Friday or the semiworshipful peasant granted license by the lord.

Another thing about doctors. They think not only that what they do is far, far more difficult and important than anything you do (which it often is), but that *they could do what you do if they merely had the desire to squeeze it into their busy schedule.* (Which they probably could not.) No matter what it is, from baking bread to designing a house (to flying a plane), they do it, or they used to do it, or they've thought about doing it, which to them is tantamount to already having done it. When I told Michael I was a bush pilot, he nodded in a familiar, dismissive way and said, "I was going to go for my pilot's license. But I got involved with other things."

Get it? "With other, *more important* things" is the implication. So I nodded back and said, "I know what you mean. I was going to take up neurological research, but I got involved with other things." He chuckled at my dry wit, and I *still* felt insulted. It was one of those vain, I-see-you're-a-saucy-wench kind of laughs.

It must be strange, being a doctor and condescending to the entire range of human experience. The exception to this, as always, is Fleischman, who makes no bones about his inability to do ANYTHING I can do. I mean Alaskan, wilderness-type things like flying and camping and hunting. Of course, he makes up for it by suggesting—no, not suggesting; by *shouting*—that these things are not *worth* doing, that the entire purpose of civilization and its march from the primal swamps has been to make cooking freshly caught salmon over an open fire *completely unnecessary.*

In my plane, I don't have to put up with this sort of thing.

Unfortunately, I do in this office, since I am now working for/with both men. By day, I serve as Robertson's interpreter as we walk around town. It's fun, actually.

Except for today, when we were visiting Chris Stevens at his trailer outside of town. Chris is a sculptor, and today we found him outside, welding old car parts together.

Things were tense from the start. He took one look at us and scowled.

"I love you, Maggie, but don't do this," he sang out, eyes on the agglomeration of tail pipes and fenders.

"Don't do what?"

"Subject me to a rationalist interrogation. Quantify my subjective experience in a way that can only falsify it."

I was flabbergasted; I thought he'd find this interesting, since he talks about science as much as mysticism or religion or poetry. Plus, Chris is one of the sanest, most polite men on Earth. But Robertson leapt right into action, utterly undaunted. He walked around the piece Chris was working on, eyeing it. I could see Chris was peeved. Then Robertson stopped and said to him, "I do sculpture sometimes. Coat hangers, tongue depressers—whimsical stuff, indoors."

Chris gave an obviously fake smile and said, "Good for you, Doctor Mike."

It was downhill from there. Robertson got his answers, which Chris gave grudgingly, and we left as it was getting dark. The doctor's parting words to the dj/artist? "Call me. I may know a good agent back East."

Chris just waved, then fired up his torch with a pop. I didn't have the heart to tell Robertson that Chris had no intention of selling his works and didn't own a phone.

Love,
M.

. . . .

4/3

Mr. Kurt Anderson
Spy Magazine
5 Union Square West
New York, NY

Dear Mr. Anderson:

First the basic info: I'm a physician, which is how we're taught to refer to ourselves to the public, don't ask me why. Maybe because there are doctors of sociology, philosophy, etc., but there are no *physicians* of sociology, etc. And, now that I think of it, there are honorary doctorates, but there aren't any honorary M.D.s. Then again, no philosophy professor was ever sued for malpractice.

I was born and bred—born and bred; bed and breakfast; bread and circuses . . . interesting—in Flushing. Bronx Science, Columbia, Columbia Medical. Typical, right? Fine.

For the last two years I have been marooned up here in— check the postmark—Alaska, in a town fully as big as Kew Gardens with a population easily as large as the sophomore class at Forest Hills. None of which is interesting, but here is what is: no one has slept in this town since the end of February. There are theories to account for this, but they are highly technical. In layman's terms, we can say that a recent "crop" of sunspots have "done a number" on Earth's magnetic field. This has "bothered" the large iron ore deposits in the mountains around Cicely, stimulating a kind of "rude backtalk" in our local magnetic field, which then "jams" the "go to sleep" signal in the "normal taking care of yourself" area of the brain.

So I was thinking: would *Spy* be interested in an article entitled "The *Real* Town That Never Sleeps"? I am thinking of something offbeat, a little irreverent, with enough firsthand medical info to lend it legitimacy and elevate it above your usual run-of-the-mill travel piece. Because I'm not only the Hair Club president, I'm also a client, i.e., I am a faithful subscriber, so I know what does and does not appear in *Spy*. As for my writing experience, it is nil, but hey, I can type.

Frankly, I'm hoping you'll be intrigued enough in this anomaly to want to run a story on it, but not so intrigued as to send one of your (admittedly better qualified) staff or customary free-lancers up here. Besides, they wouldn't like it, believe me. Remember the Exxon Valdez? Reporters from the Lower Forty-Eight paid homeowners in the town of Valdez three hundred dollars to *sleep on the floor*. (Wait a minute . . . I read that in *Spy!*) And Valdez is bigger than Cicely. Tons. Did somebody say accommodations? I don't want to say Cicely is a grueling, backward, one-moose town, but put it this way: we have no police force, but we do have a resident taxidermist. He's also the undertaker, which is a comfort.

Let me note that I was editor of my high school newspaper, got 714 in my SAT verbal, and was consistently complimented on the clarity and economy of my lab reports as an undergrad. So I like to think that I can write when I want to. What do you say? Look, it doesn't matter whether I can write or not, since you're going to re-write it anyway. I can accept that.

Write me or call with a reply (907-555-6748). I am beginning research of this whole phenom. with the eminent (trust me) Dr. Michael Robertson of the Wilson Neurological Institute of Philadelphia. So there is legitimacy here. Call his office (215-555-6002) and check it out. Or come up yourself and see what it's like being awake all the time. I'll tell you what it's like. It's like going to a class in college, and waiting for the professor to show, and waiting and hanging out, and waiting and hanging out, and finally realizing that he ain't comin'. You discover you've been handed back a piece of your own private life. Take that feeling, and multiply it times 24 hours a day.

See? I told you I can write.

Yours truly,
Joel Fleischman

PS—Look. I hope I don't have to tell you that this was written in good faith. Hubristically, okay, but still. So please don't hand it over to the guy who writes the "From the Spy Mailroom" column for his snide commentary. It would be bad enough for my friends to learn that I'm stuck up here while they're pursuing fame and fortune in more civilized surrounds. But it would be unbearable to be made fun of in *Spy*. That last sentence was rather awkward, but you know what I mean. So no, I do NOT give you permission to run this in the "From the Spy Mailroom" column or as a "Letter to the Editor." Even though, admittedly, this is a letter and you are the editor. Sorry. JF

PPS—Okay, I see I'm beginning to turn into one of those people who write coy, demanding, annoying letters to you time after time, what's their names, Halberstam or Goldfinger or DeMornay or whatever, insulting you and then six months later asking for a job as though you're expected to admire their moxie. I promise not to do that. JF

....

APRIL 4

Dear Tawni,

I am just about ready to jump out of my skin. Remember I told you about how we don't sleep here? Well, we don't sleep here more than ever! Plus, I don't know, but somehow I think it's making me smarter. Or more . . . aware of stuff. Take this guy who lives here. Ed Chigliak. I told you about him. He's our age, an Indian, a nice guy . . . but now just the sight of him makes me want to scream. He just gets on my NERVES, okay?

This morning he came into the bar for breakfast like he always does. So get this.

"I guess you want scrambled eggs, like always, right, Ed?" I said.

"No," he said, in that mopey-dopey way of his. "I'll have 'em fried."

And I want to say, WHAT IS YOUR PROBLEM?

Plus there's a new doctor in town, Dr. Robertson, from Philadelphia, who's researching this whole sleep thing. Some big shot neuro- something. Cute, like Tom Selleck without the moustache. He wants to talk to everybody, get their stories about how it feels not to sleep, when it started, and so on.

So he wants to talk to me, of course. And we're sitting at a table, me and him and Maggie O'Connell who has become his assistant, and he says to me, "Shelly, do you ever take naps at night? Do you ever stare out the window and have daydreams?"

I say, "Excuse me? Daydreams at night?"

"You know," he says, with this smoothie smile. "Fantasies."

As if it's any of his *business?* I mean, I have fantasies. But what does that have to do with sleeping? I don't know, Tawn. It's like I woke up one day—without sleeping, if that makes any sense, which I know it doesn't, although it sort of makes tremendous sense—I woke up and saw Ed as he really is, and now I have this thing about MEN. They're like a PAIN. I mean aren't they? With their hulking around and their JACKETS?

And it's like, once you realize stuff like that, the whole world looks different. I mean, as WOMEN, what is it with MEN? Maggie once asked me that, but she was kind of drunk at the time and really bummed out, and I thought, well, she's depressed, so she doesn't mean it. But now I see what she meant. Why do we have to please them all the time? Of course they try to please us, sometimes, okay. But what they do is so STUPID, why do we find it pleasing? Unless we're stupid. Which let's not be, okay?

Not Holling, of course, since he's really sweet. I mean, I can see that he's also into doing all this man-stuff, but I know him well enough to see how he's sort of stuck with it, so I forgive him. Like this morning, we were doing the breakfast rush, and the radio was on. Our local station's only dj is Chris Stevens, who does the "Chris in the Morning" show, where he talks and

101

reads and plays music. Well, it was on, like it always is, and Chris was talking about some cosmic stuff like he always does— I think he's mad at me about something—and suddenly Holling looks ILL.

"I'm sorry, folks," Holling calls out. "But I can't abide that boy these days." And he goes to the radio and CHANGES THE STATION.

Of course everybody yells out, but at least what he got wasn't Maurice playing show tunes all day like he did last year when Chris called Walt Disney a homosexual and Maurice slugged him (Chris) and fired him and took over. (Maurice owns the station.) When Holling changed the station, the only one we could get—don't ask me why, since it comes from SEATTLE, but it has something to do with the sunspots and the magnetic field, etc.—was National Public Radio. Which is like all news! And no music! And these mysterious announcements like, "The time is 21 minutes before the hour."

Now, before all this started, I would have heard something like that and just not thought about it, because I would have thought, well, it's on the radio, so it must make sense. But now, with my new outlook on things, I think: wait a minute. WHAT HOUR???

Because who gave that time report? Right. A MAN. So it makes me realize that, once you stop just believing everything men say, and start asking questions, you become a lot more intelligent.

Luv Ya,
Shelly

....

APRIL 4

Dear Lou,

Once again, thanks for your help with that Arthur B. Marone business. We have not heard from Culpepper, his lawyer, so I assume they'll just let the matter drop.

As for your other questions, yes, all of us here in Cicely have been up since the end of February. It's starting to take its toll on people. There is a young man, Chris Stevens, who in fact was once my partner on a deal I got into with him when I needed a shot of cash for the IRS. That didn't work out, and we broke it up, but there were no hard feelings. And I always liked him.

But lately he has become just about the most irritating individual I have ever met. There are some days I want to smash his face in.

The thing is, Lou, just about everyone in Cicely these days wants to smash somebody's face in. Ed Chigliak came in the bar this afternoon looking like he was shopping for trouble and was willing to pay cash. I asked him what was the matter and he said, "It's Maurice." (Minnifield, of course.) "He's getting on my nerves. I quit working for him. Let someone else go to Dr. Fleischman's house and deliver messages." When I asked Ed what Maurice had done to make him so mad, he said, "I don't know. But it must be something." Before I could inquire further, he said, "Do you know what I've decided to do?"

"What?"

"I've decided to quit fooling around. No more mister nice guy. I'm going to do it."

"Do what?"

"Make things happen. Be all that I can be. Let the chips fall where they may, because that's the way the cookie crumbles. It must be a chocolate chip cookie . . . And look out for Number One, go for the gusto, and stop at nothing to succeed.

"Ed," I said, "That's not like you."

"I know." He nodded. "It must be because I'm annoyed with Maurice."

Well, I was certainly willing to concede that Maurice could be annoying. "But you want to talk about annoying individuals," I said, "You take Chris—"

"I don't think Chris is annoying at all, Holling," Ed said.

I replied, "Well Ed, you are entitled to your opinion."

He nodded and smiled and said, "Thanks." Then he looked kind of surprised, and said, "I am?"

I know Shelly is annoyed with Ed for some reason, but I can't for the life of me figure out why.

Yours,
Holling

. . . .

APRIL 4

Ms. Kim Basinger
c/o Weisman, Miller, and Davis
1100 Avenue of the Movie Stars
Century City, CA

Dear Ms. Basinger:

I hope you don't mind my writing you, but I saw your attorney's name in an old issue of *Premier,* so I'm sending this there. I read that a year or so ago you bought a town. What a great idea. Now you can go there whenever you want and not have to worry about it being closed. If you want to open your own business, like a grocery store or a dry cleaner, you can, because it's your town. You can even have your own special Kim Basinger Day and give yourself the key to the city, although you probably don't need it since of course they give you one when they give you the town. Still, it's always good to have a spare key.

That's why I'm writing. I live in a small town in Alaska called Cicely. It's an ordinary town, except that for the past month or so no one here has slept. Not because of reasons like the neighbors play loud music, or we're worried about the economy. There's something in the Earth's magnetic field that has made us not need to sleep.

So I thought you might be interested in buying Cicely. It's great for getting things done. Of course not that many of us have that much to do. But, being a movie star, you would.

I know this is hard to believe, but it's true. Are you interested? I don't know what the price would be, but I'm sure we could work something out. You can write to me at the address on the envelope. Don't worry, I'm serious, because I have decided to be all I can be.

Yours truly,
Ed Chigliak

. . . .

APRIL 5

Mr. Jason De Brettville
Geneological DataBase Inc.
Boulder, CO

Dear Mr. De Brettville,

Thank you for your junk mail of March 24th addressed to me. But you have made a mistake. My name is not Whirl, so I would not be interested in a computerized family tree tracing my ancestors back to their possible roots in England and Wales. My husband's name is not Wind, so I would not be interested to know if he is related to Herbert Warren Wind, who used to write about college football for the *New Yorker*. I am not married. My name is Whirlwind, not Whirl-Wind.

Thank you.

Yours truly,
Marilyn Whirlwind

. . . .

APRIL THE 5TH

Dear Uncle Anku,

I hope you are feeling better. A week in Providence Hospital isn't so bad. You get to see Anchorage, although I guess you only get to see it out your window. I hear you get cable tv. The food is probably terrible, though. Oh well.

Things here in Cicely are pretty much the same. Just after you left, that Dr. Robertson came from Philadelphia. He and Maggie

O'Connell and Dr. Fleischman all came to interview me this afternoon.

I was at home, doing pre-production work on my first movie. At this stage that mainly means making lists of things to do once I have a script and some money. I'm working for Ruth-Anne at the store, helping with the mail. Everybody's writing letters and sending out for catalogues and magazines. Everybody except Ruth-Anne. She says she doesn't have time to write anything but order forms. But that's not exactly true. She wrote a sign we put in the window yesterday. It looked like this:

ATTENTION ALL LIBRARY PATRONS
GRAND AMNESTY!

All books have been taken out. None have been returned. Come on, Cicely! Finish with those books and bring them back, so others can read them, too! Normal fines will be suspended for one week starting today. Drop 'em off. No questions asked.

After Amnesty Week, a New Fine Schedule will go into effect. Every day a book is Overdue there will a charge of

Two Cents ($0.02)

Failure to pay the fine will result in a Suspension of Borrowing Privileges.

YOU HAVE BEEN WARNED!

Being interviewed by Dr. Robertson and Dr. Fleischman and Maggie was interesting. Mike asked me when was the first time I skipped sleeping, and how it felt. I told him it felt like being awake. Then he asked how I felt at night now. I said the same way as I feel during the day. He asked if I drank, so of course I said yes. He said, "Do you ever, you know, drink too much?" I said not really. He asked if drinking ever made me pass out. I said, Pass out what?

He laughed and said, "Ed. My man. I'm referring to B-O-O-Z-E."

Then I laughed and said, "Oh, you mean alcoholic beverages." I told him I didn't drink alcoholic beverages. Just beer.

There were a few more questions, and Maggie and Dr. Fleischman talked about a few things. Then Mike asked, "Ed, would you voluntarily submit to an E-E-G?" and I thought he had made a mistake. I said, "Don't you mean an E-G-G?" They laughed, and I laughed, although I wondered what it would mean to voluntarily submit to an egg. Then I realized they wanted to test my reflexes by throwing an egg at me, and I said, sure, and asked them when they wanted to do it. Mike said as soon as he could lease one from Anchorage. I said, "Lease it? It's going to get all smashed. Can't you just buy it?"

Dr. Fleischman laughed and said, "Ed, do you have any idea how much one of those things costs? Try—and correct me if I'm wrong, Mike—try fifteen, twenty, around there."

I was absolutely amazed. I said, "Twenty cents? Just for one?"

Dr. Fleischman said, "Try dollars, Ed. Try thousand dollars. Try twenty thousand dollars."

I said, "But why do you have to get it from Anchorage? My Aunt Julia raises chickens."

For a second they all looked at each other with a funny expression. Dr. Fleischman said, "What is this, a dialogue from a language lab? My Aunt Julia raises chickens?"

Then Maggie said, "Ed . . . so what?"

"Well," I said, "She can sell you a dozen for a dollar."

It turned out that they were talking about a complex piece of scientific equipment, and I was talking about eggs! We all had a big laugh over that. Then Maggie and Dr. Fleischman argued about some stuff, and Mike said some other things, and Maggie and Dr. Fleischman called each other names. All that is pretty much the usual.

I hope you get well soon.

Your loving nephew,
Ed

....

APRIL 5

Dear Jen,

No, no, *you're* the professional doing useful work in an important institution. You didn't tell me you wrote an article for *The Atlantic!* I had to consult your own footnotes to find out. I'm proud of you. (Any extra copies?)

As for me, thanks, but no—I'm not Fleischman's nurse.

Patients come in and I assign them numbers. True, sometimes Fleischman summons me into the sanctum sanctorum with a cool, professional, "O'CONNELL!" Usually he wants me to write down as he dictates notes on a patient's condition. Sample dialogue:

> FLEISCHMAN: Patient is a Caucasian male, age 34, symptoms include headache, myalgia, arthralgia, some diarrhea. Splenomegaly, hepatomegaly both possible—
>
> ME: Hold it, Fleischman, not so fast.
>
> FLEISCHMAN: Come on, O'Connell, keep up. This is life in the diagnosis lane. Pulse and respiration abnormal, traces of macular rash on torso—
>
> ME: Do you talk this fast with Marilyn?
>
> FLEISCHMAN: Marilyn doesn't do this. She refuses to record diagnoses.
>
> ME: So you go twice as fast with me, to make up for lost time?

Meanwhile, outside the office, Fleischman, Michael and I are like . . . I don't know . . . "Moonlighting" meets "M*A*S*H,"

108

which results in scenes like when we went to interview Ed Chigliak.

Ed is eighteen, an Indian, really sweet, kind of naive—at least I think so. Either that or it's a really subtle form of higher wisdom. Anyway, he was stretched out on his bed doodling. Michael asked him some routine questions, and Ed gave his usual literal/profound answers. There was some weird mixup about an EEG, which was hilarious.

At least Ed thought it was hilarious. And so did I. But the whole time we were laughing, Fleischman was watching Michael—as though for a cue? So when Michael made this obviously forced, polite laugh, Fleischman gave one of his strained, fake-good-sport grins, like the face he wears when he's asked to join a tribal dance. And then he said, "Uh, can we, can we get back on track here?"

"What's the matter, Fleischman," I said. "Afraid the scientific rigor of these proceedings will be compromised by a sense of humor?"

"Excuse me, O'Connell," he said in that prissy way of his. "But we happen to be in the middle of the most perplexing medical anomaly since Legionnaire's disease, and I think it merits a certain amount of respectful attention to the process at hand."

"What does that *mean,* Fleischman? The process at hand. Where on earth do you learn to talk like that?"

"Especially," he said quickly, "now that we've got a world-renowned authority who's come all the way up here to help us and who's time is valuable and not unlimited. I mean I know, Mike, that you can speak for yourself, but I'm sure you didn't come up here to listen to a lot of—"

"To a lot of what, Fleischman?" I said. "This better be good."

"—to a lot of . . . local . . . folk . . . ethnic . . . Alaskan rural tribal hayseed humor whose interest is at best anthropological."

"How dare you!" Mortified, I turned to Ed. "I'm sorry, Ed. Fleischman didn't mean that."

"That's okay, Maggie," Ed smiled. "I didn't understand it."

"People," Michael murmured. "Each side's argument has

merit. But may we proceed with the questions? Ed, I'm sure you're anxious for us to get out of your hair—"

"Not really. It was getting lonely in here."

"—so we'll finish up." Michael paused, then said, "Although it was quite admirable of Maggie to stand up for Ed just now."

Fleischman said, "Yeah, she's a saint. Listen, Mike, about the Reckstoffen experiment, I really think it doesn't apply."

I said, "Not that again. What is it?"

"Nothing, O'Connell."

"Nothing for you to worry about, Maggie," Michael said. "Joel, you may be right. I want to hear more of your theories."

"Great," Fleischman said. "Absolutely, Mike."

Now isn't that pathetic? To see Fleischman visibly relieved that this big-time neurologist still *liked* him, still thought he belonged on the team. Is this a man thing or a Fleischman thing? Even though his (F's) behavior had been appalling, condescending to Ed there, who everyone knows has a quite original mind of his own and is anything but a hayseed. But of course, Fleischman was embarrassed. He wanted to display to his fellow big-city physician that he was *in* but not *of* dumb, rural, folkloric Cicely. And the truth struck me like a revelation: Fleischman was a snob!

I had just begun to really absorb this, when Michael added, "Because my time up here will be brief." He looked at me. "Too brief."

Our eyes met. Fleischman saw this and starting making noises and walking around, and said, "So, Ed, about that EEG—"

Did I mention he looks like Marcello Mastroianni? A little? Michael, that is.

By the way, thanks for letting me go on like this. It's nice to have a friend to write to in the midst of all this strangeness. It is strange, isn't it? Or is it me? Don't answer.

More later,
Maggie

Dear Alexander Solzhenitsyn:

Are you ready for this? O'Connell is now working for me.

I know, believe me: weird isn't the word. O'Connell as my second-string receptionist? I can't decide whether it's a good idea or a nightmare. On the one hand, she's the smartest woman in town, and I can actually bounce ideas off her and not have them land on the floor with an audible thud (as with my patients) or have them sent back to me mysteriously transformed into ravens and moths (as with my starting receptionist.)

On the other hand, she's monumentally uptight, and (it's so obvious) *self-righteous* in that way that people from nice clean middle (or upper-middle) class homes get when they come up here and pursue The Wilderness Experience. They're fleeing the suffocating sham of their compromised, pallid, emotionally hypervigilant middle (or upper-middle) class life for the pure bracing air and clean, honest backwardness of the whole paleolithic Alaskan thing, and anyone else who has read a book or gone to the Met is a fey, crippled, neurasthenic weakling incapable of taking care of himself in any context more demanding than that of a gelateria in Soho.

She thinks I'm arrogant. She thinks I'm *conceited*. I mean, is this third grade, or what?

We go to interview Ed Chigliak. And after an amusing little interlude, in which we share a chuckle over a confusion over EEG's and eggs, I suggest we get back to the matter at hand.

Immediately she squares off. "Fleischman," she says, "What's wrong with having a sense of humor?"

Now this is the sort of "brave," "enlightened," "humanizing" question asked by many people who care deeply about the quality of American health care and who, at the same time, are idiots. It galls me that I am forced to address it.

"Not a thing, O'Connell," I am compelled to say, and go on to state that I believe a sense of humor to be a prime prerequisite for a full and satisfying life. "But this is not some unfamiliar

111

malady, like Legionnaire's disease. This is an utterly perplexing anomaly that defies laws of medicine and physics."

But she's bent on grandstanding for Mike's benefit, playing the sensible, earthy speaker-of-plain-truths. So she hits me with, "Where do you learn to talk like that, Fleischman?"

"In medical school, O'Connell," I say—we're like a vaudeville team now—and go on to deplore our excessive badinage while Mike's time is awasting. I apologize to Ed for wasting his time too, but he's having fun, sitting up against the headboard on the bed, legs stretched out, smiling and pivoting his head from O'Connell to me and back, holding a legal pad and a pencil like a tennis judge taking notes.

I'll tell you something—I just realized this, bear with me—it just hit me. What really bugs O'Connell now is the fact that THE SHOE IS ON THE OTHER PEDAL EXTREMITY. Of course! When I got here, I was the stranger in her world. She knew the lay of the land, the customs, the personalities. This was her home. She was here of her own free will, whereas I came under threat of monetary penalty and a significant period of incarceration! So of course I was a schlemiel.

But now we're involved in this medical research. Now SHE'S in foreign territory, SHE has to ask *me* what the vocabulary words mean, SHE is unfamiliar with the customs and traditions.

No wonder she's gravitating to Mike. Not that he isn't an attractive man, in some ways. He is. If you like that kind of self-conscious smouldering routine. But this is shameful. I mean the man has been here barely a week, and O'Connell is exhibiting a tropism toward him without the least regard for standards of seemliness or tact. The flirting, the bashful smiles, the wide-eyed attentiveness—I'm very disappointed. I guess . . . I don't know . . . I guess I really thought she was above throwing herself at the first handsome charming world-famous scientist that came down the pike.

I know what you're thinking, and no, it's not that I'm jealous. I don't want her. She's too . . . too prickly, and opinionated, and argumentative, and judgmental. Plus she has this very slight lisp, which infects me when I talk to her too much, and I start lisping a little, too. We're like a pair of cats hissing at each other. No, it's not that. But I'm offended. This squaring off, this me-and-"Michael"-against-Joel, this constant baiting and hectoring: do I need this?

Look, I know you don't know me. I'm a 30-year-old Jewish doctor from Queens, and you're a however-old-you-are world-famous non-Jewish Russian exile writer. But I had to write somebody. And the thought of bringing any of my friends up to date with what has happened here, even those with whom I'm already in contact, was too laborious to entertain. So when I started this letter I just wrote "Dear," assuming I'd think of someone to send it to by the time I was finished. And I did. Because I know you couldn't care less about any of this. You're above this sort of thing. SO AM I, NORMALLY, BUT I'M A PRISONER UP HERE IN ALASKA.

Just as you're "prisoner," in a way, where you are. You know, it's funny. I never thought of myself as having anything in common with Alexander Solzhenitsyn, but there's a certain situational parallel, isn't there?

Anyway, feel free to throw this letter away. You needn't write back or anything. By the way, did I spell Alexander right? Should it be Aleksandr, or something like that? What's the rule—you Americanize it while you're living here, and then revert back to all consonants if you return to Russia? Is there still a Russia, or is it called something else now?

As for how I'm going to get your address, I'm not. I'm just going to write "Alexander Solzhenitsyn, Vermont." A hundred dollars says it reaches you. Unless, of course, you live in New Hampshire. I know you live in one of them. I'd better stop now. Thanks. You don't have to be a thoracic specialist to know that it's good to get things off your chest.

Sincerely,
Anonymous

Dear Stan,

I'm sorry, but I won't be able to fly you from Prudhoe to Anchorage in two weeks as per our usual arrangement. I've been forced to take some time off. I suggest you call Len at Talkeetna Transport or Tommy at YakuTaxi.

I'll let you know about the next scheduled trip. I may be flying by then, or I may not. I don't know. I'm sorry even to miss this one trip, though. I enjoy ferrying you guys down from the ARCO station at the top of the pipeline. You look so awful, trooping out of that horrible residence building and dragging yourselves across the ice. I feel heroic, like I'm airlifting refugees.

But who am I kidding? You know as well as I do what I'll really be missing. That's right. *The pastries.* All those doughnuts and eclairs and Danishes. Still, my question is, why? Is that how they get you to sign up? "Work the Alaskan Pipeline. It's like living on Neptune with unlimited napoleons." Or is pastry important to roustabout-oil-rigger-type men in a way a woman just wouldn't understand?

Because it's not just you guys at ARCO. I once flew an engineer from British Petroleum, who handed me a bag of luscious goodies as he climbed aboard. I don't mean to propagate the stereotype of the restrained Brit any more than necessary, but here was a man who gave a woman a bag of "cream-filled Long Johns" and *didn't make any dirty remarks.* I would PAY to fly that guy again. What was his name . . . Derek. (Nice name for a guy who works an oil rig.)

So have a good vacation. I'll be in touch in a month. Sorry for the inconvenience.

> *Best regards,*
> *Maggie O'Connell*

The Postmaster General
Department of the Post Office
Washington, D.C.

Dear General:

I am writing on behalf of Ruth-Anne Miller, the postmistress, and I guess general store mistress and head librarian mistress of Cicely, Alaska. She doesn't know I'm writing to you, but actually these days, she's so busy, she doesn't know much of anything.

The thing is, usually we get a small amount of mail here. But now that we don't sleep, everybody in Cicely writes a lot of letters. And you know how it is with letters. I mean, a man couldn't get to be General of the Post Office if he wasn't an expert on letters, probably. What I mean is, letters are like seeds.

When I wrote that line above just now, I really did think letters were like seeds. But when I tried to think of why, I couldn't come up with anything. So maybe letters aren't like seeds. But what is true is Ruth-Anne needs a lot of help with the mail now. She also needs a fork lift. Could you send her one? She also needs a separate building to be the Post office, and of course if you had that, you'd need a separate Post Mistress or Mister. I'm not being too clear, but I can tell you that three months ago, we got something like three thousand letters a week for the whole town. Now we get something like fifteen thousand.

And this doesn't include all the magazines, catalogues, coupon booklets, and junk mail. What we do is dump all the Bulk Rate and Third Class stuff in a firewood bin and let people help themselves. It makes good kindling for fires now, but what will we do in the summer? So I have a request. Could you issue an order making everyone stop sending junk mail to Cicely? It would make Ruth-Anne's job a lot easier. And after all, you are the General. Thank you.

Yours truly,
Ed Chigliak

Dear Pop,

I had a revelation yesterday, and I had to share it with you. I was driving home—well, "home"—and it was raining. Up ahead, on the side of the semi-terrific road that leads from the quasi-excellent highway to my house, I saw two deer nibbling at trees. And one thought led to another until I suddenly had a blinding insight and a deep understanding of the natural world: *animals live outside all the time.*

What I'm saying is, I realized that outside is *not* animals' place of business that they go to at nine in the morning, and stay in all day, and then leave at dinner time and go to their real "home." Outside *is* their real home *and* their place of "business," which is to be an animal. If it rains, if it snows—and it does—they *stay there.* They have to! They're animals!

Do you see what I mean? The deer were getting wet in the rain, but it was not a violation of something, it did not mean that something was wrong. They were deer, they were animals, so they lived outside. What happens when you live outside? You get hit by weather. That's part of what outside is, ie, the weather.

They're there now! All over the world, animals are outside right now.

And it's *cold* here. It is night, it is dark, it is cold, and yet all those deer and moose and caribou—even if they're asleep, they're outside.

I find this tremendously impressive. I think I may have underestimated animals all this time.

I hope you and Mom are well. I'll write again soon,

Love,
Joey

. . . .

APRIL 9

Dear Katherine,

Greetings to Bryn Mawr from the 49th state. I'm sure the last person you expected to hear from was yours truly, notwithstanding the one evening we spent together that, as I said at the time, was nothing short of memorable.

You thought I was referring to our lovemaking, and I was. But what you don't know is how you affected me afterward, after you left Cicely and I returned to the problem that had vexed me until the moment I met you on Baker's Point.

I had wandered there in search of inspiration. I found it, embodied in you, sitting against a tree, your half-dome tent nearby, a picture of solitary repose over your copy of Daniel Deronda. We spoke, some current flowed between us, and I took you over to Kiniamshet Meadow to view my work in progress: a small mountain of used tires. I had assembled it over weeks, forming a giant's array of rough black grommets piled smack in the middle of the greenery. The piece, I explained, was correct but incomplete. It needed a final element.

You looked slightly repelled but said, "Well, at least it's a good use for old tires. You get points for that."

I smiled, we returned to your camp and spent an ecstatic evening in your tent. Your cries and my laughter surely kept the wolves awake. The next morning you offered a sweet good-bye and hiked off into my memory. But the seed you planted bore rapid fruit: I returned to the meadow, thought hard about your words, and decided that the last thing I wanted was "points." So I commissioned a team of Indian women to sew a patchwork tarp one hundred feet square, and staked it down over the tires, concealing them from view and completing the piece. Title: No Retreads.

I'm writing now because I was out on Baker's Point recently and could not resist the urge to violate the unwritten rules of chance, karma, and destiny—not to mention the strict gamesmanship of male-female psychology and the tricky hydrodynamics of desire—and ask if you'd care to visit me again.

I know the constraints that limit your freedom: the Bryn Mawr academic calendar, your personal commitments for the next few weeks, the not inconsiderable expense of crossing the continent. So as an inducement let me note that soon spring will be upon us here, and as it was among the ancient Celts and Druids, it is a time of fierce revelry and unpredictable passion. The very notion of which awakens, in my own consciousness, a dormant yearning for your presence. So think about it. Call me at the station (907-555-8823) and let me hear your voice.

But come quickly. The ice is melting.

With love,
Chris

. . . .

Dear Kay,

Warm greetings to Berkeley from the 49th state. If the last person you expected to hear from was yours truly, note for the record that the first person in my thoughts, upon discovering that spring is imminent, is you. The lake outside my trailer is frozen still, but you would not want to walk on it now, as its daily creaks and groans announce, with rifle shots and timber cracks, the impending thaw. Amid this tohu-bohu of melting and release, as dormant yearnings awaken and revive, my spirit encounters their mental embodiment in thoughts of you and that single night we spent together.

I recall it as a night of various passions. You had gone to Baker's Point for recreation, I, for inspiration. We met, spoke, and an electric charge built up between us. When I mentioned the project I was working on, your interest was a turn-on all by itself.

So I took you to my trailer. Outside, in the waning light, the piece hung from a scaffolding: a large, broad, dangling mobile formed of welded snow machine parts. Working title: "Snow Machine Snow Mobile." Your approval was almost sexually gratifying. And when I said that my sole remaining problem was where to hang it, you had an immediate suggestion.

"Put it up in the town hall or the church," you said. "Some place where everybody goes and will see it all the time. To establish art as a vital presence in the town."

The idea was thrilling, intoxicating. We made each other

118

drunk on the open defiance of it all. That night, in the trailer, my cries and your laughter surely kept the wolves awake. You left the next day, out of my trailer and into my memory. After watching you hike off, I contemplated the sculpture and realized what had to be done. Anyone, I understood, could hang a mobile over the ground, permitting it to turn freely and displaying it for all to see. So I dug a vast hole and "hung" it underground. I buried the thing in Kiniamshet Meadow and called it, "Snow Machine No Mobile."

Interred, immobile, does the mobile nonetheless turn? Yes. Because the Earth turns. And we are creatures of cycles. Small wonder, then, that at this stage in the seasonal round when the quiescent yields to the quickening, I discover in myself a desire for nothing so much as to repeat that time we spent together. Not to indulge in fantasies of time past, but to celebrate time present in a way we have already shared and, in my opinion, consecrated in fierce revelry and unpredictible passion.

Can I lure you up here again? Think about it, but not too long. Then tear yourself away from the constraints of the Berkeley academic calendar, personal commitments of the next few weeks, and consideration even of the expense of travel. Call me at the station (907-555-8823) and let me hear your voice.

But quickly. The lake is turning liquid.

With love,
Chris

....

APRIL 9

Dear Kimberlee,

Warmest greetings to Tacoma from the 49th state. And please don't pretend that the last person you expected to hear from was yours truly. As the lake outside my trailer announces daily, with rifle shots and timber cracks of melting ice, the impending collapse of winter's domain and the return of spring's beneficence, these sounds are answered with creaks and groans inside my heart. Small wonder that my thoughts be suddenly

119

occupied with images and memories of you and that single sleepless night we spent together.

Sleepless for every good reason. For my unbelievable luck when you stopped me on the street in Cicely and asked directions to Baker's Point. For the privilege of spending the day with you. For our lovemaking and for your cries and laughter, which surely kept the wolves and bears awake. For the artistic inspiration that you ignited and kept flaming when you looked at my latest project—a giant rocking chair assembled of two-by-fours and standing, isolated and proud, on the frozen ice of Kipnuk Lake—and said, "Hey, neat. But what about when the ice melts?"

I explained that the chair would, at a completely unpredictable time, crash through the thinning ice and sink to the bottom. You grinned and said, "Wow, cool. And so people in like fishing boats can look down through the water and see it. Like King Triton's throne."

It was the final jog to my artistic vision. As soon as you had gone the next day, driving your Jeep Cherokee into the foothills of my memory, I bought four gallons of green and brown paint and daubed the chair in camouflage. When it sank, as it most certainly did on the arrival of spring thaw, it fell to the lake floor and disappeared from sight. Title: On View.

And now it is spring again. Amid this tohu-bohu of melting and release, when ice yields to sun and earth to the rising green shoots, I must yield, too: I violate the unwritten laws of chance, karma, and destiny—not to mention the glorious paradoxes of male-female psychology and the damned, blessed hydrodynamics of desire—to ask . . . no, to demand, to beg, to hope? that you visit me again.

The lake outside my trailer, though deliquescing, is still essentially frozen. Come, let us walk on it, and dare spring's warming touch to break the ice beneath our feet and plunge us to our deaths. It won't. We will defy it with our fierce revelry and unpredictible passion.

As you once memorably said, "Everything goes in cycles." Yield, then, to this one. Tear yourself away from the constraints of the academic calendar of West Pottsville Community College, personal commitments for the next few weeks, and even the expense of travel. Let loose the dormant yearning inside you and bid it find its mate in mine, as we indulge in fantasies of time past and celebrate time present in a way we have already shared and, in my opinion, consecrated.

Don't think about it. Call me at the station (907-555-8823). Let me hear your voice. And let yourself hear mine.

But do it quickly. The icy lake is melting into liquid.

With love,
Chris

. . . .

APRIL 10

Dear Tony,

Bedtime stories and lullabies didn't work; deliberately administered tedium didn't work; and, lately, carefully selected readings from Jung, Freud, Erich Neumann *(The Origins and History of Consciousness)* and Shakespeare haven't worked. No music didn't work; boring music didn't work; and bad music hasn't worked. The upshot?

Well, the upshot is, if I don't cool it and relinquish my role as "Cicely's self-appointed guru-shrink" (so says my boss), *I* won't work. Meaning: I will be fired. So I'm back to the usual radio show—something of a relief for me, actually, since it means I can play what I like rather than what I want people not to like. And in the spirit of both timeless wisdom ("You can lead a horse to water") and Voltaire, I am about to leave the horse at the edge of the water and go tend my own garden.

I have decided that if I can't access the lightning bolts and lava flows of the unconscious unconsciously (i.e., alseep), I will try to do so consciously (i.e., in bed). By this I mean, sex. To that end I have invited a trio of women friends up for a visit. With any luck at all, one of the three will say yes. My fundamental assumption is that in the act of making love we receive a sample, a taste, of primal desires and states-of-being that come factory-direct from the unconscious.

121

Will it work? Only one way to find out. And will this electro-magnetic anomaly have any noticeable effect on my sexuality? Let's see. I'll try to take really, really good notes, but I don't promise anything.

Best,
Chris

....

4/10

Richard Marx
Siegel, Vartorella, Berger, & Knapp
812 E. 41st St.
NYC

Dear Richie,

These Foolish Things Remind Me of You Dept.

Robertson, O'Connell, and I were interviewing a tribal elder (sic; we have several tribes up here, or actually they have us; and a few dozen elders), and he said, with regard to our communal lack of sleep, "This must end. My people blame it on Exxon. They want to bring suit." Which captures the contradic-tions of modern-day . . . well, I was going to say, "modern-day Alaska," but let's just say, modern-day AMERICAN LIFE. It also reminded me of when we first met and The Most Embarrassing Moment of My Youth.

The Place: Mrs. Rosenberg's first-grade Hebrew School class at Beth Sholom. The Time: countless eons ago. The Event: Mrs. Rosenberg is explaining why each Sunday we pass around a can with a coin slit in the top and put real money therein. It's called Keh-ren Ah-mee, "which are the Hebrew words for Fund of My People." (The money goes to Israel. Whatever THAT means.) Joel Fleischman is in attendance, but Richie Marx is home with an illness.

A week later. Joel and Richie are both in class. The can is produced, and coins given to the children by their parents specifically for this purpose are clanking and clinking into it. Mrs. Rosenberg says, "Oh, Richard, you were absent last Sunday. Can anyone tell Richard what Keh-ren Ah-mee means?"

Now, my mother's chief pedagogical technique in raising me, both then and, frankly, up until last week, was to say, "You Are A Genius. You Can Do Anything You Want. Be A Doctor. And Remember. Most People Are Stupid. Stand Up Straight And Show Them How Smart You Are." So, obedient to the Prime Directive, I raised my hand until Mrs. R. called on me. "Yes, Joel? What does Keh-ren Ah-mee mean?"

"It means Fun of My People," Joel says. "Because you can use the money to have fun."

Maybe that's what they do with it in Israel. In any case, down there in Manhattan, representing Monsanto or whatever, you CAN use the money to have fun. Me, I'm writing this in Alaska. No money, no fun. Still, in either case: ve've come a long vey, boobie.

Best,
Joel

MINNIFIELD COMMUNICATIONS
CICELY, ALASKA
907-555-8610

4/12

Ms. Kim Basinger
% Weisman, Miller & Davis
1100 Avenue of the Stars
Century City, CA

Dear Ms. Basinger:

My associate, Mr. Ed Chigliak, has forwarded to me your letter of 11 April in which you express tentative interest in the purchase of the town of Cicely, Alaska. Please permit me to express my extreme pleasure and gratification at this news.

You will appreciate that Cicely is a very small town. Therefore to your query of Mr. Chigliak, "With whom should we negotiate?" let me reply, with myself. We have no formal government to speak of, apart from a mayor (whose exercise of her power is largely imaginary) and a sort of defacto, informal mayor, who happens to be a good friend of mine. Indeed, as the chief businessman and principle property owner of the town, I am for all practical purposes the powers that be.

I will therefore take it upon myself to do the legwork and legal investigating to determine how (and, quite frankly, if) Cicely can be sold. Rest assured, by the way, that the electromagnetic anomaly of which Mr. Chigliak wrote you is still very much with us. We are awake day and night, with no ill effects save for swollen electric bills!

In return I would ask two things. One, that this remain strictly confidential for now. Not all of our residents are as worldly or sophisticated as you, an international cinema personality, and myself, a fomer astronaut. What I am saying is if Cicely is indeed to be bought, I will have to figure out a way to sell the idea to its citizens. Among us rugged individualists, such a level of general civic agreement is not to be taken for granted. But it is not, I assure you, unattainable.

My second request is that I be the sole legal representative of the town of Cicely and that the sale be contingent upon my receiving a commission, the terms of which will be negotiated between me and the town's authorizing body. Lawyer talk, but not all that unfamiliar to you, I am sure. In closing, let me again express my delight in your interest and my confidence that, when you and your people do come up to visit, you will be anything but disappointed. Please contact me at your pleasure to arrange a date for your inspection of the property.

Yours truly,
Maurice Minnifield

· ·

ARPIL 12

Dear Phyl,

This letter-writing has become a habit. Do you mind? If so, tell me, and I'll write you a letter of apology.

What did I tell you about Michael Robertson? Did I say he was a self-adoring know-it-all? If I did, forget what I said. I forget what I said, but whatever it was, forget it.

(Before I forget: You're kidding! Raoul is a saint. But next time, no molly bolts. Also, make the doilies out of zinc, dip the babies in chocolate *first,* and play Puccini.)

Now: Michael Robertson is possibly the most intelligent man I have ever met. And it's fascinating and something of a privilege to be working with him.

Even though . . . Okay. The work I'm doing is not exactly creative. Or the most intellectually satisfying. Or even physically satisfying like maintenance on my plane. What I'm doing is I'm typing up (well, inputting; he has a laptop) Michael's notes. But it's amazing how many notes he's taken already! And we have a couple hundred more people to talk to! He's asked if I would be willing to transcribe the taped interviews, and I said yes.

I know it's tedious. I know I'm being reduced to a secretary, without even a secretary's paycheck. But I don't know how to explain it, he's just very compelling. At first I thought he looked like Marcello Mastroianni, but now I see traces of Barry Bostwick. Did I say he isn't married?

This came out earlier this evening. The two of us and Fleischman had dinner at the Brick. Then Fleischman had to see some patients, so Michael and I dropped by the office Maurice has

125

donated for the research. He sat at the desk and I sat on the old couch. Michael opened the drawer and pulled out two glasses and a bottle of Fundador. He poured me a little and I took it.

"To Alaska," he said. I nodded and took a sip. "So tell me, Maggie. Why?"

"Why what."

"Why Alaska? Why Cicely? What's a nice woman like you doing in a place like this?"

"Escaping from Grosse Pointe," I said—a little glibly, but it's not as though I hadn't answered that question a hundred times in the past six years. "Escaping from other people's expectations."

"Good for you."

"Michael," I said. "Don't patronize me."

"I patronize everybody," he said. "I'm a doctor."

And I can't help it, Phyl: I laughed.

Then he said, "But I take your point. It's a bad habit. Worse than that. It's insulting. I apologize. But that's what I get for going into research. My bedside manner has completely atrophied."

"You're forgiven," I said and drank a little more brandy.

He said, "I bet Joel's bedside manner is alive and well, isn't it?"

And there was something insinuating in the way he said that, so I bristled and said, "What's that supposed to mean?"

He laughed. "Just that. Ease up. I mean, he's probably good with patients."

"Yes. He is. A little too cerebral, a little condescending and superior, but yes. He's good with patients. He respects them." I smiled, and added, "He doesn't *understand* them, at least a lot of the ones up here. But he tries to respect their quirks."

"Of course he does." He took a big gulp of brandy. "He's of the next generation. It's one of their *things*. Humane medicine. Every ten years a new wave of interns wants to reinvent the profession. I did, too, but I outgrew it." He looked at me suddenly and said, "Are you and he a . . . an item?"

"ME? and FLEISCHMAN? Absolutely not!"

"I didn't think so. He's too . . ." And then he shook his head and waved a hand, as though to cancel the thought.

So naturally I prodded him and told him you can't start a sentence like that and not finish it. He shrugged, finished the brandy, put the glass down with a little knock, and leaned forward over the desk toward me. He spoke softly. "Strictly entre nous? Just between you, me, and the fax machine?" I nodded and suddenly felt odd. My stomach churned. Michael said, "Dr. Joel suffers from an acute case of Terminal Entitlement. You see this a lot among young hotshots. You hear it in the way he speaks. That self-conscious verbal style. Every pronouncement is an official statement."

Now I'm not sure why, but I said, "Well, he wants to be precise—"

"Oh, absolutely. I'm not being critical. And what you must remember is it really isn't his fault. First-generation professional—he wasn't raised in the tradition. He *can't* take it for granted. So he tries too hard. Feels he's aspiring above his station, and it makes him self-conscious."

"Well, he is a bit much sometimes, but—"

"Still, in some ways I envy it. If I had that . . . that fantastic verbal brio, I might be more successful."

"Head of your own institute? I'd call that pretty successful."

He shrugged. "It's a plateau. There are other plateaus above it. But actually I meant, successful with women."

"Come on." I grinned, and looked into my glass, and grinned some more, and said, "You're not going to convince me you're unsuccessful with women."

He sat back. "I have my moments. But why am I still alone?"

What could I say? I looked away, and he looked away, and then, for whatever reason, I mean I know you *know* what reason, I said, carefully, "You mean you're not—"

"Not what? Married? No. I notice you're not married either." Before I could say anything, he leaned back and looked past me, into the distance, and said, "Why aren't we married, Maggie?"

Is this what magazines call The New Flirting? Take a come-on

127

line men *used to* pretend was "sincere," although it wasn't, and now deliver it with no pretense? I've been up here in the bush so long, I wouldn't know. Or did he think I was buying this retail? Not that I was. But I had to say something, and it came out, "We, uh . . . we haven't met the right person?"

"That must be it. We haven't met the right person." He sat upright again and looked sharply at me as though I'd just suggested something brilliant. "I haven't met her in Philadelphia, and you haven't met him in Alaska."

"Yet," I said.

And he smiled. "Yet."

> *Don't ask me what this means,*
> *Maggie*

MINNIFIELD COMMUNICATIONS
CICELY, ALASKA
907-555-8610

12 April

Dr. Robert Barlow
NASA Planetary
Houston, TX

Now, Bob—

You have got to try to bear with me on this. Yes, the magnetic field anomaly is still with us, and yes, I have been awake since I last wrote you. But no, you cannot come up and investigate, and I'll tell you why.

I have a deal pending here with an individual that would be jeopardized by the presence of you and your team. I cannot disclose the identity of the individual at this time, but I will tell you that he or she is a well-known, bona fide celebrity. It's my feeling that he or she would be put off by a group of scientists and engineers popping up all over the place.

However, I do think, once I complete the deal with him or her, that he or she might be flattered by the Agency's request to set up shop in Cicely. Just bear in mind I haven't asked him or her about this. His or her interest in Cicely involves the obtaining of a certain amount of privacy, which he or she might feel to be imperiled by a NASA research project dropping in. In the end he or she may say okay, come on up. I don't really know him or her well enough to venture a guess. It would be up to her. Or him.

What I'm saying is this is business. As soon as I can square it with the potential buyer—of what I'm not saying—I'll get back to you. Meanwhile, just sit tight. The wheels are turning. Better yet, the line is out, the fish looks interested, and I expect a strike within a couple weeks.

Best regards,
Maurice

. . . .

APRIL 12

Dear Mr. Salinger,

I don't know where to start. I mean, it's not as though I haven't read, like, BOOKS before. In fact I was just finishing the *1977 World Almanac* when somebody sent your book to me in the mail. (I don't know who sent it, somebody in Gainesville, Florida. I entered this chain letter.) Well, now, just now, I just finished reading *The Catcher in the Rye*, and it's like I KNOW you, and you KNOW me. I mean not really, but it's like Holden says—after you read a great book, you want to call up the author

129

and tell him how great it was. So I did. At least, I tried to call you at the publisher's office in New York. But the girl who answered the phone didn't know who you were, so she said you didn't work there or that maybe you were a temp.

So I decided to send this to the publisher's office, so you can pick it up when you come in. Or they can forward it to you. (I mean, I KNOW you don't *live* there!)

Anyway, I can't tell you how neat that book was. Holden is EXACTLY LIKE this kid in my class at school, Brian Lacombe. Do you know him? He has red hair and was always sort of quiet and mischievous. I once thought he was cute for about five minutes, but then Billy McGee shoved him against the lockers and he started to cry, which was a turn-off.

I live in Alaska and have never been to the Lower Forty-Eight, but some day I'd like to visit you and just thank you personally for writing such a fantastic book. Please send me your address and I'll ask Holling (my boyfriend) when we can set up a trip. But don't worry. I'll make sure he reads the book before we go! (He's 63, so even if he read it, it was probably a long time ago and he doesn't remember a thing about it.)

Your biggest fan,
Shelly Tambo

....

12 APRIL

Dear Ingrid,

I'm sorry we won't be enjoying the pleasure of your company this year. My old friends from the Canaveral days are in some ways the dearest and most special of them all. We Mercury boys felt that you, and people like you, were with us all the way. When we were sitting on our rockets waiting to go up, we felt as though you were there, sitting on our rockets, too. Still, as you say in your recent letter, if your husband's been shifted from tagging snowshoe hares to monitoring Dall sheep, c'est la vie. Maybe next year.

Then again, perhaps it's just as well. Something peculiar

130

seems to be happening up here, which I can only ascribe to that bizarre sleeplessness I wrote you about before. Now I am not one to shrink from confronting the dark side of the human animal. I know what Man and Woman are capable of. I know that our psyches are repositories of turbulent emotions that to our ancestors represented the difference between obtaining, and being, dinner. So when, as occasionally happens, someone in this community goes on one kind of a rampage or another, I may deplore it but I am not surprised.

But the kind of psychic upheaval afflicting Cicely these days is, if you'll pardon my politically INcorrect French, more appropriate to a salon full of cat-fighting interior decorators and sullen nancy boys than a town of hardy Alaskan pioneers. Everybody, regardless of age or sex, seems to be infected with a highly selective but virulent form of crabbiness. That sounds more venereal than I intend. I mean crankiness, grouchiness, irritability.

It turns out that just about everyone finds someone else preternaturally annoying. I myself have developed a distinct intolerance of none other than Marilyn Whirlwind, the Indian girl who works as the receptionist for Dr. Joel Fleischman. I almost went into business with Marilyn last year; I had some idea that the colossal eggs produced by her pet ostriches might fetch a pretty penny on the open market.

But the more I involved myself with the enterprise, the more it became apparent that those ungainly creatures simply did not like me. In fact the ostriches hated my guts. They stopped producing eggs the size of honeydews and starting cranking out skimpy little things no larger than lacrosse balls. So I cut my losses with no hard feelings, and Marilyn and I parted ways.

But now I can't abide the sight of the woman. And it has nothing to do with the ostriches, the eggs, or anything else. It must be the lack of sleep, although like everyone else, I feel normal. It seems to me that Marilyn harbors similar feelings toward Holling; Holling can't abide my disk jockey, Chris Stevens. Chris is provoked by Holling's girlfriend. She, in turn, is irritated by Ed Chigliak, the boy who works for me. Or used to, I should say, since—of all people!—the one human being whose very existence offends young Ed is . . . yours truly. Similar daisy-chains of annoyance can be traced throughout our community.

Which is bad enough. But lately I have been promoting the bejesus out of Cicely, sending letters to some of the most eminent thinkers, do-ers, developers, and hotshots of our time. I mean, am I insane, or is a town where sleep is unnecessary not THE place where you want to hold your next convention, retreat, conference, or peace negotiation?

And I'll tell you another thing. Somebody is interested. I am not at liberty to disclose who, but I will say that this party—who comes equipped with an international reputation—has a solid record of commercial involvement with towns like Cicely.

Thing is, though, this deal won't fly if our citizenry is engaged, twenty-four hours a day, in a round robin of bickering and sneering and grudge holding. Which leads me to conclude that what we need is a joint project, something the entire community can commit to and get behind, to break down these petty barriers and foster a more general sense of collective harmony. Beats the hell out of me what, though. Can't have a picnic. Not in this weather.

My best to your husband, and I expect I'll be writing you about this later.

Fondly,
Maurice

. . . .

4/12

Steve Cohen, Lawyer of the People
PittsPa

Dear Steve,

Not to be premature, but I am LIKE THIS (holds up two fingers next to each other) with Dr. Mike Robertson, which means that my, okay, *our* monograph in *Nature* or *Lancet* or *JAMA* or *Science* is practically in galleys. Yes, it has yet to be

132

written. Yes, our conclusions and theories have yet to be fully articulated. Yes, the research on it has yet to be summarized, or even evaluated, or even concluded. But I approach this with renewed determination and confidence. Why? Because this morning, over a "working breakfast" at the Brick, while O'Connell labored in the project office transcribing interviews, Mike and I had a guy-type chat and discovered a ton, a host, a slew of things in common. Basketball—he is, predictibly, a Sixers fan, but I can respect that—beer (domestic: Sam Adams. Imported: Pilsner Urquell), and, well, not to put too fine a point on it, women. Which he brought up, as follows (all dialogue not guaranteed verbatim, but accurate in, uh, thrust):

"But seriously, Joel. What do you do for fun up here?"

"I dunno," I said impressively. I nibbled at a piece of toast. "A lot of people drink. But, me, I'm not a big drinker."

"So what else is there? That *Last Picture Show* theater across the street. And what? Indian Bingo?"

I laughed. "For the Indians, yeah—"

"Or do you have a girlfriend?"

"Well," I said, "Let's just say I had one, back home, but we ended it."

"Ouch. That hurts. Mutual consent?"

"Ultimately, yeah."

He slurped coffee and put his cup down with a clink. There was something stagey about it, but of course I knew why: here was this six-foot, good-looking, well-groomed stranger with a smooth urban manner and soft city-boy hands, whose main job was to snoop into the lives of every grizzled man, woman, and child in Holling's bar. So he was seeking to strike the common note. Then he looked sly and said, "Or is there something going on between you and Maggie?"

You can bet that if I had been sipping coffee at that moment, I would have executed an immediate Danny Thomas turbo spit-take right into his face. "ME? and O'CONNELL?" I laughed. "Did she tell you that?"

"Good Lord, no. We didn't discuss you. Not that I'd blame you. She's a beautiful woman."

"Well," I allowed. "Yeah, she's . . . she's got a face." Then I added, "But come on, man, her personality. Talk about confrontative . . . talk about critical. Maggie O'Connell is without question the most brittle, most repressed, most emotionally defended and moralistically sanctimonious and aggressively self-righteous individual I have ever had the misfortune to encounter."

"Nice body."

I pretended I had not thought about O'Connell's body before and looked pensive, then said, "Well . . . yeah . . . if you like . . . you know . . ."

"Bodies."

"Right." Then I said, "Whoa, Mike, do I detect a note of interest?"

"I assure you, doctor, my interest is strictly professional."

We traded leers, man to man. Then he said, "Jesus Christ, I'm glad you're here. Imagine if I had to drag my ass up here and do this without an ally."

"You would never have come," I said. "I'm the one who contacted you, remember?"

"Exactly. It's good to have a peer on hand."

I grinned. "That's great, Mike. I mean, it's terrific. Our working together, I mean—"

"So you wouldn't object if I . . . how to put it . . . set my sights on Ms. O'Connell?"

"Uh . . ." And for a second it felt a little weird, don't ask me why. I mean, sure. I know why. And I know you know I know why: because I was jealous. Which I freely admit. I was. But I consciously reminded myself that Mike's expression of interest in O'Connell was by no means repudiation of or a threat to his friendship with me. So of course I said, "I give you my blessing. Essen gezundteh heit."

"Which means. . . ?"

"Go for it."

Okay, I admit there's a kind of lockerroom macho tone in that exchange that I probably, if I really thought about it, don't·like. On the other hand, he was right to ask if there was something between O'Connell and me. And if something blossoms between them, some kind of affair or romance, fine. Because a) maybe it'll make her a happier person and she'll relent in her unceasing campaign to criticize and scorn me and b) there are more important things at stake than my relationship with Maggie O'Connell.

I am fully aware, as I am sure Mike is, that the research we have commenced into this anomaly could make my career. We are on the verge of a major scientific breakthrough. What if we could locate the exact area of the brain causing our sleepless-ness? And what if, therefore, we could learn to synthesize a chemical—or better yet, construct a radiation device, which would probably, once we learned the basic principle, be as easy to build and market as a microwave oven—that could eliminate the need for sleep? Or defer it? The financial possibilities are staggering.

So, is it okay with me if Michael Robertson puts some moves on Maggie O'Connell? I think it is, yeah.

Gotta run. More news when it happens.

Joel

. . . .

12 April
Samuel French, Inc.
New York, New York

Gentlemen:

I am interested in staging an amateur production of one of the following shows:

    1) *The King and I*
    2) *My Fair Lady*
    3) *Guys and Dolls*

4) *Oklahoma!*
5) *The Music Man*

Kindly let me know which of these shows come under your purview and your fees for scripts, royalties, scores, etc. I say "amateur," but I may sell tickets, although then again, I may donate the proceeds to charity, but bear in mind that if this production turns out to be as problematic and hair-raising as I have a feeling it will, the charity so designated may be not much more than my account at a certain package goods and wine store in Anchorage. In other words, let me know the various forms of payments you require for various kinds of money-making or eleemosynary productions.

Thank you very much.

Yours truly,
Maurice Minnifield

. . . .

12 APRIL

Sgt. Barbara Semanski
Alaska State Police Precinct 7
Tok, AK

Dear Barbara,

I am communicating with you this way, rather than by telephone, because I want you to consider carefully what I am about to propose. It is very important to me, and I admit to a good strong pang of anxiety about popping this particular question. I am afraid, in fact, that you will think I'm kidding. Believe me, Barbara, I am in earnest. Just let me try to assure you from the get-go that I am perfectly serious, that I believe together we can work out any difficulties that might be inherent in this setup, and that I am certain it can result in great fulfillment for us both. So I'll just come right out with it:

Will you be in my musical?

I am contemplating staging an amateur production of a classic Broadway show to be cast from people in and around the greater Cicely area for the sheer hell of it. Who'll come? Whoever's not in it. I will fund the production myself, foot all the bills, and cover my expenses at the end from whatever gate receipts there are.

Why? Because ever since we lapsed into this nonsleeping period from about the end of February, Cicelians have been increasingly at each other's throats, sniping and snapping for no good reason. Now I know that you know I am not a humanitarian. The general state of human comity in the town of Cicely, Alaska, is of merely passing, theoretical interest to me. I go about my business and I expect others to go about theirs. I'm no liberal sob-sister moping over why people are sometimes mean to each other or don't recycle their Q-tips.

But what I *am* is an explorer and a businessman, and all this free-floating antipathy is bad for business. How can I invite a Michael Eisner or a Charlie Rouse or a Steve Jobs up here and urge them to plunk down two, three hundred million dollars if the entire town at the hub of this thing is evincing a group state of PMS?

So I thought, Hey—let's put on a show! Because I don't care what your age, socioeconomic background, or taste in entertainment is, I don't care who you're peeved at or what kind of mood you're in: you work on or sit and watch one of these splendid examples of musical theatre, and I defy you to leave the auditorium without a song in your heart, a tear in your eye, and a smile on your lips. A project like this will bring the whole town together. What amazes me is the fact that I didn't think of it sooner.

I am going to hold open auditions for all roles, although I can confide in you, off the record, that I have certain assumptions about which of our citizens will probably be cast in which roles.

Let me now tell you what roles I see you in and describe them so you'll appreciate the snug fit:

1) *The King and I*—Lady Thiang, the King's wife. Shunted aside, neglected, world-weary, but oh, so wise. Has a dandy solo number, "Something Wonderful." ("He may not always say/ What you would have him say/But then sometimes he'll say/ Something wonderful . . .") This show is my own personal favorite.

2) *My Fair Lady*—Mrs. Pierce, Higgins' main maid. Proper, unflappable, she has some sweet lines in "I Could Have Danced All Night" and—this will appeal to your sense of irony—gets to have Higgins talk-sing to her, "Mrs. Pierce, you're a woman. Why can't a woman . . . be more like a man?"

3) *Guys and Dolls*—The Captain of the Salvation Army. A can-do military woman and type-casting, if you ask me. No songs, though.

4) *Oklahoma!*—Aunt Eller. No-nonsense, good-natured aunt to the leading lady. A person of gumption. No extended solos, but gets to strut her stuff in "The Farmer and The Cowman Should Be Friends."

5) *The Music Man*—Town lady, can't think of her name, who leads the others in the sprightly, irresistible gossip song "Pick a Little, Talk a Little." There's the role of Marion's mother, but better suited to a more mature woman.

Now I ask you: is that a selection of theatrical plums? It occurs to me that you may not be familiar with all of the above shows, their scores or plots. Feel free to audition my cast albums at any time, although I will have to insist it be done in my music room. I don't want to let those babies out of my sight. Meanwhile, let me know if any of this tickles your fancy. And don't tell me you don't have any theatrical experience. For one thing, you're a police officer, i.e., a public servant. You play a role every time you strap on the holster. For another, no one here does. I have never directed a show in my life. Why let that stop us? This is Alaska!

> *Very fondly,*
> *Maurice*

. . . .

APRIL 17

Matthew Miller
Flanagan, Bender, and Zipperstein
265 Michigan Ave.
Chicago, IL

Dear Matthew,

You don't know me, but I'm a friend of Ruth-Anne Miller. She's your mother. She asked me to write to you to bring you up to date on what's going on here in Cicely, because she is so busy she doesn't have time to write. She says not to worry, she is fine. And I'd like to add that she is fine, but she really doesn't have time.

She was even too busy to talk to Dr. Fleischman and Dr. Robertson and Maggie O'Connell last night when they came by to interview her for the scientific paper they're writing to win the Nobel Prize. It's about why we're not sleeping.

Maggie asked Ruth-Anne if she could take about a half hour off to answer some questions, but she said no, she had to shelve three cases of Progresso soup and then said she had a question for them. She asked them if they thought she should sell appliances.

Dr. Fleischman said, "Ruth-Anne, absolutely, what a superb idea! Get some popcorn machines, some blenders . . . I mean, not to drive Holling to the poorhouse, but that would make a lot of people self-sufficient."

Then Maggie said, "Fleischman, only you would think that being able to make your own popcorn in your own popcorn machine, both of which have been flown in five hundred miles, makes a person self-sufficient."

Dr. Fleischman said, "Sorry, O'Connell. Not everyone is a crackerjack homemaker like you. Did she cook for you yet, Mike?"

"Why as a matter of fact she did," Dr. Robertson said. He looks like the man in a movie who seems like a great guy but ends up disappointing the protagonist.

"And what did she make? No, don't tell me—"

"Fleischman—"

"—lasagna?"

"You know, Joel," Dr. Robertson said, "She did make lasagna, and it was abs—"

"And the Caesar salad, right? With the coddled egg? Say what you will about Maggie O'Connell, she knows how to coddle an egg."

"Michael," Maggie said, "I'll talk to Ruth-Anne later, when she has time. Let's go back to the office, and we can start organizing the transcripts."

Dr. Fleischman said, "Forget it, O'Connell. Mike and I are setting up a conference call with a geologist in Seattle."

"Joel," Dr. Robertson said, "You call him. Lay the groundwork, explain the situation. Then set up another call for next week, and I'll sit in. Maggie, on the laptop, boot up FoxPro and find a file called Outline. Break down the transcripts according to those categories."

"Okay. Uh—how?"

"Oh, then just do it from DOS. I have some calls to make."

"Huh?"

Dr. Fleischman said, "Mike, it's four in the morning."

"I know. I'm calling Rome."

Then Ruth-Anne reminded them she needed some input about whether or not she should stock appliances. Like maybe ice cream makers.

"Ice cream makers?" Dr. Robertson said, and he laughed and looked at Dr. Fleischman. "Like sending coals to Newcastle, isn't it?"

Ruth-Anne said no, selling ice cream makers wasn't like sending coals to Newcastle. It was like sending a coal-burning stove to Newcastle, which they probably did all the time. It would only be like sending coals to Newcastle, Ruth-Anne said, if she was talking about selling snow.

So as you can see, she's fine.

Yours truly,
Ed Chigliak

....

Mr. Barney St. John
State Farm Insurance
338 Fifth Street
Anchorage, AK

Dear Barney:

How are you? I'm fine, as is Shelly. The reason I'm writing is I want to know if there is a more extended kind of insurance coverage I can buy for the Brick that would cover widespread acts of destruction. Lately, everyone in town has grown so irritable, we have been plagued by incidents of accidental breakage. The amount of glasses and plates that have fallen on the floor has gone through the roof. A case in point was last night.

Maurice Minnifield came in at about seven o'clock with a poster he tacked up on the bulletin board. The place was packed. Maurice called for quiet and announced that he was going to put on a production of *Guys and Dolls,* starring Cicely's most talented. He then invited everyone to auditions, starting the day after tomorrow.

"I've thought about it," he said, "And I have concluded that Frank Loesser's classic is best suited to our purposes. We can fake the costumes, we don't need English accents, and there's unlimited room for men and women in the chorus."

Well, as you can imagine, this left us all a bit confused. He told us how he would make copies of the script available, and he'd personally tape the album for whoever didn't have it. Then he gave us one of his great big smiles, spread open his arms, and said, "So how about it? Are you interested?"

There was absolute silence. People looked at each other. I thought, well, these are wilderness people, most of them haven't seen a play. Maybe one or two of them have been up to the dinner theater near Sourdough, but that's about it.

Maurice was getting an earful of nothing, so he squinted and glared around the room and said, "I have a lot of time, effort, and prestige riding on a group of invitations I have sent to some of the biggest movers and shakers in the nation. A movie star, whom I am not at liberty to identify, may come up here any day now with checkbook blazing. I want these people to see a united, happy community. Now you all know how much we have been getting on each other's nerves. Staging this show will be good therapy for one and all."

Then Don Galen, a mechanic, stood up and yelled, "How come we can't do *Mame?*"

People nodded and murmured, "Hell yes, I love that damn show," like that, until Maurice waved for quiet. "Because we need a show with an equal balance of men and women," he said. "For God's sake—*Mame* is two gals and a little boy!"

"That's not why," someone said. Maurice looked around and found who it was. It was Ed Chigliak, who has been especially peeved with Maurice these days.

"Well, Ed, suppose you tell me why," Maurice said.

"We're not doing *Mame* because you don't like it," Ed said. "You told me so yourself, Maurice. You once said, 'I respect the hell out of Angela Lansbury, but that Jerry Herman score is like a cheap wedding cake. All icing, no substance. All flourishes, no flavor.' That's what you said, Maurice."

At that everybody started talking at once. *"Camelot* is very colorful." "I like *Sweeney Todd.*" *"South Pacific* or count me out!" *"La Cages Aux Folles?* That's for . . . well . . . *gay* people!" and so on.

But the loudest of all was my own Shelly! "Pipe DOWN, Ed," she said, coming around the counter with a tray of five glasses of beer. "Honestly, so Maurice doesn't like *Mame*—who cares?"

Ed, who is a mild-mannered young man, looked wounded and said in his hangdog way, "I was just reporting the truth."

At that Shelly dropped the tray! And the glasses shattered, the beer flew every which way, and she screamed, actually screamed, "Stop moping! Just stop it! I can't stand that mopey-dopey look of yours!"

"Now hold on—" Maurice said. But just then who should stand up at his end of the bar, but Chris Stevens, our local radio personality. I have found his very presence intolerable lately, so when he said, "A man's look is a man's soul, Miss Tambo. Men don't tint their faces or paint their lips," I saw red.

Shelly said, "Huh? What's that supposed to mean?"

I stepped in and said, "Chris, I'll thank you to leave these premises."

"What for, Holling?" someone said, and it was Marilyn Whirl-wind, a local Indian woman. "What Chris said is true."

"Marilyn," I began to say.

But at that moment Maurice pointed to her and said, "Damn! You going to let her talk to you like that, Vincouer?"

By then everybody was yelling, standing up, shaking fists, stuff was falling off of tables, glasses were breaking and crunching underfoot—and the thing was, Barney, it wasn't a brawl. Nobody threw a single punch. Instead I heard random shouts from people like, "Will you please wear a different belt for once in your life!" and "I hate your beard! Do you hear me? I hate it!" And, one by one, people stormed out of the bar. As they left they did more damage—upending chairs, knocking glasses off tables, and so forth.

Finally, when only about eight people were left and the place was a complete shambles, Maurice looked around, and it was perfectly silent, and he said, "Sign-up sheet in my office tomorrow. Character descriptions to be posted nearby. Scripts available on request. Come on, people . . ." He stopped to brush some mustard off his jacket sleeve, then said, "Let's make some magic."

Is there some kind of coverage I get for that? Let me know. Call any time. Thanks, Barney.

Yours,
Holling

. . . .

18 APRIL

Mr. Charles McDevitt, CPA
3383 Fourth Ave.
Anchorage, AK

Charley—

Thanks for getting that tax extension. Every day we keep their cut in our hands is a victory for our side.

Another question: as part of my continuing promotion of Cicely as a site for commercial development, I am contemplating staging a musical. Are the expenses I incur in so doing deductible? Duly documented, of course. I intend to use local talent, but as our community lacks a suitable venue for the performance of a full-dress theatrical production, I may decide to undertake improvements in one of my properties, e.g., one or two storefronts I own or even my own home.

Would such a remodeling qualify as capital improvement, deductible only over the long term if I sell the property, or can I claim the expenses as legitimate business investments? I know it's a grey area. But believe me when I tell you that I'm doing this strictly to promote community harmony and thereby get Cicely in the proper mood to receive visiting developers. Because somebody had better do something. This town is in a snit like you wouldn't believe.

Regards to Bonnie.

Best,
Maurice

Mr. John Newton
KZAK
Anchorage, AK

Dear John:

I know I could call, but I wanted to put this on paper so it can sit on your desk and haunt you until you do me the following favor. Without going into the whys and wherefores, which are considerable, suffice it to say I am planning a production of *Guys and Dolls* down here in Cicely, to go on the boards probably around the end of May. Local people in all the roles.

As the purpose of this project is more therapeutic than aesthetic, I have no need of an orchestra or pit band. In fact, all I have in mind is a single piano. Now, we have a gal in town who can play the hell out of the instrument; can't sight read perfectly, but give her some practice and you'd get your money's worth.

Problem is, John, lately I have grown inexpressibly irritated with her. The whole town's like that: everybody hates somebody sometime, but it's not "hate" so much as a kind of irked antipathy. Well, I am irked by this gal and would sooner shave with a chainsaw than ask her to play piano in my show. So I'm writing you to ask if you know anyone in Anchorage who'd be interested. We both share an affection for the American musical theatre, so I know I can trust you to pick the right kind of pianist.

I am willing to pay for the musician's time and will put him or her up in my guest room. Rehearsals would commence around Mon., May 4, and last four weeks or so. The run itself would probably cover the first week of June.

It won't be a cake walk; the whole town is feeling ornery and temperamental. Even in the best of times we are talking about a cast and crew of surpassing amateurish incompetence, so your suggested musician had better bring along a sense of humor. But having said that, let me add that I believe in Cicely and know

that my fellow Cicelians will extend themselves to make him or
her feel at home. All except that Marilyn Whirlwind.

> *Best,*
> *Maurice Minnifield*

....

My Dearest Mother—

I'd ask "How Are You?" but who am I kidding? I don't
REALLY CARE.

I'm fine.

Not that I'm sleeping. No, we don't "do" that here any more.
Have you any idea what torture it is to be trapped in my superior
consciousness twenty-four hours a day? The acuteness, the pain,
the limpid clarity—just FORGET IT. If you're wondering whether
a friend in Singapore sent me a case of coconut milk, the answer
is yes. I'm doing curries. Simmering. Simmering! At the lowest
possible heat, so that the bubbles, the thing bubbles, I'm micro-
adjusting the stove so that I get at most one bubble every twenty
seconds. *You will be interested to note that I have installed a
seven-inch-diameter ten-pound lead flywheel to the right front
burner in order to calibrate its level with maximum precision.*
Then I sit there and stare at the simmering curry and DARE a
premature bubble to surface. Of course this takes time. But now
I have time in abundance. Yesterday I sat and dared the bubbles
for eighteen hours until I was sure it was under control. Then I
simmered the curry for another twelve hours. In this way, the
coconut milk reduces to almost a GLAZE.

The result was acceptable.

Then I went into town. Why? PERHAPS IT HAD SOMETHING
TO DO WITH THE FACT THAT THE LEAD FLYWHEEL FELL ONTO
MY NAKED "FOOT" AND CRUSHED MY TOES.

So I went into the office of the doctor, Dr. Fleischman, as his
name is. Present at the desk in the front was Maggie O'Connell.
I KNOW YOU DON'T KNOW THEM. I was surprised. But in the
current situation, as it develops, Maggie is the day receptionist

and Marilyn, the magnificent totem-head, the one woman I actually RESPECT in this miserable town, is the nighttime one. And now, an evocation of what transpired——

Dr. Joel emerged from the back room. He saw, among other waiting patients, me. His greeting? A curt, blunt "What."

Naturally I disdained to give him the satisfaction of knowing my pain. "Nothing," I replied. "I was in need of entertainment, so I came here."

"Fleischman," Maggie said from the desk, broadcasting disapproval. "The man limps in here with bleeding toes, and all you can say is 'what'?"

Fleischman laughed, the swine. "Is that what he told you, O'Connell? Bleeding toes?"

"No, he didn't 'tell' me," she riposted. Riposted! "He didn't have to tell me, Fleischman—"

"Because you're psychic?" He addressed the line of impassive Indians and grousing loggers and sullen MORONS and all the other worthy ladies and gentlemen in attendance. "Madame Maggie. Palmistry, tea leaves—"

"Fleischman, I happen to know for a fact he has bleeding toes—"

"And how, O'Connell?"

"Because he's not wearing any shoes."

Fleischman looked at my feet. I HEREBY CONDEMN THE WOMAN FOR REVEALING MY SECRET. "Adam," he said. "What happened? Did you—"

"Did I what?" I said, unshakeable in my conviction, whatever it was.

"Did you WALK here with your foot like that?"

"No," I sneered. "I flew. With love's light wings did I climb these walls."

Dr. Fleischman made a face. Of inconvenience! I will destroy him one day. And yet the love I feel for this man . . . "Let me dress this," he said. To the others in the waiting room he said, "Does anyone mind? He's visibly bleeding . . ."

No one did, and as the noble physician led me into the room, his receptionist said, through tight teeth, "You owe me an apology, Fleischman."

I wheeled on her, I rejoined thus, saying, "Touchy touchy, Nurse Margaret?"

"What for, O'Connell?"

"That crack about being psychic."

"I apologize."

"Say it like you mean it."

"I don't mean it."

"You are unbelievable, Fleischman! Why do you always have to have the upper hand? If it's not with your patients, then it's with me and Michael. It gets to you, doesn't it? That he and I are working so closely together."

"O'Connell, you have become seriously delusional! Do you honestly believe that your role in the project is in any possible way comparable to or on a par with mine? That my working relationship with Dr. Robertson could possibly be eclipsed or rivalled by your inherently secretarial role?"

"CHILDREN!" I cried. "WHY CAN'T WE ALL JUST BE AMERICANS AND LOVE ONE ANOTHER?"

They didn't listen. They never do.

All my filial love, naturally. I need money.

> *Madam, I'm,*
> *Adam*

. . . .

APRIL 20

Dear Jen—

Well, it happened.

We were in the office (Michael and me) working. (I'd say "working late," but around here 2:30 in the morning just means it's dark outside. There is no "late.") I was typing on the laptop, he was . . . well, at first he had been reviewing data, but suddenly he was leaning over my shoulder. Maybe he really was reading what I was typing. At any rate, he said, "Maggie."

148

I stopped typing. His face was four inches from my neck. "Uh . . . Michael?"

"Seriously. Haven't we been coy long enough?"

"Uh, really . . . ?"

Of course I knew what was coming, and I guess I could have moved away. Part of me wanted it to happen, which didn't surprise me, but part of me didn't want it to happen, which did surprise me. In any case, he kissed my neck, which was nice. And then he kept doing it. But as soon as I got ready to be swept up in it, something shut down inside. So I pulled away and said, "Not here."

He paused and nodded. "Your place?"

"No . . ."

He looked puzzled. "My place?"

I laughed. Some "place." He's staying in a room in Ella Capaldi's house. She's a snoopy, paranoid old biddy who rents out rooms, and it had taken a phone call from Fleischman, a *prescription*, to convince Ella to give Michael a key so he could come and go at will. The notion of us going there was absurd.

So I shook my head and said, "No, not there. Not . . . I guess what I'm saying is, not now."

"Not yet?"

"Yes. No. I don't know. Just *not*, for now."

At which he shrugged, nodded, and we went back to work. After a few minutes I said, "Michael?"

"Yes, Maggie?"

"What's the Rockstoffen experiment?"

"Nothing."

"Is it—are we in any danger—"

"No. Forget it. Hey, why don't I give you a back rub? I'm told I have a certain touch."

"No, thanks."

"Suit yourself."

Did I do the right thing? Please advise.

In knots,
Maggie

Dear Aunt Ilene,

How are you? I am fine. I thought you would be interested in something happening here in Cicely. We are doing a production of *Guys and Dolls,* which will probably be performed starting Sunday night, May 31. Maybe you would like to come. I will be playing piano for it.

I almost wasn't. But Maurice Minnifield, who is in charge of it, came to see me at the doctor's office where I work. He said how lately he had been very irritated with me. I said I knew, that I was very irritated with Holling Vincouer. He said we were all victims of irritation and that the economic future of Cicely depended on our overcoming it, which depended on doing this production of *Guys and Dolls,* which depended on my playing piano for it. So he said he was willing to overcome his annoyance for the sake of Cicely's future and asked me to play piano. I said, that depends. He said, on what. I said, on one important thing. He said, well, what is it. If it's whether or not he'd be in the show, the answer is no. I said, that isn't it. He said, then what? I said, Will Holling be in it? He said, well, possibly.

Auditions are going along fine and he could promise that Holling would not have a lead role. But if it came down to Holling or you, Maurice said, Holling is expendable.

I told him I would think about it. But I think I'll say yes. It sounds like fun. As long as Holling won't be sitting next to me at the piano, turning the pages.

Love,
Marilyn

Mr. Kurt Anderson
Spy Magazine
5 Union Square West
New York, NY 10003

Dear Mr. Anderson:

I note with a faint but palpable pang of dismay that you haven't yet responded to my letter of whenever it was. Which is fine. In it, as I'm sure you have no need to be reminded, I offered to write an article for *Spy* about the small town in Alaska where I live. "Cicely: The Town That Never Sleeps" was the suggested title, which at first glance seems to offer no more than a typical *Spy*-ish slice of irony, but which in fact is meant to be taken literally, in dead, dead earnest or, if you prefer, deadly deadly earnestly. What I'm saying, or failing to say, is that, because of sunspots and magnetic field fluctuations, we residents of Cicely, AK, have not slept since Feb. 28.

I now hereby amend the offer. I am currently collaborating with Dr. Michael Robertson, of the Wilson Neurological Institute in Philadelphia. We are undertaking a scientific examination of the sleeplessness phenomenon and will be submitting in due course a paper to one of the leading medical journals.

That's how legit this whole thing is—which is why I feel that the subject is extremely *Spy*-worthy. In fact Dr. Robertson's involvement has already drawn some (mainstream) national media attention. Just this morning—by which I mean 4 AM local time—Dr. Robertson was interviewed via telephone by Robert Siegel, of "All Things Considered," on National Public Radio for a taped segment to be broadcast in a few days.

I was in the office when Mr. Siegel interviewed Dr. Robertson, consulting primary sources with regard to a theory (my own, actually) positing the site of the disturbance as being somewhere in the neuronal link between the midbrain reticular formation and the circadian mechanism of the hypothalamus.

Sound impressive? I hope so. It did when Dr. Robertson enunciated the hypothesis to Robert Siegel, without, I noted, crediting the theory's originator.

What I have in mind for *Spy* is a sort of James Watkins/Double Helix behind-the-scenes story, which is still unfolding, of course. I would therefore be both unable and, frankly, unwilling to write the article until this anomaly is solved, ideally (I didn't say "hopefully"; I believe in using "hopefully" correctly) thanks to the work of myself and Dr. Robertson.

Look, I know *Spy* likes to cover stories about true-but-wacky science. Here's a true-but-wacky phenomenon, experienced by wacky-but-true Alaskans, being covered firsthand by true, non-wacky scientists. It's not a home run, but it's a clean double, isn't it?

I await your reply.

Yours truly,
Joel Fleishman, M.D.

MINNIFIELD COMMUNICATIONS

CICELY, ALASKA

907-555-8610

GUYS AND DOLLS

Official Cast List

Sky Masterson	Chris Stevens
Nathan Detroit	Joel Fleischman
Sarah Brown	Maggie O'Connell
Miss Adelaide	Shelly Tambo
Nicely Nicely Johnson	Ed Chigliak
Harry the Horse	Dave
Big Jule from Chicago	Holling Vincouer
Salvation Army Captain	Barbara Semanski
Various Gamblers	TBA

The Hot Box Girls .... TBA
Salvation Army People .... Ruth-Anne Miller, TBA

Piano .... Marilyn Whirlwind

Entire Production Produced and Staged by
Maurice Minnifield

....

APRIL 24

Dear Tawni,

Look at this list! COULD YOU DIE!! Do you believe I am one of the LEADS in our new show? (I told Maurice, who is putting it all together, that it would be nice if the guy I was playing opposite was Holling, but that I understood how it had to be someone more my own age. So it's Dr. Fleischman, who as a matter of fact *is* kind of cute. Although it'll be real weird doing, like, love scenes with your DOCTOR.)

Anyway, my part is this real hot night club dancer! I can't wait. Plus I have a couple songs. One is a SOLO about catching a cold (!!), the other is with Dr. Fleischman. I mean I am PUMPED. I asked Maurice who is going to teach us the dancing, and he said he was working on it.

The only problem is Ed Chigliak is in the cast, and he gets on my nerves. But I don't think I have any scenes with him. Of course, by now we've all realized that each of us gets on the nerves of somebody else. Maurice says that's the point, that's why we need to do the show.

Can you come? I mean, I know you're 700 miles away. But try to. You can stay with us for a couple of days and we'll have a blast. And you can meet Holling who (ask Cyndy) is totally bitchen. (I can't wait to see him in costume! Are you ready for this? Holling is actually going to wear A SUIT!)

Let me know.

Shells

153

Dear Jack,

Remember the letter I sent you two days ago, which you probably haven't received yet but which you will certainly have received before you receive this one, unless for some reason you don't? Well, ignore it. Here's what's new:

I arrived at Fleischman's office this morning. He was already there. He was already there. It was whatever it was—9:00. He said, Where were you? I said, What do you mean, where was I? He said, We were supposed to meet here at 7:30. I said, I'm sorry. You're right. I forgot. I was working with Michael.

This is hard to follow, isn't it? How about this:

> F: Doing what?
>
> ME: What do you think, Fleischman? Transcribing interviews.
>
> F: Why does he have to be there? Can't you just listen to a tape and type what's being said?
>
> M: We discuss what's relevant. And what do you care?
>
> F: I care because if you miss appointments with me, I can't get away in time to do *my* work with him, which, if you'll excuse me for saying so, is just a little more important than the transcription of tapes.
>
> ME (OUTRAGED): Fleischman, you are unbelievable! I have witnessed your arrogance over the past two years, and there have been times when I was tempted to phone the *Guinness Book of World Records* to make sure you got recognition for it. But this—!
>
> F: O'Connell—what do you think this is? Grad school, where everyone gets a session with the prof? This is SCIENCE, okay? This is real professional research. Where everyone has to do his OR HER job, and meet commitments, and not turn every work session into playtime—

ME: WHAT?

F:—and not cadge an extra hour with "Michael" because it's so cosy and such fun leaning over the laptop together.

ME: How dare you—! No. No. Fleischman, I am not going to lose my temper. Because I can see very clearly what is happening here. You are jealous. Daddy is spending more time with sister than with Joel, and it makes you mad.

F: Oh, slick. Very slick. Reduce everything to The Berenstain Bears Enter Analysis. Frankly, O'Connell, I'm surprised. That sort of stuff is not worthy of you. Or maybe—maybe you're just not clear about your sense of priorities.

ME: Meaning what?

F: Meaning that maybe you have to choose which is more important: the health of the community or your own private . . . personal life.

ME: Fleischman, is this the delayed effect of not sleeping? Massive, sudden breakdowns of rational capacity? Are you going insane before my very eyes?

F: I need you here. In this office. Cicely needs you here. It's hard enough for me, working double shifts here AND helping Dr. Robertson get to the bottom of this thing—

ME: Excuse me, Doctor Selfless. I tend to forget that you are in fact a saint and are working with Michael strictly out of disinterested altruism and with no thought at all of career advancement.

F: No, no, but if Cicely is going to enjoy proper medical care, then the doctor's staff must be on call and on duty and on time. So—

ME: So what? What are you saying, Fleischman? Spit it out.

F: I'm saying you have to choose. Him or me.

ME (STUNNED, GAPING, GASPING FOR AIR):——
???? What?

F: You heard me. I can't run a proper office if my day receptionist is off somewhere. Either you work for Dr. Robertson or me. Pick one.

ME: No. I'm not going to pick one. That is without a doubt the most ridiculous, the most pathetically insecure—

F: Fine. You're fired.

ME: Fleischman, PLEASE don't be this way.

F: I'm not being any way. I'm trying to be professional.

ME: You really are jealous, aren't you? That's . . . kind of sweet in a sort of infuriating, repellent way—

F: I'm very busy, O'Connell. Excuse me.

—and he went into his office and slammed the door behind him.

What does it all mean? It means that I'll go back to helping Ruth-Anne at the General Store and Holling at the Brick. Which is fine. It means that Fleischman and I will probably avoid each other like the plague, at least until this blows over, which I doubt that it will. It means that Michael will be in the middle.

And it means I will not be able to take part in the show. The idea of sharing a stage with him, even though Nathan Detroit and Sarah Brown are rarely in scenes together, and even though we don't literally have a stage, is just too much for now.

Otherwise I'm fine. How are you?

Love,
Maggie

. . . .

4/25

Dear Mom,

I'm sorry, but you'll have to cancel your reservations. I'm not going to be in *Guys and Dolls* like I told you on the phone. It's a long story, but it just isn't going to work out with my other medical responsibilities. I know you and Pop were looking

156

forward to visiting me here, but the show will go on without me. So maybe put it off until something else comes up.

Otherwise, thanks for the pastrami. And the lox, although there's so much fresh salmon up here maybe you can find a recipe, and I can make it myself. The Eskimos dry it in the sun and eat it as finger food. It's called Eskimo candy. And if you think that sounds bad—it isn't, really—wait till you try Eskimo ice cream. Somebody offered me some and I thought, Oh, like an Eskimo pie, vanilla ice cream covered in chocolate. Well, not really. It's actually whipped seal oil mixed with very bitter berries and snow. But don't be misled—it's actually worse than it sounds.

So as you can see, I'd love for you to visit, but not only is there nothing to eat, I'm not going to be in the show. Regards to Pop.

Love,
Joey

MINNIFIELD COMMUNICATIONS

CICELY, ALASKA

907-555-8610

GUYS AND DOLLS

Revised Official Cast List

Sky Masterson	Maurice Minnifield
Nathan Detroit	Chris Stevens
Sarah Brown	Barbara Semanski
Miss Adelaide	Shelly Tambo
Nicely Nicely Johnson	Ed Chigliak
Harry the Horse	Dave

Big Jule from Chicago .... Holling Vincouer
Salvation Army Captain .... Ruth-Anne Miller

Various Gamblers .... TBA
The Hot Box Girls .... TBA
Salvation Army People .... TBA

....

APRIL 27

Dear Tawni,

Big changes here. Maggie and Dr. Fleischman had a fight and they dropped out of the show. So Maurice is going to play the lead, and Chris will play opposite me. Which is cool, at least with me. But another new problem is, just like I get really annoyed with Ed, Chris gets really annoyed with me. We all know there's no real reason for it, but we still feel like we want to scream. So Maurice will have his hands full. (He's still directing, as well as starring.)

Still, come on out. Even when these shows are terrible, it turns out to be fun. Remember the Drama Club's production of *Macbeth?* What a hoot! But I still think my big scene would have gone over better if the nuns hadn't refused to let me say "damn" onstage. Because A, it's Shakespeare, right? and B, saying "Out, out darn spot" sounds so, like, lame.

Still, it was fun. So this will be too. Call me!

Shelly

....

4/30

R.M.
S.,V.,B, &K.
Address
NYC

Dear Richie—

Thanks for the books. I plan to be seen in public reading the Stephen King and, if it's all the same to you, will keep—

hide—*Chutzpah!* under my pillow to be savored alone, in private, under the covers. But both are appreciated. Our local "library" consisted of three empty shelves until one of our ditsier residents, Ms. Shelly Tambo, took part (against my express advice) in a chain letter for which the currency was books. Result: she and her boyfriend (sic; he's 63) bring them in for general circulation by the boxful, by the hundreds. And not all of them are worthless!

I said "under the covers" above, but I mean it as an idiomatic, or in my case, idiotic expression. I spend virtually no time under my covers. I don't sleep, and God knows I don't have a sex life. The only benefit of such a routine is that I never have to launder my linen or, indeed, even make my bed. Is it worth it? A resounding no. But it does afford me more time for my work, which in this case means seeing almost two full shifts of patients a day AND pursuing a crash research project with a Phila. expert on sleep disorders and brain functioning. He told me half an hour ago that he has to go back to Philly for two weeks, leaving me to carry on the good fight. (My God, an innocent typo and it would have said, ". . . to carry on the food fight.") Leaving me with time to read more, too.

And, with time to bicker with Maggie O'Connell, about whom I may have told you. Apparently now we hate each other's guts. But I don't take it personally. Still, these next two weeks may be interesting as re her, too. And the rest of the town? Thanks for asking. They'll be appearing in a production of *Guys and Dolls*. I turned them down for one of the leads, so when you call for reservations, don't mention my name. They're still mad.

Yours in Chutzpah!,
Joel

PART THREE

AND
SO
TO BED

Herr Kriminal Wolfgang Puck
Spago/Chinois/Eureka/Whatever
Los Angeles, CA

Puck—

I'm still WAITING. Waiting for you to behave like a man of
HONOR, instead of the loathsome pipsqueak we both know you
to BE. Waiting for you to respond to my just claim and remit the
money that is rightfully mine. Waiting for you to ADMIT TO THE
WORLD THAT IT WAS I WHO INVENTED THE DUCK SAUSAGE
PIZZA, AND NOT YOU, you detestable but charismatic little
genius/copycat.

Shall I refresh your ego-clouded memory? That afternoon at
Ma Maison all those years ago? When in a fit of appropriate
indignation I stormed back into the kitchen and WITH MY OWN
LIVING HANDS fashioned the scraps and remnants of the (serviceable, no more. SERVICEABLE) fowl into the item for which
you have become so ill-deservedly famous? Oh yes, it all comes
back to you now. The minced ginger. The touch of (fresh)
coriander. The insufferable Terrail hovering, hovering. I'm WAIT-
ING.

You know my terms. A dollar for every duck sausage pizza you
have served since you opened. In CASH. You reply: "But Adam,
why cannot I send a check, dear boy?" Because I don't TRUST
you, no, you or your very lovely, very talented wife.

I hear the two of you laughing, crying, groveling. Get up. You
embarrass me. "But my dear Adam," you protest. "How can I
possibly know how many of your originally conceived duck

sausage pizza pies I have sold since opening?" Do what school-children do, maestro. ESTIMATE.

But be utterly accurate or face the consequences. A buck a pie. Act now. Rates go up after Memorial Day.

Irreproachably yours,
Adam

· ·

MAY 2

Dear "Mother"—

My own beloved Eve is heavy with child. There is life in the woman, "Ma," life which will out. I know you join me in wishing me and her all the best. Certainly everyone else does. Have I mentioned what happened yesterday? When I was forced, com-pelled by a sense of fatherly-to-be obligation, to enter the repellent premises of Ruth-Anne Miller's "General Store" be-cause the mother of my offspring declined my offer of a maple sugar crème brulée because she wanted a ZAGNUT?

I entered the establishment and beheld a singular tableau: our own Dr. Fleischman, who as you know is my personal physician, and Margaret O'Connell, who as you know is my personal pilot. These two were elaborately ignoring one another in that stylized pas de deux in which people seek to indicate a passionate unconcern for individuals in whom they are inordintely inter-ested. Naturally I challenged them on the spot.

"So here we are," I sneered perceptively. "The sensitive young doctor and the spirited young pilot. Abie's Irish Rose with a college education. What's the matter, campers? Having a spat?"

"Butt out, Adam," Fleischman replied.

"How's Eve?" O'Connell asked.

"Changing the subject, Margaret?" I countered. "And what of the handsome Dr. Robertson? Still his slave? Still typing his notes like a grad school wife?"

"I don't need this," O'Connell said. "Where's Ruth-Anne?"

"Busy with the mail in the back," Fleischman said. "But wait,

164

I think he's on to something. That's a very perceptive comment, Adam. Grad school wife. Very trenchant."

"As though you can talk?" I wheeled on the doctor and fixed him with my baleful gaze. "While you labor on his behalf, like an unnamed apprentice in a master's studio?"

"Touché," O'Connell said.

"No, not touché. Wait a minute—"

I seized the relevant candy bar and glared at him. Holding up the confection, I said, "Pay for it. Put it on my tab." Then I turned on my heel and strode out.

I still need money. I am contemplating working.

Yours,
Adam

....

Dear Tony,

From the Be-Careful-What-You-Wish-For,-You-Just-Might-Get-It File:

Of the women I mentioned I had written to, all three accepted. And arrived en masse on April 29. On the same bush plane from Anchorage.

It sounds like a bad sitcom premise, but you should have seen it, man. Three women stepping out of the plane down onto the field and looking around, like a rock group on tour, airlifted into the next small town and gearing up to make the best of it. Except *pissed*—each bristling with grievance, in search of something or someone (me) to explain and assuage. These three good-looking ladies, in their flattering jeans and brightly colored ski jackets, their hair brushed out and just a bit of makeup for traveling, saw me coming and struck annoyed, arms-folded, this-better-be-good poses. And while of course I was eager to rush forward and offer my heartfelt apologies, I had to stop and just dig the scene for a moment.

Because, while I had essentially the same thing in common

165

with each of them, it was still an eerie thing for me to see them *with each other.* It was as though three pieces of my inner emotional being—the separate feelings of connection I had with each of them—had been taken out of me, set up fifty feet away, and transformed into feelings of connection they had between each other.

Get it? People from separate incidents of your life commingled in an unlikely juxtaposition? A piece of the inner emotional state embodied objectively over there in a striking (and not unerotic) sight? What I'm saying is: it was like a dream.

So already I was hitting paydirt in my effort to regain access to the unconscious. Sadly, that sensation lasted about as long as it took for me to reach them and give greeting. Will you be surprised to learn I was the only one smiling? Katherine, the intellectual, said drily, "You overbooked."

Kay, the political activist, added, "This is insulting."

Kimberlee, the artist, summed it all up. "This is real gross, Chris."

The scene went on from there, part low comedy, part high indignation. But I wasted no time finessing. I played my trump card immediately and no one could top it: I said that Katherine, Kay, and Kimberlee were about to experience something utterly new and unique. ("Oh please" and similar snorts of derisive skepticism.) I apologized about getting my logistics snarled, but promised these women that they would, at midnight tonight, be as awake as they were now and would remain so indefinitely. ("Oh really?" and similar expressions mistaking our town's objective fact for my own subjective sexual vanity.) I apologized, I begged forgiveness, I winked saucily—I did what needed doing.

Finally I told them that they could either get back on that plane or arrange a different flight out tomorrow—by which time they would see what I was saying was true. So why not chance it and stay the night?

After a brief huddle, in which their sisterly solidarity was demonstrated for my benefit, they agreed.

Next we needed accommodations—not for sleeping, mind you, but for washing, changing clothes, "sitting," etc. This called for two rooms, since I offered to share my trailer with one of them under whatever conditions they thought appropriate (I was admirably deadpan when I said this and may actually have meant it.) We went to town, where I prevailed on Maggie O'Connell and Joel Fleischman to let the women use their homes. Joel's barely accommodates one, and Maggie's is spare as a monk's cell, since all her things were destroyed when her mother burned down her cabin. But it doesn't matter; ever since we've stopped sleeping, homes have become more like locker rooms—places to change, grab a bite, take a breather, and then leave.

Maggie and Joel both agreed, but in a distracted, cursory way. They are each working for a scientist up from Philadelphia and seem to be vying for his favor. It's been four days now, and Katherine, Kay, and Kimberlee all attest that while Maggie and Joel are outwardly courteous, neither seems to be in much of a mood to play host to visiting strangers. (If you must know, yes, my three visitors and I have established a rotation, so that at any given moment one stays with me and the other two with my neighbors.)

So soon we will have to find alternative accommodations. That aside, the ladies find anomaly-plagued Cicely interesting and a life without sleep fascinating.

As for me, well, yes, it is an exhausting routine. But I have significant data to report. The anomaly has had no noticeable effect, positively or otherwise, on my sexuality. (Afterward we are tired, but we don't snooze. We rest.) I can report a marked drop-off in artistic production. But is that the result of replacing sublimation with outright nooky or simply the result of spending more time in bed and less wielding the acetylene torch? It's not clear.

So I guess I'll just have to keep investigating, won't I?

Selflessly,
Chris

Dear Tawni,

Guess what! We started rehearsal for *Guys and Dolls!*
Or, at least, we started to start. But we may not do it now.
Which is a real bummer, because my character, who I thought
was just a sort of bimbo night club singer, is a STRIPPER.

I have this fantastic song called "Take Back Your Mink," which
is about how supposedly I'm mad at this guy for giving me all
these presents, and suddenly one night he wants to take advan-
tage of my accepting his gifts and cash in and DO IT with me? (I
like totally missed all this the first time, but Maurice explained
it to me. He's the director.) So I give all the stuff back! GET IT? I
take off the mink coat and throw it in his face. I take off the
dress, the shoes, the necklace . . . and, see, not only am I taking
off my clothes, but I'M TAKING MY CLOTHES OFF.

I don't know how far we'll go with this . . . but then, I also
don't know how we'll even get started. At our first read-through
Maurice explained everything to everybody, and how we would
work on separate scenes, so there would be a rehearsal schedule
posted, and all of that. Then he asked if there were any questions.

Then Ed Chigliak—who else??? I mean, Mister Pain—raised
his hand and asked, "How will we work on the songs?"

Maurice shrugged and said, "Well, listen to the record, then
learn by doing."

Then Ed said, "Uh, Maurice? Could you try not to embarrass
me? I mean, what about the vocal arrangements?"

Maurice looked annoyed and said, "Well, hell, son, you've got
two ears. You listen to the singing and you recapitulate it."

"But what if we're not skilled recapitulators?"

I mean is that typical or what? Why does Ed have to say
recapitulators? Why can't he just say singers? Anyway, then
Maurice looked at Marilyn, the piano player, and made a face,
because he's been as p.o.'d at her as I am at Ed, and said, "Now
Marilyn, I just want you to answer one simple question. Will you

do that for me? With a minimum of Native American inscrutibility?"

"Okay."

"Can you or can you not work with the singers and do the arrangements?"

"No."

"Hey, Maurice," Chris said. "As I recall, in Act Two the men and I do a dance to "Luck Be a Lady." Are you going to choreograph that?"

So everybody turned to look at Chris, who's sitting there with—get this—THREE girlfriends. I mean I know we're not sleeping so everybody has extra time for—you know—everything. Maurice said, "Son, what I know about choreography you could inscribe on a peppercorn and still have room for the Lord's Prayer."

So I stood up and said, "Then who's going to teach me how to strip?"

At this point Holling stood up and said, "I don't know that I want *anybody* teaching you that, Shelly," and that was the signal for everybody to start talking at once. Maurice tried to quiet everybody down and reassure us that he knew what he was doing, but it seemed to most people that the point of the meeting was to prove that he DIDN'T know what he was doing.

In fact, by the time the meeting broke up, everybody was totally disgusted. Barbara Semanski said, "Maurice, if you can't mush the team properly, don't hitch up the dogs."

Afterward, at the Brick, everyone was saying too bad, it would have been fun. Like it was already a dead issue.

But I'm learning my lines anyway, just in case. (When I asked Maurice how I was supposed to speak, he said, "Hell, this takes place in New York, doesn't it? Ask Fleischman.") Holling says he's not going to let me strip, but I told him I won't go all the way (because I mean YUCK!), but just enough to get some reaction from the audience. He said what reaction. I said some hollers. He said what kind of hollers. I said nice ones. He said he'll think about it.

You know that chain letter I sent you? If you sent it out, better make room on your shelves. So far I've received 642 books. Ever hear of *Foucault's Pendulum?* We have thirteen copies. Ask if anybody wants one, but tell them it's impossible to read. Also, what the heck is *THE QURAN?* We have eight.

Well, I gotta go slice pickles. We could buy them sliced in bulk, but what about the people who like them whole?

Luv ya,
Shells

....

MAY THE 4RTH

Mr. Sydney Pollack
c/o Mirage Productions
Universal City, CA

Dear Sidney,

I know I haven't written to you for a long time, but to tell the truth, I was so disappointed with *Havana* that I couldn't bring myself to write.But I don't blame you. I think that the Cuba section of *Godfather II* was so good, it used up all the movie-energy for that subject. (I have a theory that there is a kind of energy in the atmosphere that helps people make movies about different subjects. It's sort of a private hunch, really, and not all that scientific. Still, did you see the movie *Cuba* that Richard Lester directed with Sean Connery? So there you are.)

The reason I'm writing is we have an interesting situation in our town of Cicely that could use someone of your skills. Because of sunspots, the magnetic field of the earth is making it so that none of us can sleep. We all get a lot done, and so forth, but we also get on each other's nerves. One of our citizens, Chris Stevens, says this comes from not sleeping. He's sort of a philosopher/disk jockey, so he's used to thinking about the big picture.

"Ed," he said, "we're all looking down the business end of a double whammy. First, each of us is busy being ourselves twenty-four hours a day. We're about a third again as much ourselves as normal." (There isn't really much you can say when someone says something like this to you, so I just nod and he keeps going.) "Second, none of us has the benefit of sleep in which to digest and metabolize our experiences. That's what's causing all this annoyance. We're being all that we can be, twenty-four hours a day, in each other's face. We're being ourselves. Only more so."

I don't understand this, but it sounds right. So, to bring the community together, and also so we'll be in a good mood if Kim Basinger wants to buy the town (that's a secret, so don't tell anyone yet), we are staging a production of *Guys and Dolls.* The problem is the man who says he's going to direct the show is Maurice Minnifield. He may have been a good astronaut, but he's a terrible director. So the whole production is falling apart because no one wants to work with Maurice, who doesn't know what he's doing anyway.

That's why I'm writing. You are excellent with actors. Can you offer some suggestions as to how Maurice can work with us? I will convey to him your suggestions, although he is so irritating I can barely bring myself to do it. Still, for the good of Cicely, I'll try.

Or, what would be even better is, if you could come up here and direct the show yourelf. Oh, I know what you're thinking: won't Maurice complain if you show up here wanting to take the show out of his hands? Maybe. But all he really cares about is getting the show done. He told me, "Hell, I have no ambitions or vanity about my abilities as a Broadway director. But we have got to instill some community pride and civil decorum in this town if we're going to clinch the deal with Miss Basinger."

So Maurice probably wouldn't mind if you took over. Besides, he knows that if someone doesn't help him with this soon, there won't be any show anyway. By the way, we can't pay you, but we can show you what it's like to never have to sleep. It's weird.

Your fan,
Ed Chigliak

171

Dear Michael,
   Like this card? Anyway, I was just thinking. When you get back, let's go on a hike! Overnight—tents, "gorp," campfires, etc. So I can show you more of AK than just Cicely. Telling you now so you can bring any nec. gear from Phila. (No telling when we'd wake up, though. Or if we'd sleep at all.)
   Til then . . .

                                    Maggie

PETERSBURG—"Little Norway"
Located on Mitkof Island, this town of charming and beautiful is home of the state's largest halibut fleet.

Mike—
   Note, obverse, bear. In this picture, he is looking for me so he can kill me. An idea: as long as you're fetching an EEG, what about static elect.? Any chance of a Van Der Graff generator? Or is that electroplating the lily? Just a thought. See you next week.

                                    Joel F.

THE BLONDE TOKLAT GRIZZLY is one of Alaska's most dangerous animals. When running, grizzlies can attain speeds of up to 40 mph.

. . . .

                                    5 MAY

John Newton
KZAK
Anchorage, AK

Dear John:

   You said you wanted to kept apprised of our production of *Guys and Dolls,* well, get ready. Yesterday was our first read-through—mumble-through, is more like it, although I shouldn't complain, because in the end something of a miracle occurred. Early on the cast inquired of me who was going to be vocal coach and choreographer. Will you believe me (and will you keep it under your hat) when I say that until that moment I hadn't thought about it? Oh, I knew in the back of my mind that somehow the singing would have to be spruced up and the dancing managed into more than the kind of writhing modern-dance free-for-all you see on PBS. But so great was my enthusiasm, that I failed to come to grips with these basic fundamentals.

I paid for that, I can assure you, in the hard currency of loss of face. For a while, at least. There we were, in the Cicely church, my flagrantly amateur cast, most of whom had never seen the show and some who had never even heard it (and, in one case, heard *of* it). This is our second meeting, and I have already had to personally beg some people to stay aboard. My Miss Adelaide is asking me, "Who's going to teach me how to do a strip-tease?" and my Nicely Nicely Johnson is demanding, "Who's going to show me how to sing this?" I had started to give blanket assurances that sounded hollow even to my own ears, when my Nathan Detroit, Chris Stevens, the young man who works as my drive-time dj, took me aside. I asked the cast to take ten and joined him.

With him, as it happened, were three young ladies who at his invitation had come up to Cicely to visit. Katherine from Bryn Mawr, Kay from Berkeley, and Kimberlee from some community college in Tacoma. Chris introduces them and says that they are about to save my amateur theatrical bacon.

"Now you can call this sheer luck, Maurice," Chris says. "But after a point, you have to wonder where luck ends and destiny, a conscious imposition of energy by some superior force, begins. Katherine here, it turns out, is a dancer. Kay arranges voices for a community choir. And Kimmee here is a graphic arts major."

I gaped and then said, "Which means—"

"Which means, my friend, that if you play your cards right you've got your choreographer, vocal arranger, and scenic designer staring you in the face." Then he laughed and said, "Don't look at *me,* man! I'm as shocked as you are!"

"Well," I said, smiling at these attractive ladies, "What's the game, and how do I play my hand properly? If it's a question of money—"

"We don't want money," Katherine says. "We need a place to stay."

"To *sit,*" Kay says.

"In shifts," Kimberlee says.

"They're at Joel's and Maggie's," Chris explained. "But the atmosphere is tense."

I won't bore you with the combinations and permutations. Suffice to say, bad planning had resulted in these three gals being up here all at once. So in exchange for providing room and board, I've got a crackerjack creative team the likes of which they can only dream about over their German chocolate cake up at DeConcini's Dinner Theatre. This works out tidily for all concerned, not the least of whom is Chris, who is now able to rotate his houri's like a sultan. You may be wondering if, in the private confines of my own lavish home, I ever look upon these gals with a covetous eye, but frankly, they're too young. I'm too old. And all I care about at this point is the show.

But I'm being just a tad coy with you here, John. I have another reason for being indifferent to these youngsters.

Did I tell you I'm Sky Masterson? When my first string quit, I could no longer resist temptation. Well, my Sarah Brown is Barbara Semanski, a state trooper from up north whom I might confess has been an object of my interest in times past. How she wangled time off to take part in this venture is just one more mystery in a springtime rife with enigmas. She stunned me by accepting the role, but in casting terms it's less of a stretch than it looks. Sarah Brown is punctilious, strict, a stickler for rules, and officious to the point of obsession. As I told Barbara, this is the role she was born to play.

You know life is a funny thing. I conceived of this project as a selfless businessman, as a way to unite the community. Now, suddenly, I'm center stage, doing classic dramatic scenes with this magnificent specimen of femininity!

I appreciate your interest. Look for comps when the time comes.

Best,
Maurice Minnifield

....

MAY 8

Rudolph Miller
% Oregon Freight Inc.
Portland, OR

Dear Rudy,

Ruth-Anne Miller, who as you know is your mother, asked me to write you to let you know she is okay. But she said she can't bear to look at a pencil and paper at the end of the day, so she can't write you herself. She asked me to tell you she apologizes for using me to do it. If that's not okay, and you want to communicate with her directly, just let me know and I'll tell her.

She asked me to bring you up to date on what's going on here in Cicely. So let's see. People are writing a lot of letters. A lot of people are reading. We're doing a Broadway show called *Guys and Dolls*. Ruth-Anne has a part in it, but she says she only hopes she can get away from the Post Office long enough to come to rehearsals. Maurice, the director, asked her if she was willing to wear a big bass drum for one scene if he could get one. She said no.

Let's see, what else.

Shelly is getting thousands of books in the mail. This is funny because she's more of a tv or magazine person. Every day two or three planes fly them in. Maggie O'Connell, our grounded pilot, looks sad when she sees them.

Oh, here's something. Dr. Fleischman's friend, Dr. Robertson,

175

is back. Maybe he's Maggie's friend, actually. No one is sure. Anyway, he came here to study why nobody is sleeping. He had to go to Philadelphia for a while but now he's back, and he has brought with him an EEG machine. (There was a big mixup with me and the EEG, but you don't have to worry about that.) Now he wants to study everybody's brain waves. I asked Dr. Fleischman if it would hurt, and he said no, it was more like a lie detector. You hook it up to your head and monitor activity. I said I was impressed that now they had a machine that could tell if you were even thinking about a lie, but what was the difference between that and just imagining something imaginary? Dr. Fleischman slapped me on the back and said not to worry about it and to have a nice day.

I hope this answers your questions, if you had any. Ruth-Anne sends her love.

Yours truly,
Ed Chigliak

....

5-10

Dear Anita,

I must say things here have gotten somewhat stranger. For one thing, we're all getting electroencephalograms. Did I spell that right? I'd go back and check, but looking over that word feels like walking onto a patch of tundra after rain. Anyway, the EEG.

That Dr. Robertson from Philadelphia has brought in an EEG machine, and we have been asked by Joel Fleischman to voluntarily submit to a brief test to have our brain waves recorded. The office that Maurice gave Dr. Robertson now looks like a cross between a barber shop and Frankenstein's laboratory, with people waiting around on chairs, reading and chatting, while someone lies on a table and has electrodes glued to their head.

Earl Farner asked for a copy of his test and now everybody wants one. Each time the paper comes spooling out of the machine with its jagged trace lines, Maggie has to tear it off, run across the street, and send it through Ruth-Anne's coin-operated Xerox machine. She gives the copy to the person and the original to Dr. Robertson. People stop each other on the street to compare patterns and argue whether this peak or that one proves that one person is smarter than the other.

Edith Merkle started shouting this afternoon that her EEG looked exactly like the west face of Mt. Alyeska. She was in the throes of a religious experience until Ed Chigliak pointed out that she was looking at it upside down. Every home in Cicely now has EEG readouts hung up like Christmas bunting, held up by cheeseburger magnets on refrigerators, or stuck up with duct tape on mantlepieces.

As if all that isn't odd enough, I am going to be in a musical! Maurice is staging a production of *Guys and Dolls,* and he has cast me as a big-time gangster from Chicago. I'm a little nervous about it, but at least I don't have any songs. What concerns me more, to be honest, is Shelly. She has been cast as a strip-tease dancer. Everyone assures me that nothing untoward will happen.

I was tempted to ask Shelly to drop out of the show, but after Joel and Maggie did that—and they were cast in leading roles—I wouldn't dare. Everyone in town is still disappointed that they dropped out. Worse, the two of them are feuding with each other. And this is more than the usual back-and-forth they do, this seems more angry. It probably has something to do with Dr. Robertson, but I don't know.

I do know that the atmosphere in that office is somewhat strained. You've got this tall, debonair doctor from Philadelphia fiddling with electrodes while Maggie and Joel joke with the patient and snarl at each other. Then the patient lies down, the needles on the machine start leaping around, and Maggie and Joel each try to talk to Dr. Robertson and get him to ignore the other. It's enough to give anybody a case of brain waves.

Let me know if you want to come up and see the show. I don't think Maurice really knows what he's doing, but he seems to be surrounded by people who do. So it's shaping up.

Fondly,
Holling

177

Dear Jen,

Well, I started out as a part-time secretary/assistant to Michael Robertson, and now it's full-time. I've quit the other jobs at the store and the cafe and am working with Michael twelve, eighteen hours a day. Of course, I'd chuck all this and be in the air in a minute if I could, but for now it's really very interesting work. We interviewed everyone in town, and now we're taking their EEG's. Michael is superb, very friendly, and easygoing. He puts the suspicious locals and nervous children at ease.

Unfortunately, Fleischman is ever-present, running over from his office to insert himself into the process in a transparently desperate effort to impress Michael—who, of course, takes this in stride. I think the only reason he agrees with Fleischman is to placate him.

When Michael was in Phila. I sent him a postcard proposing we go for a hike some time soon. He hasn't mentioned it, but I noticed that he did bring back hiking shoes and a backpack. What will happen . . . or, rather "happen" on such a trip, I have no idea. But presumably something will. Which is fine. Something happening, I mean. I think. It all depends on what we mean by "something" and "happening." So long as it doesn't happen—depending on what it is—in town. For some reason the notion of something happening in town makes me queasy. ("In town" means at the office, at my house, at anyone's house . . .) On the trail, in the bush, fine. Maybe. Depending.

Poor Fleischman! So eager for this mentor's approval, so naked in his attempts to elicit it! It really is rather sad, in a way. In another way it's infuriating, and I wish he would just leave us alone. Which is petulant and childish, I know. But Fleischman brings that out in me.

Of course, one way to fly again is to move out of Cicely. It's inconceivable. But it's something to think about.

Love,
Maggie

Steve Cohen, etc.
Etc.
Pittsburgh, Etc.

Dear Steve—

Not that you asked, but in about ten minutes I will be able to qualify as an authority on electroencephalography. Or at least, on electroencephalography as a combination diagnostic technique/home decorating style. We're doing readings of the whole town. One guy thought we were doing a polygraphic screening of the citizenry. He was very nervous, very reluctant, and when we finally got him on the table and wired up, the machine made a single beep and he broke down and confessed he had stolen his brother-in-law's Vise-Grip. I let him off with a warning.

But we are getting data, all of which is (ARE. DATUM IS, DATA ARE) providing excellent support for my theory about this elec. magnetic condition and its effect on what up here passes for the human brain. I won't bore you with the details now. Wait until I write it up for a prestigious medical or scientific journal under my and Mike Robertson's name; *then* I'll bore you with the details. But in sum, all is well, and we're still awake.

All is well with me. It's O'Connell that I worry about. She has so plainly transferred feelings of an inappropriate nature to Mike, it's a little embarrassing. What's the word—transference? You know, the psychological term for transforming an ordinary, adult, boss-employee relationship into an idealized, eroticized Daddy-daughter analogue. The way she gazes adoringly at Mike—it's unhealthy, it's perverse. She does any and everything he asks of her, from the most tedious secretarial stuff (typing notes, transcribing interviews) to running for coffee. Which is useful to the project, yes, until I ask her . . . then she tells me to do it myself. Why? Because "she's not my secretary"!

As for what Mike thinks of it, well, naturally he likes it and has confided to me certain intentions about which I have no feeling

179

whatsoever, none. It is absolutely none of my business. But what if I told him that *her last FIVE boyfriends of record have met with unexpected and in some cases violent ends . . .*

But that would be unthinkable. She would be angry with me for interfering in her budding relationship with Mike. He would be peeved with me for distracting him with information that is both inflammatory and irrelevant. No, instead I should do the proper thing, which is to write him an anonymous note. Maybe tie it to a rock and throw it through his computer screen. Or do they have programs now that can do that automatically? Ha ha. More later.

Living life to the fullest,
Joel

. . . .

MAY 13

Dear Bernard,

Well, the onset of high spring, of indubitably mild breezes and balmy temperatures, has done less than nothing for our current plight. Cicely remains awake by day and by night; the closest any of us come within whispering distance of blissful somnolence are the glazed stares of the kids being subjected to the more egregiously boring classes at school. I had thought the progress of Mother Earth in her orbit might, by now, have moved us out of the zone of anomaly and into the arms of Orpheus; but no such luck.

I still find this very disturbing. A few Indian elders do, too, and have tendered up special sacred dances to appease whatever Native American deity has clout with Apollo and his spots. But, thus far, to no avail. Not that things are a complete disaster; for one thing, the population seems essentially okay. The musical I mentioned on the phone is slouching toward readiness, and my own performance in the (ill-chosen, if you ask me) part of the comic lead has received any number of polite, unconvincing compliments.

Interestingly, the lady cast opposite me, Shelly Tambo, whom

180

I had lately found to be almost metaphysically annoying, has begun to seem, as the architect once put it in describing the generic Main Street, "almost all right." Shelly's unself-conscious glee, her sincere naivete—they inform her character (a nightclub "canary") in a way that makes me LIKE her again. The result being that our scenes together are not the exercises in torture I had feared they would be. At the end of the show, when I decline yet again to marry her, and she reads me the Runyonesque riot act, I sing "Sue me/Sue me/Shoot bullets through me/I love you" and there's something in her look—tight-lipped but yielding, implacable but tempted—that strikes a chord.

I am ready to forgive her. All I have to do now is figure out what for.

Best,
Chris

. . . .

MAY 14

Dear Tawni,

Well, my life is now totally upside down.

For one thing, there's my normal work at the cafe. We're still open 24 hrs/day, and now we're one person short since Maggie O'Connell quit. I don't know what's wrong with her, but she seems preoccupied. I think she has a thing for that neurotic from Philadelphia that Dr. Fleischman brought in. (He took my brain waves yesterday with one of those machines that they plug into your head?) When Maggie is alone she's normal. But if that new guy is with her, like if they come into the Brick for lunch, she turns very artificial and cool. So when she quit work here to work with the new guy full time, I wasn't surprised.

Also I'm in the show, like I wrote you before, and it's going great! I have a song about how I have a cold because my boyfriend won't marry me—I sing, "In other words, just from waiting around for that plain little band of gold, a person can develop a cold." RIGHT? So, this morning we're working break-

181

fast, and I come back to the counter and sneeze. Holling looks at me and says, "What's that supposed to mean?" (!!)

Of course, the only reason things are going well is Chris's three girlfriends all have theatrical experience. Maurice isn't much help. I mean, I know he's the star as well as the director, so he gets to yell at everybody. But that's all that he does. Ed, who gets on MY personal nerves and is still irritated with Maurice about . . . well, everything . . . has a scene with Chris and Dave. Ed asks Maurice, "Am I Nathan Detroit's employee or his friend?"

Maurice looks disgusted and says, "For God's sake, Ed, this is musical theater, not some Hungarian Greenwich Village psychodrama."

Ed nods, in that dorky way of his, and says, "Maurice. Until you learn the difference between an employee and a friend, I'm not going to work for you again."

"Fine, Ed," Maurice says like a big old sourpuss. "Just hit your mark and read your lines. I am making an effort with this production to bring the community together, and I can't do it if we're going to stand here all day gabbing about friendship."

Luckily just then Katherine and Kay came over and said that Nicely Nicely Johnson (Ed's part) is an employee who likes his boss. Ed's face lit up and he nodded, then he looked mopey again and shook his head at Maurice and said, "I think we can all learn a lesson from this."

Meanwhile the sets are being built—no problem for some of these guys, who built their own cabins—and painted, and some of the women are putting together the costumes. Marilyn is great on the piano. Kay just says something like, "From letter D after the chorus," and Marilyn just nods and turns to the right place in the sheet music and plays it. I didn't know human beings were capable of something like that. But she's an Indian, so she has a deep spiritual life, so the spirits must help her. You can see that even Maurice, who has been mad at her all along, is impressed.

Ed has a solo number that he sings to all the men and to Ruth-Anne and the other Salvation Army officers called "Sit Down, You're Rocking the Boat." And, as much as I'm actually into metal and Maurice's show tunes that he sometimes plays on the radio make me want to puke, I have to admit that when Ed stands up there and sings it's extremely moving. He sings, "And the people all said sit down, sit down you're rocking the boat." It's a dream of him being on a boat to Heaven, and everyone else in the boat is telling him to shut up. And I believe it! When Ed does his songs, no matter how horrible his voice is, everybody stops and listens. So maybe I've been wrong about him.

Gotta run. PLEASE try to come out and see it!

Luv,
Shelly

....

MAY 15

Dear Bernard,

I played "She Blinded Me With Science" this morning, and nobody laughed. (That might have been because possibly nobody heard it. Holling still refuses to play my show in the Brick. The luck of the annoyance draw has been such that I am his bête noire, his summum malum. Breakfast customers therefore get a steady dose of "Morning Edition.") I had science, and blindness, on the brain, because it was my day to visit the office of Dr. Michael Robertson. Dr. Mike had brought his own EEG machine and is seeking cerebral autographs from tout le Cicely.

I showed up as requested at the appointed hour. Present were Dr. Mike, Joel, and Maggie—the latter two lately conspicuous in their absence from our local theatrical endeavor. Joel asked me to let him attach the leads, and I said, "Gee, guys, I don't think so. It's against my religion."

"Come on, Chris," Maggie said. "Everybody's doing it. Michael says we need a complete sampling of the town."

"Sorry," I said. "I changed my mind. And any use of my brain's broadcast without the written consent of major league baseball is prohibited."

"Chris," Dr. Mike said, all manly baritone and movie star eyes.

183

"I've heard your radio show. You're an enlightened person. Not—"

"Not like the rest of Cicely? Is that what you mean, Mike?"

He smiled with beautiful emptiness. "You don't like me, Chris. Why?"

I shrugged and smiled back. "I don't like exploiters, I guess."

"Whoa," Joel said and stepped forward. "Chris, believe me, I can echo that sentiment, and I'm sympathetic. But we're not arrogant anthropologists here, invading a habitat and upsetting the balance. I'm here, Michael is here, to gather data. That's all."

"Come on, Joel!" I laughed. "That's what they told the natives of Bikini Atoll. Then they shipped them off and dropped the H-bomb."

"Chris," Maggie pleaded. "Don't be like this. Michael says—"

Inspired, I held up a hand: halt. "Has Dr. Mike had his skull tapped?"

Dr. Mike said, "I'm not a resident."

"Then what about you, Maggie? And you, Joel?"

"Hey," Joel said. "You want me to do it? Fine. I have no problem with that. Come on, Chris. I'll show you my EEG if you show me yours. Deal?" I nodded. "Great. O'Connell, care to do the honors?"

And so he lay on the table, Maggie made a flurry of faces (anxiety, distaste, concern, exasperation) as she affixed the electrodes. I watched and an interesting scene unfolded.

The rule, apparently, is that the subject cannot speak. So I was witness to a conversation between Maggie and Dr. Mike in which Joel, lying inert between them, was unable to participate. What complicated feelings exist between Maggie and Joel is a topic of endless speculation around Cicely; everyone has their theory (and I have mine), but no one really knows what's going on with them. So I will report the dialogue and make no attempt to elucidate the subtext.

"Frankly, Fleischman, it'll be a significant piece of data if we record that you have a brain at all," Maggie said. Joel gave a fake smile and twirled a finger.

"Now come on, Maggie," Dr. Mike said. "Don't tease my chief assistant."

Joel frowned. Maggie saw this and smiled at Dr. Mike and said, "He's an excellent assistant, isn't he?"

"First-rate."

"Yes, we're so lucky that he's helping us. By the way, Michael, did you get the postcard I sent to your office?"

"I certainly did, Maggie, and I accept your invitation."

Joel frowned at this. Then, seeing I was watching him, he flashed a quick smile that utterly lacked credibility. Maggie saw this, too, and said, "Great! Then let's set a date."

I couldn't take it. Like an arrogant anthropologist, I upset the balance and said, "Set a date? Hey, are you two kids getting married?"

Mild amusement. Maggie said, "No, no, I've persuaded Michael to let me take him on a hike."

I said, provokingly, "Day hike?"

"My God, I hope not," Dr. Mike said. "I mean, you can't really *do* anything on a day hike. Don't you agree, Maggie?"

"Absolutely. We'll do an overnight," she sighed and moved from the deadpan Joel to the machine to gaze at the skittering pens and the Brooks Range of tracings they were inscribing. "I mean, we'll take tents . . . and sleeping bags . . . although whether we'll actually get far enough away to fall asleep remains to be seen. Maybe you'll tell me what the Rachtstoffel experiment is."

Dr. Mike said, "Oh, that's not important. We'll talk about more urgent things, I would think."

"We'll see," Maggie said slyly. "How about the day after the show?"

Dr. Mike allowed as how that sounded perfect to him, and Joel's EEG—a profile, if you ask me, in anguish—was complete. They then urged me to take a turn, but I demurred until Maggie had complied. She assumed the position and Joel, with utter professional cool, applied the leads.

Can you hear what is coming, brother? Right. It was Maggie's turn to lie there and be still as the two docs conferred above her, and the needles jumped.

"So, Mike," Joel began. "I think we're ready to proceed with the preliminary paper. Let's set aside some time to knock out a first draft."

"You do it," Dr. Mike said. "You're a better writer, Joel."

"Sure. Why not." Joel then fake-smiled down at Maggie, who was already fake-smiling up at him, and said, "Say, Mike, mind if I use your secretary?"

"Maggie?" Dr. Mike said. "Not at all."

Maggie looked miffed and glared at Joel, who smiled with fatal politeness. "Of course, I don't know," he pretended to wonder. "I'm not sure I could get the caliber of work out of her that you do. Do you think she would do for me what she does for you?"

At that Dr. Mike gave forth with a downright salacious laugh and said, "One way to find out." The two physicians shared a chortle at this, and then Dr. Mike said, "No, no, I'm joking. Of course she will. I mean she certainly will if I tell her to. Won't you, Maggie?"

"She'd do anything for you, Mike," Joel said.

"Oh," Dr. Mike murmured. "That remains to be seen."

Maggie looked stonefaced. Joel, over at the machine, held up her readout, waggled it playfully, and said, "Got her."

Then they did mine. Maggie asked me if I wanted a copy, but I said no. Do you blame me? With all these nasty spirits adrift and amok in the ether up here? I repudiate any electromagnetic signature my mind might issue under these circumstances. Life without sleep is counterfeit life. Those tracings are a forgery.

Kesho,
C.

Marx
Law Firm
NY

Ricardo—

Hip-deep in writing the prelim. paper we plan to submit about the so-called (by-me) "Cicely Effect," in which electromagnetic blah blah, induced by solar hoo-hah, affect the brainstem and etc.

Meanwhile, Mike is reviewing the EEGs and doing statistical breakdowns of the patterns. Totally outside my realm of expertise. He and O'Connell (cf. prev. correspondence) plan to take a "hike" in two weeks. I can't help wondering what this means. Not that it "matters," but okay, I admit I am a little worried. Not that I feel the need to compete with her for his attention, but what does she think this is? Is it all an elaborate ploy to go to bed—or, perforce, sleeping bag—with him? So go already. Is she then going to follow him back to Phila. when his work is done? (Because surely she doesn't think he's going to stay here indef.) I hope not. He's not her type. For a hike, okay. For anything more, absolutely not her type.

Of course, if she does accompany him back to Philly, the plane will crash, she will miraculously escape unscathed, he will die in a particularly showy and bizarre way, and she can come back. So maybe it doesn't matter after all. Still I'm against it. Although it is her business, of course. Not that it should be necessarily; Maggie O'Connell is living proof that even if women ought to have been given the vote by the whatever-it-is amendment to the Constitution, not all women should be so enfranchised when it comes to selecting their own boyfriends. But never mind. I've got work to do.

Methodologically,
Joel

MINNIFIELD COMMUNICATIONS

CICELY, ALASKA

907-555-8610

21 May

Ms. Kim Basinger
co/Weisman, Miller, & Davis
1100 Avenue of the Stars
Century City, CA

Dear Ms. Basinger:

I am in receipt of your letter of the 15th and can confirm that Monday, June 1, will be eminently suitable for your arrival in and inspection of Cicely. My attorney tells me he has forwarded to you his comments about the legality of your purchase of the town of Cicely and the procedure that must be followed. As I read it, we've got smooth sailing ahead of us.

As regards the attitude of our population toward selling the town, I have not yet broached the subject with them. I have decided to do so after your visit. I will, of course, account for your presence on June 1st by saying that you are interested in investing in Cicely. I can assure you that you and your entourage will be afforded every courtesy.

I look forward to meeting your plane at 12 noon and to our future business together. Many thanks.

Yours truly,
Maurice Minnifield

Col. Robert K. Semanski
Edwards Air Force Base, CA
9352-5000

Dad—

Just a quick update on what's up here in Cicely. We got off to a rocky start on the show, but Maurice had the sense to delegate. Three gals from the Lower Forty-Eight stepped in with dancing, singing, and artistic expertise. So we're on track. Acting-wise, it's catch as catch can, but we find our way. Maurice is willing to take my suggestions, at least. Just between you and me, he's terrible. Still, working for the Alaskan state police, how often do you get a chance to act in a Broadway musical? Not too damn many, believe you me.

People tell me how surprised they are to hear me sing. Well, YOU wouldn't be. Not after my Vera in our high school *Mame,* right? Dancing, that's another story. But Sarah Brown isn't much of a hoofer, and I can move on my feet okay. Long as Charley back home is feeding the dogs, I'm having fun.

Of course, that's not the real story up here. It's this sleep thing. I haven't had shut-eye since I left home first of the month. Feel fine is the funny thing, except for a stab of annoyance at the hash slinger who works the grill at the local dive. Guy named Dave. He shuffles out of the back room with a sack full of fried spuds and I have to reign in my urge to apply the choke hold.

But everybody has somebody they can't stand. Ask me, if you've got to sacrifice your universal love of humanity and hate one individual's guts in exchange for a continual state of alertness nonstop, hell, I say: do it. Make the trade. Maybe I'll stay here. Depends on what the Captain would say about a transfer.

But maybe it's easy for me to say, since I've only been down here three weeks. The others have been up continuous since March 1. I think it's taking a toll. We're at rehearsal yesterday— I'm up next, so I'm loitering on the periphery—and Chris Stevens, our Nathan Detroit, is out onstage with a gal name of Shelly Tambo, your basic teen queen bopper, doing Adelaide. Their final number: she's going to leave him, reads him the indictment of his malfeasances, and his response? "Sue me/Sue me/What can you do me/I love you." And so on, and on, and he replies, "Sue me/Sue me/Shoot bullets through me/I love you—"

Suddenly Stevens waves everyone quiet. Starts to address the group, not just little Shelly waiting innocently for her cues. "YES!" he says. Nods, like he just grasped a vital point, and starts to sermonize to those present. "We all know how Miss Adelaide feels, friends," he says. "She's mad, and she's hurt, and she's disappointed. But don't you see? This scene isn't about how she feels. It's about how NATHAN feels! And how he feels is, he's just being himself! He's saying, this is who I am. Take it or leave it. But remember, I love you." He starts talking to himself as much as to everybody else. I've seen this sort of behavior before, of course. In my experience, it's the intense introspective phase before an individual goes psycho. So I'm primed to intervene, and he says, "Take it, leave it, or sue me. Take me to COURT, okay? For being myself. Because of that, I am guilty. And THAT, friends, is what we have to say to each other now, these days—"

Maurice clears his throat and says, "Stevens, you want to save this sort of thing for the radio, and let's get on with it?"

"In a minute, Maurice. Because this is important. Sue me, is Nathan's message, and Mr. Abe Burrows's and Mr. Frank Loesser's and Mr. Damon Runyan's message to all of us. If we were sleeping, this all wouldn't be necessary. But since we're not, and since we're subjected to each other's unflagging subjectivity all the time, then we have to give each other some slack, and say, take me as I am. Otherwise—sue me."

Now in my experience, a man makes a speech like that, it's an even bet he's on the edge. But these people must be used to this kind of thing from Stevens, because everyone just nods and agrees, and they all go back to work. Later, when Stevens does his radio show, he plays "Sue Me" from the show's album three times in a row and repeats the message, so the citizens who weren't at the rehearsal will not miss the benefit of his insight.

Maybe I won't move here after all.

Hope you're well.

Love,
Barbara

. . . .

MAY 27

Dear Phyl,

What am I doing? Do you know? If so, kindly reply by return mail.

I have been working intensely with Michael for weeks now, performing the drudgiest kind of work and fending off his . . . do we still say "advances"? Not because I'm not attracted to him—hell, we're set to go off into the foothills for a night soon—but because I can't bring myself to do anything here in town. I feel terribly guilty: I ignore my friends, I dropped out of this show everyone is doing, which is the biggest thing around here in ages . . . I'm bickering with Fleischman like a bratty sibling . . .

I don't ask that this thing I'm in the middle of with Michael be "love," but can it at least be palpably different from nausea? The past, as usual, is no help. I'm not sure when I started out with Dave—I mean, yes, it was love. No. But it was romantic. But he was writing a book, we were going to Alaska—the entire gestalt was romantic, waking up and getting dressed was romantic.

Glen, yeah, I felt love. I think. If you only think, is it love? Never mind. Bruce, well . . . next question. Harry, oh, I don't know. It was that kind of love that looks convincing as long as you don't look at it. And then Rick. And yes, I would say definitely that that was love. Of a kind.

With Michael? I'm not sure, but my hunch is, this is not love. This is pastry. Here's my latest analogy: You're walking down the street and you stop before a bakery window. And you see the most baroque, most touristy, most overdone sugary dolled-up cake imaginable. Puff pastry filled with cream AND icing everywhere AND arbitrary nuts, dried fruits, chocolate sprinkles, sugar roses, etc. At first you want it; the very muchness of it looks "good."

But then you know, you consciously *know* that it's bad for you, which, admittedly, sometimes doesn't matter. A lot of things that are bad for you are good for you. But with this, you also know that you'll feel stupid and faintly sick and self-loathing afterward, and that you can have just as good—no, better—an experience with something far less elaborate and pandering.

Well, I'm standing at the bakery window, and the thing looks good. No matter what I "know."

I wish everything would go back to normal. Cicely would go back to sleeping, I would go back to flying, Fleischman and I would go back to our mildly acerbic needling, Michael would go back to Philadelphia. Is that possible? Kindly reply by return mail.

> *Yielding to Temptation,*
> *Maggie*

....

MAY 30

Dear Anita,

Well, it's about 3 AM on Sunday, the 31st. I have just come from our dress rehearsal, and I must say it went very well. The costumes are wonderful. It's funny how putting on a costume gives everybody a lift and makes them feel more in character. In this show, the men all wear big wide pinstripe suits and dark shirts and light neckties. You can imagine how strange and otherwordly I felt.

We ran through the whole show only stopping for minor adjustments. I found myself in the wings with Katherine, one of Chris's girlfriends who taught us the dancing. She seemed to be trying to conceal her laughter at the scene on the stage, and when I asked her how she thought the show was turning out, she said, "Holling, it couldn't be any better."

I must say that Chris Stevens has performed admirably in a

role none of us thought he was suited for. And his scenes with Shelly are very touching. I happen to know—the whole town happens to know—that Chris had suddenly found Shelly almost intolerable. But tonight he told her she was terrific and he apologized.

And she is terrific. Maybe it's the experience she had competing in the Miss Northwest Passage and other beauty pageants, but she is a natural on stage. When she sings "Marry the Man Today," about how she and Barbara Semanski should marry Chris and Maurice now and worry about changing them later, she really seems to mean it.

Now I know you won't believe this, and you'll think it's only because he apologized to Shelly, but I found myself tonight feeling far more kindly toward Chris than I have in a long time. In fact ever since the end of February, when I first started to detest him. Watching him do these scenes tonight and doing a very funny one with me, where I intimidate him as Big Jule from Chicago, I suddenly found myself relenting. All the things that had bothered me about him—his overly poetic way of speaking, the preachy way he talks about figures from stories and myths, the way he lectures you on the outlooks of other people as though your own outlook is pretty shabby, the way he has of calling Beethoven "Ludwig" and Freud "Old Siggy" and so forth—I found myself forgiving all that. Don't ask me why.

Of course, at the center of all this is Maurice. He had originally cast Chris to play Sky Masterson, the leading man, and Joel to play Nathan Detroit. But when Joel dropped out, he shifted Chris to Nathan and took over Sky Masterson himself. Now I have known Maurice Minnifield for twenty years. I know that he is a person of broad capabilities and that he can accomplish pretty much anything he sets his mind to, but playing Sky Masterson may not be one of them. I don't want to dwell on this, so let me just suggest that maybe he's being thrown off by the fact that Barbara Semanski is playing opposite him as Sarah Brown, the Salvation Army lady. Maurice has had a sort of unrequited passion for her. And it sneaks in.

Still, he has managed to engineer this out of nothing. One day

193

we were just an ordinary town in Alaska whose people stopped sleeping. Now we're on the verge of Opening Night. I take my hat off to him.

If I see you here tomorrow, this letter will be unnecessary. If not, I hope I see you soon another time.

Fondly,
Holling

....

5/31

Steve Cohen
His Firm
City, State

Dear Steve,

It's done. I finished the preliminary paper and gave it to Mike for final vetting. Supposedly he's sending it out tomorrow with a cover letter. Just before he and O'Connell go on their hike. She's home, in fact, cramming in last minute work before tomorrow, which means she'll miss the show. But it's supposed to run all week, so she—and I, I think—will catch a later one. I don't really feel like mixing it up in society tonight.

Besides, the presence of O'Connell or me might put a damper on things. The good residents of Cicely have not been reluctant to imply that they felt betrayed at our abandoning the show. So I've been cleaning up, seeing patients, killing time. As with any big project, when it's even tentatively finished there's a big letdown. I'll have

I'm back. There was a hiatus there for about five minutes as Ed Chigliak, a local young man with a deep aversion to knocking, suddenly materialized here in my office with his trademark wave and grin. It happens every time. I'm writing or reading or daydreaming, I look up, and he's *there*, black jacket and all, like he's just beamed in from the *Enterprise*. I keep asking that he knock, but he just says, "Indians don't do that, Dr. Fleischman. It's rude." Oh.

Ed said he came to give me "something important," reached into his pocket, and came up empty. He left it in his costume, you see. So he's gone to fetch it. What is it, I asked. A postcard.

It strikes me that if something comes of this paper and the more rigorous one we will follow up with, I may be in demand. I may be summoned for meetings. I MAY HAVE TO GET THE HELL OUT OF ALASKA AT LAST!

Be still my beating heart. Will you excuse me while I go eat dinner? Maybe I'll cave in/muster courage and take in the show. If they don't stone me for a traitor when I arrive. Not that I would blame them. But science requires sacrifice, right? I'll tell the angry mob you said so.

On the brink of stardom,
Joel

....

JUNE 3 (!!!)

Dear Jen and Phyl,

Sit down, both of you. You'll note this is a xerox. I don't have much time to write this, let alone to tell it twice, so get ready for installments. One day all three of us will get together, and you two can meet. You'll have lots in common, starting with the following:

The last time I wrote either of you was a day before the big opening here of *Guys and Dolls,* two days before my hike into the hills with Michael Robertson. So let's pick it up there. Curtain was scheduled for 8:00 PM. I was not going to attend; first, because I felt guilty for having abandoned my friends and quit the show, second, because Michael asked me to input into the laptop a letter and introduction he had handwritten to be mailed the next day. So I was home, alone, typing, all night. Michael had other work to do, calls to make, etc., and would join me for a final review of the introduction at about 10:30.

These times matter. Take notes.

At about 9:30 there was a knock on the door. Michael, of course, so I opened it in a good, if slightly anxious, mood. But it wasn't Michael. It was Fleischman. He looked lousy—pained, lackluster, hesitant. But of course as soon as I saw him I bristled, ready for combat.

"What, Fleishman? I'm very busy."

"I know . . ." He had that baffled look he gets when he's not in control of things.

"I want to finish inputting Michael's letter tonight so we can go on our hike with no loose ends."

"Yeah . . . can I come in?"

I paused, looked less than thrilled, then moved out of the way and let him enter. He moved like someone carrying a safe.

"Well what?" I said. "Look, I know we haven't been getting along lately, so just . . . let's just—"

"I don't think you should go on that hike tomorrow," he said.

I felt like I do when the keyboard freezes on the laptop: mentally I'm still winging ahead, but something fundamental has shut down and I don't realize it yet. All I could say was, "What makes you think you have a vote, Fleischman?"

"Never mind do I have a vote, O'Connell," he said, pacing around. "I have an opinion. And in my very considered opinion, just please don't go on that hike with him."

And then I got it, and said, "You're jealous. You don't want him to LIKE me more than he LIKES you. Fleischman, I'm just the secretary, remember? You're the colleague. We're not competing. We have different interests here. So what is the problem?"

"He's not what you think he is. He's . . ." He huffed, he shrugged, he looked defeated. "Okay, let's put our cards on the table. You're taking sleeping bags, right?"

"So?"

"And you'll be gone overnight, right?"

"At least."

"At least, right. So am I correct in assuming that there will be a physical consummation of the relationship? And don't get disingenuous with me, O'Connell, because I happen to know

196

that a physical consummation of the relationship has been on his mind from the start."

"And how do you know that?"

"He told me."

I laughed. "Fine! I'm flattered! And maybe I feel the same way! And having said that, let me now say that none of this is any of your business!"

"I know. I know. Just let me ask you one more question." I didn't say anything. So he said, "What are your intentions? Are you like in love with this guy or what?"

"Fleischman!"

"Well?"

It was the one question, of course, I didn't want to be asked. So in a stupid way he got points for asking it. I had to look away and shrug and say, "I don't know. I mean, no. But it could happen. One thing could lead to another." I turned to him and, as though all this—the whole sleepless thing—were his fault, said, "Because if Cicely is going to stay like this, I don't know if I can live here. If I can't fly, I'll have to go somewhere and do something else."

"Somewhere, where is somewhere—like Philadelphia?"

"Philadelphia qualifies as somewhere."

He looked away. He walked around. He started muttering. "I've been walking around town for an hour now wondering how to handle this."

"There is nothing for you to handle, Fleischman. Thank you for your interest, and drive safely."

"No, you're wrong, because this is a very delicate situation. Ethically very delicate, very complex. My motivations are not unambiguous. I ask myself, why am I doing this? I say to myself, O'Connell? She's an adult. She's responsible for her actions. She is capable of making her bed, she is capable of lying in it, ba-boom, end of story."

"Thank you."

"But I don't want you to get hurt. I may have a ton of other motives and secret agendas, but I don't want you to get hurt."

Dryly, very dryly, I said, "How kind of you. Can I go now?"

197

"Ed—" He paused, then reached into his jacket pocket and pulled out something. "Ed gave me this to give to Mike. It came two days ago and got lost in the shuffle at Ruth-Anne's."

He handed it to me. And what the hell, I took it. It was a color postcard of the Empire State Building. And all at once Fleischman started laughing nervously and saying, "Of course maybe I'm making this up. Maybe you already know. Maybe it doesn't matter whether you know or not."

"Know what?"

"Read it."

"Fleischman, this is someone else's mail—"

"It's a postcard, O'Connell, Nothing private happens on post-cards. Read it. I'll . . . I'll be in the next room . . ."

So he wandered into my bedroom, I shrugged, and turned the card over. It was addressed to Michael care of General Delivery (ie., Ruth-Anne's store). A man's sharp handwriting. Dated last week. And I read it . . .

I had to read it again while my brain caught up with my body, because I had started, if you can believe it, *blushing*. Growing hot and red and feeling—not ashamed, and not even angry, but deeply embarrassed. Of course I understood now what this was all about. I must have stood there for a minute or so and then somehow drifted into the bedroom. Fleischman was there, reading or pretending to read the text on the laptop screen. He looked at me.

He asked, "Did you know?" I shook my head. He asked, "Does it matter?" I nodded. He winced, took the card from my hand, and read it aloud. " 'Dear Mike: Alaska? Unbelieveable! Take pictures. Hey, your wife tells me you and she will be in NY end of June. Dinner? Call and let's arrange. Wendy sends regards. Stay warm. Hal.' " He looked up. "I'm sorry, O'Connell."

"Please go."

"Yeah. Sure." He sat down on my bed.

"Please."

"I will, I just—"

"Fleischman—!"

"I just have to finish reading this," he said. "Something's

198

weird." He bent over the laptop and scrolled the text and kept reading.

I have to stop here. More in another letter. And believe me, there *is* more. This isn't the half of it.

> *Love to you both,*
> *Maggie*

....

6/3

Marx
Etc.

Dear Richie,

And suddenly we reach a climax.

On the night of *Guys and Dolls,* i.e., Erev the schlep into the hinterlands of O'Connell and Mike Robertson, I am leaving the Brick after dinner. How can the cafe be open, when Holling and Shelly and even scary Dave are in the show? Because Adam, the world's greatest crazy/craziest great cook, has deigned to "prepare a cold collation" for spare money, of which he is in significant need now that Eve is pregnant. Which means I am well fed.

I can't decide whether to see the show or not, but am spared any need to ruminate on it because, clad in his big double-breasted suit and dark shirt and white tie (his costume), Ed Chigliak comes running out of the church where the show is to be performed (thus shattering some presumed taboo about being seen by the audience before curtain) and buttonholes me on the street. "Doctor Fleisch-man!" he cries, like a kid in an old MGM movie. "Doctor Fleischman!" And hands me a postcard to give to Mike, who is otherwise engaged. "Ruth-Anne said this got stuck inside Maurice's copy of Forbes." The mail must go through. I take it.

Q: You are handed a personal postcard addressed to a famous, or at least noteworthy-in-your-field, person. What do you do?

A: You read it.

Which I did and proceeded to wander around town as the opening night crowd gathered excitedly before the church, looking very much like a New York theatre crowd would look if you took every member of the New York crowd, forced each one to gain thirty pounds, dressed them in old flannel tops and lumberjack shirts, made the men all grow beards, made the women all grow beards, got all of them drunk, and required them all to openly display either hunting knives, dogs, or tattoos. I'm exaggerating. Twenty pounds.

They shuffled into the church as I read the card. The card—well. Suffice to say the card was from one of Mike's friends in NY, mentioning his (ie, Mike's) wife. Q: Did O'Connell know he was married? A: I didn't know. But I assumed not. Q: Should I tell her? Good Q.

Actually I felt bad for her, but wasn't sure what my motives would be if I *were* to tell her. Wasn't she an adult, responsible for her own actions, capable of making her bed, capable of lying in it, ba-boom, end of story?

But I realized that underneath that position was something else. Something disturbing but indubitably there. *Pleasure.* There was something satisfying in this turn of events. Why? Because, after all of O'Connell's taunting, all her attitude, all her smug little displays of territoriality, it turned out that she had been merrily shanking her Titleist into the biggest, the oldest, the most obvious sand trap on the course.

But I also felt bad for her. I don't mind seeing people proved wrong, but I don't like seeing them get hurt.

So I went to her house—the new one; her mom had visited a few months before and burned down the old one. You know how it is—and after the inevitable jousting, gave her the card. She read it and grasped the implications. It was terrible. I had hoped she would be angry, but I wasn't prepared for her to be humiliated. That got to me. No more pleasure.

She asked me to leave. And I would have, although arguably it would have been worse for her to be alone. And, while presumably there may have been a few dozen other people in Cicely she would have preferred to go to for solace, the fact was they were either in or watching *Guys and Dolls* at that moment.

So as I say, I would have gone. But.

After I gave her the card, I let her absorb it alone. I went into her bedroom. On a little table was the laptop that we had been using on the project. She was in WordPerfect, writing a cover letter from Mike. So while I was waiting for her to read the card and react, I read the letter.

And I couldn't believe it. So I finished it, zapped back to the top, and read it again, just as O'Connell came in—numb, reddened, a wreck.

"Please leave," she said.

"I will," I said, tapping like mad on the keys. "I just—" I got to the top and read the letter."Is this what he told you to write?"

She looked dully at the computer. "I'm typing in what he wrote." She showed me the handwritten original.

I gaped like an idiot and said, rather eloquently, "But—" Then I zipped out of the letter, stored it, and called up the file of the report. My report. The one I had written. It came on the screen. "I CAN'T BELIEVE IT!" I yelled. "HE TOOK MY NAME OFF IT. HE'S CLAIMING ALL THIS IS HIS!"

Poor O'Connell stumbled forward, blinking at the screen. "What?"

"He deleted my name from the file! And look—" I called up the letter again. "My work . . . several assistants and I . . . I know all too well my conclusions in the following . . . et cetera, et cetera. Your Pal, Dr. Michael Robertson!" I—have you ever actually "stormed around a room"? I did that. Try it. It's aerobic. "That THIEF! That GONIFF!"

"Fleischman, I'm sorry," O'Connell said, looking like someone with a hangover. She turned and moved toward the window. "I didn't know what your arrangement was with him. I just wrote what he gave me."

"I know. It's not your fault, O'Connell." I started gasping again. "What did he think, that I wasn't going to find out?"

"I know," she said quietly, staring out the window.

"Did he think I wouldn't MIND? That he would EXPLAIN it?"

"I know."

"That I would UNDERSTAND? That it was an OVERSIGHT?"

"I know."

I simmered down, or tried to, sitting on the edge of the bed. The alarm clock on the night table showed 10:16. I shook my head. "O'Connell?" I said. "You want to learn some Yiddish?" She walked over and sat down beside me. The bed creaked. "Let's start with the word 'schmuck.' As in, You and I are a couple of schmucks. Now you try it."

"You and I are a couple of schmucks."

"Not bad. But give it more self-awareness, self-disgust, self-contempt."

"Schmucks."

"You and I—?"

"You and I are a couple of *schmucks.*"

"Excellent."

We sat there, the clock ticking, a little tiny hum coming from the computer. I looked at her. She was what, two feet away? One? And the funny thing is, I've been up here two years, and at that moment I felt as though I had been looking at this woman my whole life. I said, "Are you okay?"

She nodded. "You?"

I nodded. I said, "He lied to you. At least implicitly."

She said, "He stole from you. Almost."

"I'm sorry I had to tell you."

"I'm glad you did."

We looked at each other. And it seemed appropriate for me to put my arm around her shoulders and sort of draw her to me in a comradely way. Because that's what we were, wasn't it? Comrades in betrayal. So that's what I did. I put my arm around her and drew her to me. And she . . . you know . . . she let me, she *helped* me by drawing closer.

I'm stopping here. You want to learn what else happened? Do what I did, boychik. Pay your dues. COME TO ALASKA.

Joel

202

Dear Jen and Phyl,

And now the conclusion of our drama.

The reason Fleischman refused to leave when I asked him is, he had discovered that Michael had intended to submit the preliminary paper under his (M's) own name, with only a vague reference to Fleischman who, remember, had written it. So we were both victims. Fleischman stormed around a bit, and I tried to stop thinking and feeling. Finally Fleischman sat on the edge of my bed and said we were both schmucks. He was right. I sat next to him.

He asked me if I was okay, and I said yes. He said, "I'm sorry I had to tell you."

I said, "I'm glad you did."

He said, "He stole from me. Almost, anyway."

I said, "He lied to me. Implicitly."

We sat there. We looked at each other. Then he put his arm around my shoulders, and I leaned toward him—it was brotherly/sisterly, almost. And he held me like that for a few seconds, and then we both sort of fell back onto the bed, on our backs, and turned to each other.

"Why did you do that?" I asked. "Lie back like this?"

He blinked and said, "I dunno, all of a sudden I'm tired. It's been a rough day."

"Me, too."

"O'Connell, uh . . ."

"Fleischman . . . ?"

He said quickly, "You know, I don't believe in wallowing in self-pity or in feelings of victimization. I mean, I *do* it. All the time. But I don't approve of it."

"Neither do I," I said. "I believe in honest, sincere emotion."

"Exactly. Honest sincere."

"But self-pity, victimization—"

"Forget it. Don't believe in it. Never did, never will." I nodded, and we looked at each other. Then he said, "But it's hard. It's

203

hard to be betrayed. It hurts. It's hard to be hurt. It hurts to be hurt. I'm a doctor, I can tell you with institutional authority— pain hurts."

"It does," I said. We were like two drunks growing philosophical. "Pain hurts."

"So," he said carefully, "It's nice, and I think it's perfectly legitimate, when in pain, to seek analgesic relief."

"Solace, succor, comfort."

"Comfort, exactly," he said, and then he did an odd thing. He yawned. "We can mutually provide comfort, due to the symmetry of the pain, the hurting pain, in which we are bilaterally *in* right now, don't you think?"

"That would be nice," I said, and because he had yawned, I yawned, which made him yawn again. So we yawned at each other for a few seconds, and then he put his hand on my hand— our eyes were tearing from all the yawns—and said, "Can I just . . . stay here with you for a little while?"

I said, "Yes, that would be good. Oh hell."

"What? Oh hell what?"

"The time. Michael is due here in about five minutes."

By then we were locked onto each other's eyes. "So," he said, "If he comes here, he'll find us here. He'll walk in the front door, which is unlocked because this is Cicely, and he'll swagger right on in and encounter us here. Together. Explicitly seeking succor and being blatantly comfortable. Alone. Here. Together."

"Yes. He will."

Fleischman's face drew closer to mine. "Hey," he said with a wicked smile. *"Let* him . . ."

And that's all I remember about that night. Honest.

Very truly and sincerely yours,
Mary Margaret O'Connell

Cohen

Dear Steve,

And so, to conclude:

At one point the clock on O'Connell's night table said 10:31. She and I had a nice tête-à-tête, and the next thing I knew, the clock said 3:12. Light outside, so it was the afternoon of—what? I felt like Rip van Winkle. My beard was not the usual scratchy sandpaper of an overnight's sleep. It was soft and thick. Next puzzle: I was under the blankets, fully clothed, as was she. She was still asleep—ASLEEP.

I got up, turned on the radio, and got nothing from Maurice's station. And for a few seconds I was absolutely at a loss. I had no idea what day, time, or even year it was. I was like a character from an old "Twilight Zone" who suddenly realizes he has amnesia. So I groped for the phone and called information. I asked what time and day it was, and—after arguing with the woman, since they're only allowed to use a vocabulary of about six words—that's how I learned what had happened.

We had slept for a day and a half.

Presumably, during this epic snooze, each of us managed to crawl under the covers. And, of course, I was starving. I washed up, made coffee, ate whatever was there (Cereal. Trust O'Connell to have only Raisin Bran.) and waited for her to wake up. Maybe I made a little more racket than was absolutely necessary. Finally she did wake up, and we looked at each other with an eerie combination of embarrassment and mystification.

She said, "Did we—?"

I said, "No."

She said, "Oh."

I said, "But almost . . ."

She said, "Well, we were so . . ."

I said, ". . . hurt?"

She said, "Confused."

I said, "Disoriented."

She said, "Vulnerable."

I said, "Feshtoodled."

Then we sat there like two old geezers, nodding in the silence for a bit. Finally I said, "O'Connell, I don't know . . . don't take this personally, but lately I have found you so . . . how to put it . . . not *hateful*, exactly—"

"Annoying?"

"Yes."

"Fleischman, you have been unbelievably irritating for the past three months." She paused and shrugged. "But now . . ."

I said, "It's passed, huh?"

She nodded. More old geezer reveries. Then she said, "Fleischman? What's the Rackstoffen experiment?"

I had to make a decision. But after all this, I couldn't not tell her. And it didn't seem to matter any more. "Rechtschaffen. Allan Rechtschaffen. Sleep researcher. Did a major experiment in 1983 on sleep deprivation. He gave two rats unlimited food and water and identical living conditions with one variable. One rat was allowed to sleep at will. The other poor bastard was jolted awake as soon as he dropped off. There were some interesting results . . ."

"Well?"

"The rat denied sleep ate more and more but suffered drastic weight loss. Total metabolic dyscontrol. Finally he failed to regulate body temperature and died."

A respectful silence descended, as we thought about a dead rat. Then O'Connell said, "Michael was right. It isn't relevant."

"MICHAEL? I was the one who said it wasn't rel—"

"Oh my God."

I said, "What?"

She looked aghast and said, "Michael. He was on his way here when we fell asleep. He never made it."

"So?"

"So, that means he fell asleep when we did. IN HIS CAR. Which means—"

I winced. "You lost another one?"

206

"No! That's not fair! We hadn't done anything. We had no relationship whatsoever."

I shrugged. "You almost did, though. Maybe it's the thought that counts. To know, know, know him is to kill, kill, kill him."

"Fleischman!" She leaped up, grabbed her jacket, and tore outside. I had to hustle to catch up with her. We drove toward town and found him a quarter mile away. His car had gone off the road and plowed into a tree. He was groggy; he had sustained some cuts to the face and neck when the windshield shattered; but he would be fine. We drove him to town, where people were staggering around out on the streets like the survivors of an atomic war.

There's more, but I think I'll let it go at this for now. (Time for some shut eye.) Oh yeah—at my insistence we submitted the paper under both our names. Robertson pretended to apologize and I pretended to accept it. I expect the paper to be rejected, but anything's possible.

In pajamas,
Joel

. . . .

JUNE 4

Dear Tony,

And then came the night of May 31. The premiere of the Maurice Minnifield production of *Guys and Dolls,* with none other than our own Chris Stevens in the role made famous by Sam Levene and made strangely anticlimactic and irrelevant by Frank Sinatra.

It was on that night that an extraordinary thing happened . . .

I found myself on the streets of Cicely, where I—and, indeed, everyone I knew—was dressed in a rummage sale version of Depression-era Broadway finery: big-shouldered, double-breasted baggy-trousered suits, dark shirts, and light ties for the men; racy, tight dresses and lots of hot-cha, kiss-me-but-don't-muss-me-darling makeup for the women. But of course, it was show night, and we were dressed to kill or at least to knock 'em dead. And, naturally, as everyone on the street seemed to be going to the same place, I followed the crowd.

Our destination proved to be the church, where I have been known to give the occasional nondenominational sermon and where town meetings are held. This was where we had performed the show. Somehow, though, the show was over—I both already knew this and was surprised by it—and the stage had been dismantled. What remained resembled more a courtroom than a church.

But a stylized courtroom, to say the least: there was no gallery for onlookers, and no ordinary jury box. The jury box *was* the gallery. Indeed, the entire population of Cicely, all in their killer Broadway duds, was seated in the jury box. At the front of the room, elevated on the bench, sat the judge: Dr. Michael Robertson, the Philly doc I've told you about, clad in robes, yes, but the white robes of the lab scientist. Still, he had the gavel, so we knew he was the boss.

Below him and to the side, where the witness box should have been, was a table—padded, as though from a doctor's office. And even as all this struck me as increasingly weird, I nonetheless knew that I had a prominent role in what was about to unfold, and so, waving greetings to the jury/gallery, I proceeded to one of the main tables opposite the "judge."

In fact I was defense counsel. But for what and for whom?

It became clear immediately. Holling Vincouer, one of our most venerable citizens and until recently the actual Mayor of Cicely, left the jury box, went over to the padded table, and lay down on it. The judge said, "You may proceed, Mister Prosecutor."

I looked to my right: up stepped Joel Fleischman, our doctor. "Thank you, your honor," he said. It was then that I noticed an electroencephalograph standing near the witness table. Joel attached the electrodes to Holling's head, turned on the machine, and the needles recorded Holling's brain activity.

"We will prove, your honor, that Holling Vincouer is guilty," Joel said. Grave, concerned looks among the 800 or so "jurors."

208

Then Joel tore off the EEG trace, held it up to the judge, and said, "There you have it, your honor. The prosecution rests."

I found myself leaping to my feet and crying, "Objection! Holling is just being himself."

Dr. Mike, the judge, nodded. He said, "Not guilty," gave his gavel a firm rap, and said, "Case dismissed."

Everyone (including I) applauded as Holling—dapper in his dark pinstripes and carrying his oversized hat—got off the table and returned to the jury box, where he shook hands and traded smiles and laughs. Somehow we all felt vindicated, except maybe for Joel, who scowled at the machine, kicked its stand, and said, "I can never get any decent equipment up here in the sticks."

Then Judge Dr. Mike rapped his hammer again, said, "Next victim!" and Maurice Minnifield left the box and reclined on the table. Joel hooked him up, demanded a guilty verdict, I objected, and again, the judge ruled for the defense. This process went on and on, each resident of Cicely being judged not guilty for being him or herself, until I woke up.

That's right: woke up. Old Sol has cleaned up his act, the spots have receded, and Cicely is sleeping again. With exquisite pleasure we take leave of each other at night, head for home, and submit to that voluntary extinguishing of consciousness that is the brain's hard-won legacy over ten million years of evolution. The "anomaly" is over.

For good? Most likely. Maurice's contact at NASA says its focus on our town came in at odds of roughly one to one-and-keep-writing-zeroes-until-I-say-stop. What have we gained from it? Hard to say. A lot of people got a headstart on new hobbies. Shelly managed to receive upwards of 12,000 books, some of which are worth reading. Most Cicelians got their brain waves measured and received copies of the result suitable for framing or, if you prefer, for sticking on your refrigerator.

None of which is all that extraordinary. No, what I alluded to at the top was the fact that when sleep did descend, and felled us all like a scythe through ripe wheat, all of us—or, at least everyone I have spoken to, and who has called in to my radio show this morning—had the dream I described above. The same dream, with the same setting and events, at the same time.

Now, I have always been ambivalent about Jung's notion of the collective unconscious. Patterns persisting in myths, yes. The stages of human life reflected in stories separated by oceans and centuries? No problem. But in the actual brain cells of individuals? The Lamarckian flavor of it leaves a bad taste— because doesn't it imply that? The inheritance of acquired characteristics, which is as bogus as Piltdown Man? Besides, one knows too well how much Carl Gustav had a stake in creating and promoting his own psychological system at the expense of old Siggy's. But the evidence is the evidence. Eight hundred loyal Cicelians and true, dreaming a single coherent dream as though attending the same drive-in movie in their heads. *That's* entertainment.

We know of mass delusions and the madness of crowds. We know of states of communally induced ecstasy, of religious visions. We know, in other words, that there are more things in Heaven and Earth than are dreamt of in Freud's (or Lamarck's) philosophy.

Besides, neither of those two gents had the experience of staying awake with their friends and neighbors for three months straight. Who's to say that in that time we didn't become some advanced form of volvox, that communal creature formed of thousands of individuals linked together in a spiky ball, that moves, eats, and, for all I remember of high school bio, lives and dies en masse?

Kay told me of a summer in which her sister worked as an actress in a dinner theatre production in North Carolina. Far from their homes and routines in New York, the small cast of the show began after about three days on the road to dream about one another. And women, we know, will start to coordinate their menses when they work together for any length of time. Given all that, after so much intense and unfathomable experience together, why should not the residents of Cicely share on the occasion of their reunion with Orpheus the same dream?

Easy to say. Vexing to contemplate. I leave the hard-science theorizing to Drs. Robertson and Fleischman and the other professionals. As for me, I could use a nap.

Let's stay in touch, Teach.

Best regards,
Chris Stevens

MINNIFIELD COMMUNICATIONS
CICELY, ALASKA
907-555-8610

5 June

Ms. Kim Basinger
c/o Weisman, Miller & Davis
1100 Avenue of the Stars
Century City, CA

Dear Ms. Basinger:

I hardly know where to start, other than to beg you to accept my apology for the reception you received, or rather did not receive, on the afternoon of June 1. I can well imagine your discomfort and perplexity upon debarking from the plane. There you were with your entourage, expecting to be met, as I had promised, by me and my entourage. Instead, no one was there.

The explanation is, Ms. Basinger, that we fell asleep—suddenly, totally, the entire town. Which means, as you no doubt have inferred, that the sunspot anomaly that had kept everyone awake has abated. It seems to have disappeared forever, or at least thus far, which means that once again we are sleeping and waking normally.

I am under no delusion that a normal Cicely in which people hit the hay at nighttime like everyone else in the world is as attractive an investment possibility to you as the previous, anomalous Cicely. But let me add that what we now lack in electromagnetic brain-altering potential we more than make up for in gorgeous scenery, ample outdoor recreational attractions, and a congenial local population the likes of which I guarantee you won't find within a two hundred-mile radius of Los Angeles. Believe me, I have spent time there visiting JPL, and I know whereof I speak.

If that sounds good to you, either for investment or personal recreational reasons, then do not hesitate to contact me. I promise to meet your plane next time. And thanks for your interest in our town, Cicely, the Saint Tropez of the Alaskan Riviera.

Yours truly,
Maurice Minnifield

. . . .

JUNE 7

Dear Rudy and Matthew,

Well I hardly know where to start. In any case, you'll notice that this is a xerox. I have no intention of writing this twice, and I don't want either of you to feel slighted. So I'm keeping the original and you *both* get copies.

I know my good friend Ed has been writing to you boys, keeping you up to date on the events of the past three months. I'm sorry I couldn't do it myself, but you will have to believe me when I say that this is my first free moment I have had. Running the Post Office alone has been a full-time job, and by "full time" I mean during this period. I mean 24 hours a day. People were writing letters like you wouldn't believe—which is not so bad for me, of course, since all I have to do is sell them stamps and fill up the canvas bags. But they have also been getting mail, magazines, and catalogues. Poor Leon, who flies in the mail from Anchorage, pulled a muscle in his back unloading one of the bags and is filing for workman's compensation. He deserves it.

So do I, although I have had help. Ed, Maggie, and others have been just wonderful. The store has been besieged—when you're awake twice as long, you use up supplies twice as fast. Especially snack foods and light bulbs. And all that incoming mail has to be sorted, you know.

One of our girls joined some book club and has been receiving hundreds, thousands of books. They're piling up in boxes in the back. And this is a girl who rarely reads anything more challenging than teen magazines. I've been nominal librarian of Cicely's nominal library, but until now it's consisted of three shelves of remainders and paperbacks. Suddenly we've got a catalogue bigger than the Anchorage Public Library. Fortunately Maurice Minnifield said he would contribute the storefront where Dr. Robertson had set up shop. So Cicely will be getting a new library, all thanks to Shelly Tambo. My god, life is peculiar.

Speaking of Dr. Robertson, he's gone back to Philadelphia. I don't know what if anything will come of his research. Maggie O'Connell is flying again and is just delighted. And speaking of Maurice, he strikes me as looking rather sad. He claims he almost arranged for Cicely to be bought by Kim Basinger, the actress! But the deal fell through when she and her entourage arrived on the 1st.

You should hear Maurice describe what happened when Miss Basinger and her people came to inspect Cicely. We were all still asleep. So no one met them at the landing field. Somehow they made their way into town and discovered the entire population just snoozing away. Maurice says Ms. Basinger thought that we were all dead. She took one look at all the bodies lying around on the street and in the church and deduced that there must have been so much opposition to a Hollywood movie star buying Cicely that we all committed suicide, like at Masada. Her assistant said something like, "My God, it's another Jonestown," and they all fled. I wish I could have seen that.

Still, I'm not really sure it actually happened. Most people find the very notion of anyone (let alone Maurice) selling Cicely to be so outrageous, they simply don't believe it. It's probably a good thing for Maurice they don't.

Another thing that was hard to believe was our production of *Guys and Dolls.* I had a small role as the commander of the Salvation Army. It gave me an ideal perspective from which I witnessed what was certainly the most absurd and ridiculous theatrical production in history. And I include in that the version you were in, Matt, of *Death of a Salesman,* in high school, and Rudy, your famous Thanksgiving Pageant in 4th grade. Or was it vice-versa? Did they do *Death of a Salesman* in fourth grade? Even if they did, this was worse.

For one thing, Maurice cast himself as Sky Masterson, the dynamic and sexy gambler who wins the heart of cold, upright Sarah Brown, a Salvation Army sergeant. And he cast Barbara Semanski, a state trooper he's sweet on, as Sarah. It was a prescription for musical comedy disaster. Maurice may be dynamic, and there may be some who consider him sexy (I don't think Barbara does), but he cannot act his way out of a paper bag, and his singing compares unfavorably with the mating call of the moose who walks through town once a month.

Sky has a song, "My Time of Day," with an odd, modern-type melody. Well, Maurice must have decided the hell with it, that he would do a Rex Harrison and just talked it. It came out like one of his blowhard monologues—terrible. Now Barbara has a surprisingly serviceable voice. But she has to giggle drunkenly and say, "Ask me how do I feel" at the start of "If I Were a Bell." Well, her "ask me how do I feel," delivered in her gruff state-trooper voice, came out like a dare, as though if you did get up the nerve to ask her, she'd sock you in the chops and tell you it was none of your damn business.

When they sang a duet, "I've Never Been in Love Before," people in the audience just looked at each other. Backstage, I realized that if I gave in and started to respond to this performance with the laughter it deserved, I might never stop laughing for the rest of my life. They would have to cart me away. Still, it might have been worth it, for a laugh like that.

It got worse. Chris Stevens tried hard, and for a second or two did make us believe he was Nathan Detroit; and Shelly, opposite him, was just darling as Miss Adelaide. But the supporting men were dreadful, and their dance in "Luck Be a Lady" was like watching men do aerobics at gunpoint. The women in the chorus behind Shelly ("The Hot Box Girls") sang "Take Back Your Mink" and danced in their chorus line like little girls playing dress-up.

And then . . . well, a little into the second act, I began to notice that the response from the audience was getting less enthusiastic. I had thought that was due to people realizing what a travesty they were witnessing, but when I had a scene onstage I looked out, and sure enough: some people in the audience were asleep!

I can't tell you how strange that was. At one point, everyone in the cast realized what was happening, and we all knew it was a race against time. *We had to get to the end of the show before everyone passed out.* So people began rushing their lines, motioning "come on, come on" with their hands, fighting off yawns . . . Those who managed to get through a scene with all the characters still awake would beam delightedly at each other, then run off and make room for the next scene. Chorus members and people without lines would simply collapse onstage, like soldiers being shot. I mean they would simply crumple without warning and lie there. Pretty soon the bodies were falling faster than stage hands could drag them off. At one point Maurice, who was the director, stopped in the middle of a line, yawned like a great big lion, stepped up to the edge of the stage, and spoke to Marilyn, who was at the piano.

"You're the lynchpin, Marilyn," he said grimly. "We can do without anyone except you. Stay with me, little lady. We can beat this thing." Marilyn just nodded and kept on playing. You know, it reminded me of that movie, *A Night to Remember,* about the sinking of the Titanic. The orchestra kept playing even as the ship listed terribly and sank faster and faster. Well, that was Marilyn—game, stalwart, a trouper to the end. Finally, Maurice himself couldn't take it any more. He sat down on the stage, leaned up against some scenery, and said, "Marilyn, I take back everything I said about you. You've been superb," and fell asleep.

Ed Chigliak did a heartfelt rendition of "Sit Down You're Rocking the Boat" with exactly two people backing him in the chorus, yawning and leaning on each other and wiping their eyes. After the final crescendo he turned to the audience, arms out, and four people clapped. They were almost drowned out by the snores. Ed shrugged and lay down on the stage and then he was gone, too. The last thing I saw before I dropped off was the few visitors we had—two of Shelly's friends from Dawson City, John Newton from an Anchorage radio station, Chris's brother Bernard from Portland—standing up in the audience and watching as everyone around them snuffled and snored away. The stage was covered with bodies, like the end of *Hamlet*. Marilyn closed the cover of the piano keys, folded up the sheet music, and put her head down.

Needless to say, there was no curtain call.

We all slept for a day and a half, and it felt wonderful. We had all thought that our continually being awake was not having any adverse effect on us, but things did seem nicer after that long sleep. Looking back I think we were all under a strain whether we knew it or not. Everyone was surly, irritable, and carped about things concerning other people they normally just ignore or don't even notice. Did I mention that we all had the same dream? That was unusual.

As for me, I'm glad it's over. I'm finally cleaning out the store and the post office. I found some junk mail that I "forgot" to sort, some old magazines, and oh, there was one thing I do feel badly about. It was a letter written by Joel Fleischman the first day he ever came here. It was addressed to his fiancé (at the time), Elaine, and it has me wondering whether their relationship might not have endured if I had not misplaced it. I guess we'll never know. Perhaps it might have ended sooner! I have no idea what is in it. I intended to give it to Joel, but when I asked

Ed for it he said he sent it out with the rest of the outgoing mail. So maybe Elaine will receive it after all. I wonder what she'll think?

I'll tell Joel what happened, but how he'll react I haven't a clue. I would not even begin to try to fathom his personal affairs. Now that we've returned to status quo, the whole town has shook hands and made up. But Joel and Maggie keep right on bickering—not as harshly as during the past three months, but still. It has always struck me as somewhat unfortunate. The entire town can see that they're made for each other, but they refuse to acknowledge it. Maybe that's the new way.

But what do I know? You'd think that the older you get, the wiser you become, and the more you understand life. The opposite is true with me. All I see now are contradictions of what I assumed a wise person would "know." Is that my wisdom? That, in the end, wisdom itself is baloney? It looks like it. All I can say after this whole odd experience is you boys do yourselves a favor: get old, but take nothing for granted. Nothing. Not even sleep.

Love,
Mother

....

6/12/90

My Darling Elaine,

This is unbelievable, a total outrage. They've stuck me in this cabin, this hunting lodge in the middle of nowhere, I'm like a defector in a Le Carre novel, in a safe house somewhere in the German woods. My landlady is this snippy girl pilot, you know, Annie Oakley/Amelia Earhart—who, okay, I made the mistake of speaking to her thinking she was a hooker, so she was conceivably justified in being offended . . . Actually you would have been pleased at my response to her, something like, "No thanks, honey, I happen to be engaged to a knockout." Which you are.

But this is a nightmare. Waiting all day for your call at that cafe—I felt like a leper, no, check that, I felt like a healthy

217

person *surrounded* by lepers. Of course the owner did bring me a sandwich, gratis, without my asking, which was nice of him. But this is not my scene. These are not my people. Lumberjacks with beer bellies and flannel shirts? I didn't sign up for this.

So, seriously, I know you're busy, but please, pull every possible string, make every possible phone call. We're talking about four years! You have got to get me out of this. This two-block main street with storefronts and moose antlers all over everything! This cabin—you heat it with a wood stove. And the natives, my God, what a group, they will eat me alive. YES. IT IS A QUESTION OF PERSONAL SURVIVAL. A runty, fast-talking Jew from New York is going to ask them to take off their clothes (and their *wives'* clothes!!) and touch them? And play doctor? This is all wrong. For everyone's sake. Everyone. Help. For God's sake, honey. I'm in big trouble here. Help.

> *I love you.*
> *Joey*

PS—I don't mean to be obnoxious. But there is just a complete mismatch of doctor and community here. I can't even approach it like an anthropologist and be "interested" in the primitiveness of it all. Not for four years, my God. Quaint for a day, okay. BUT FOUR YEARS! It would NOT be "good" for me, like that duplicitous, disingenuous, lying jerk Pete Gilliam said. It would be bad for me. For everyone. Very bad. These people don't want me, and I don't want them. If they can't trust and feel comfortable with their physician, what's the point?

And as for me, my God. What can I possibly learn from these people?

A Selected List of Fiction Available from Mandarin

While every effort is made to keep prices low, it is sometimes necessary to increase prices at short notice. Mandarin Paperbacks reserves the right to show new retail prices on covers which may differ from those previously advertised in the text or elsewhere.

The prices shown below were correct at the time of going to press.

☐	7493 0003 5	**Mirage**	James Follett	£3.99
☐	7493 0134 1	**To Kill a Mockingbird**	Harper Lee	£2.99
☐	7493 0076 0	**The Crystal Contract**	Julian Rathbone	£3.99
☐	7493 0145 7	**Talking Oscars**	Simon Williams	£3.50
☐	7493 0118 X	**The Wire**	Nik Gowing	£3.99
☐	7493 0121 X	**Under Cover of Daylight**	James Hall	£3.50
☐	7493 0020 5	**Pratt of the Argus**	David Nobbs	£3.99
☐	7493 0097 3	**Second from Last in the Sack Race**	David Nobbs	£3.50

All these books are available at your bookshop or newsagent, or can be ordered direct from the publisher. Just tick the titles you want and fill in the form below.

Mandarin Paperbacks, Cash Sales Department, PO Box 11, Falmouth, Cornwall TR10 9EN.

Please send cheque or postal order, no currency, for purchase price quoted and allow the following for postage and packing:

UK	80p for the first book, 20p for each additional book ordered to a maximum charge of £2.00.
BFPO	80p for the first book, 20p for each additional book.
Overseas including Eire	£1.50 for the first book, £1.00 for the second and 30p for each additional book thereafter.

NAME (Block letters) ....

ADDRESS ....

....

....